WHAT DOES A MISSING C(
AND THREE DEAD RESEA ___ _____.... .....,

HAVE IN COMMON?

Private investigator Chance Sunday is hired by Carol McIntyre to find her missing daughter and prove her innocence. Soon after he starts his investigation one of Laurel's best friends is murdered. Sunday is afraid Laurel may be next. He must sort through the misdirection and lies of Laurel's friends to find the truth.

Praise for A Chance on Sunday

"Really enjoyed the read. Characters and story were well developed and the pacing was a good speed overall."—*Debra Hartman, Professional Book Editor*

"Loved the characters and especially Boomer. I think this is the best book you have written."—*June Jones, Avid Reader*

" Loved the story. It was well written and kept me turning the pages. I fell in love with the dog, Boomer."—*Kay D, Avid Reader*

"The story felt like talking to an old friend. I could imagine sitting at the bar in the Do Drop Inn and listening to Mr. Sunday tell me about his latest case over a beer."—*Patricia C, Avid Reader*

I took out my pad and pencil. "Ma'am, let's start from the beginning. Er...first, what's your name?"

She poured the cola I'd offered into the glass and watched it fizz before she gulped a drink. This appeared to revive her. She sat back in her seat, sighed, and raised her head. "It's Carol...Carol McIntyre."

"Pleased to meet you. My name is Chance Sunday. Now, how may I help you?"

"My daughter, Laurel, is missing. It's been over three weeks now with no word. It's not like her not to call or text me. We used to talk almost every day."

"I take it you reported her missing to the police. What did they say?"

"I didn't have to report her missing. They say they haven't been able to find her either. They want her too, Mr. Sunday. It's not because she's missing. They think she's an accomplice." Her eyes became larger as she spoke.

"An accomplice to what, Mrs. McIntyre?"

"To m–murder!" She sat up straight in her chair. Her eyes glittered. "But I assure you, she didn't do it. She's scared, and that's why she ran away. Please, if you can't help me, I don't know what I'll do. I'm so worried I can't sleep or eat. I can't go on like this not knowing if she's alive or...dead."

She slumped in her chair, breathing heavily. Boomer moved in closer and laid his head on her lap. She put her hand on Boomer's head. I waited until she looked up again and started breathing more easily. She took another sip of her cola.

A Chance on Sunday

Brenda Bell

Moonshine Cove Publishing, LLC

Abbeville, South Carolina, U.S.A.
1st Moonshine Cove Edition December 2020

ISBN: 978-1-945181-962
Library of Congress PCN: 2020922543
Copyright 2020 by Brenda Bell

Cover image public domain, cover and interior design by Moonshine Cove staff.

Dedication

To June in Montana, a friend across the years and across the miles

About the Author

I was born in the shadow of the Blue Ridge Mountains in Western North Carolina. I met my husband, a Canadian, while skiing in Montana. We have lived in many different

 locations across the United States and Canada. We finally settled in West Virginia with our dog Wesley, but now we have moved for the last time to Western North Carolina. I worked as a network analyst for a major bank in West Virginia. I am enjoying my time off to write and do research. Under the pen name of Amanda Balfour, I have published three historical romances: *Rumors Among the Heather. The Call of the Raven,* and *Too Hard to forget.*

https://brendabell.net

A Chance on Sunday

Chapter 1

My name is Chance Sunday. New people I meet typically ask if that is my real name, and then I'm obliged to tell my story. My great-great-grandfather came from Germany. His last name was Sonntag. He decided it would sound more American to change it to Sunday. My mother's doctor told her she had one chance in a thousand of ever having a child, so when I was born, she named me Chance. What can I say? I'm stuck with the whims of my relatives.

On my way to work each morning, I turn in at the old Community Church. The small, white clapboard building has an old-fashioned open steeple and an ancient cast bronze bell. The bell has a deep, rich tone when the pastor calls the faithful to church on Sunday. There are three arched, stained-glass windows depicting a scene from the Bible on each side of the church. The hundred and fifty-year-old windows came from a church in Athens, Ohio, though no one knows for sure how old they are since the records only went back to 1865. At the back of the church, behind the pulpit, is a small stained-glass window depicting Jesus holding a lamb. When the sun shines on the stained glass in the mornings and the rays reflect on the path to the cemetery in the back of the church, you feel as if you are standing on sacred ground.

I stop by the cemetery most mornings. It's not as morbid as it sounds...or maybe it is. I have no idea, but I can't pass by without stopping. I buried my wife and son alongside my parents in that church cemetery almost one year ago. Sometimes I talk to them, and often as not, I sit without speaking. I don't know why, but I always feel better when I leave.

Sitting here in the peace and quiet, I remember the good times. I have periods of depression, anger, and bitterness, but not here in this place. Sometimes the pastor comes by and sits with me and my dog, Boomer. Rev. Hoyles doesn't talk—he just sits with us, providing company for a short time. When he gets up to leave, he pats me on the back and gives Boomer a scratch behind his ear. I watch him walk away with his stooped shoulders and a bowed head.

As I sit on the bench in the cool of the morning and look across the cemetery, I hear birds singing and bees buzzing around the rhododendrons enclosing this place. Wisps of clouds glide across the bluer-than-blue sky. What a beautiful day. Here in this place of eternal peace, I have time to think, time to remember. Maybe today will be a good day.

Sometimes I wonder if my wife holds me responsible for what happened to her and my son. I hope she will find it in her heart to forgive me. I look down into Boomer's big eyes, and he gazes back at me as if he knows the answer. If he could talk, would he tell me? So much for the thoughts of a seeker or a mad man. Some days I can't tell the difference.

After someone killed my family, Boomer was there for me. He gave me a purpose, if for nothing else than to feed and water him. I poured my heart out to him. From the look in his eyes, I sensed he understood. He saved my life, but I don't know for what purpose. I was ready to end it all. I had the gun pressed against my temple, trying to get up the nerve to pull the trigger. Boomer whined and laid his head on my lap. One look into those wise eyes and I laid the gun on the table. I couldn't do it. I couldn't let him down.

The day we found Boomer will always stand out in my memory. We had been on vacation, and our neighbor had collected our mail and newspapers while we were away. We were going through Sunday's paper, and there was Boomer's picture in the animal adoption section. My son wanted a dog. We had not decided if we should get a pedigreed dog, one small or large, or one from a breeder or the animal shelter.

Our three voices in unison said, "Look at that face. Let's go get him."

It had been more than three days since his picture was in the paper, so I was afraid someone had adopted him, or a worse option came to mind. We took the paper with us and showed the picture to the lady at the animal shelter, who also wasn't sure if he was still there.

We started a tour through the place. It was hard to get past the kennel odors and, worst of all, the many hopeful faces standing by the doors of their cages. Boomer was in the next to the last cage we looked in. He was even more handsome in person than in the newspaper's picture.

The lady at the shelter told us he was a ten-month-old keeshond. I had no idea what a keeshond was, but he is a medium-sized dog with a plush two-layer coat of black and silver. He has a lion-like mane and rimmed eyes giving him the appearance of wearing spectacles. He has small, dark triangular ears. His tail curls up on his back. The kennel lady told us the Dutch used the breed on their barges, as a patriotic symbol during times of unrest.

Right away, we could tell he would be a great family dog. He was smart, agile, and playful. At first after we got him home, he wouldn't eat. I took him to the doctor, and it turns out he had tonsillitis. I didn't know dogs could get tonsillitis. Next, he had an ear infection, then an eye infection, and last of all, hookworms.

Boomer and I came in from a run through the neighborhood one morning before it was time to go to work. I found my wife in the kitchen fixing breakfast. I sat at the bar, and Boomer lay down beside me, resting his head on my foot. He was such a well-mannered dog. I said to my wife, "I wonder why someone would give away such a nice dog?"

She reached down and scratched him behind his ears before looking up at me with a gleam in her eye. "Maybe they couldn't afford the vet bills." She laughed and smiled fondly at Boomer.

I know dogs can't smile, but I'm positive he looked up at me and smiled. Scientists say dogs aren't that smart, but I think they're wrong. As crazy as it sounds, I think I would credit Boomer with ESP.

In my business, you have a lot of acquaintances but few friends. My wife was my best friend. My other best friend, my dog Boomer, comes to work with me most days. He waits patiently while I talk to my family here in the cemetery. From the sad look he gives me, I think he understands why we come to this place. I sense he misses them too. Reluctantly, I leave this place of peace and we head back to my truck, Boomer trotting along beside me.

I'm a private investigator in Parkersburg, West Virginia. Parkersburg is situated along the banks of the Ohio River. It's a city but still has a small-town feel. Almost everyone knows everyone else, or at least who their mothers or fathers were.

My office is in an ages-old brick building on Sixth Street, over a barbershop. In this era of nondescript unisex hair salons, it's amusing to see a "barbershop" with an authentic turning barber's pole by the front door. My office consists of two rooms. The outer office looks like I have a receptionist, although my operation is too small to justify the expense. There are four brown faux leather chairs, a metal desk with a laptop, and a filing cabinet against one wall. The floors are oak hardwood.

When I first moved in, linoleum covered the floors. I removed the linoleum and discovered the beautiful original oak floors underneath, which I had refinished. The walls were covered in cheap paneling. After I tore the paneling off, perfectly preserved plaster walls were revealed. The ceiling still had the plaster detail around the light. I had the walls painted a muted green and trimmed in light oak. I've been told green has a calming effect. Some of my clients could use several days in a green room.

The outer office is all for show. I don't know why I keep up the pretense of a receptionist, since I don't have to impress clients. I'm the only private eye in town. There are two other security firms in the area, but I'm a one-man operation. I have a corner office with a huge window overlooking Sixth Street. The window covers almost an entire wall of my private office. The other wall has a large window with views of the Ohio River.

My office name is printed on the windows, "Mid-Ohio Valley Confidential Investigations, PLLC." I thought about calling my business 'Sunday Private Investigations,' but that sounded as though I only worked on Sunday. My desk sits catty-cornered to the file cabinets, and the window gives me an unrestricted view of the Ohio River. I enjoy watching the barges navigate up and down the river. On summer weekends, the river is full of boaters and fishermen.

The beginning of our spring season has been soaked with rain almost every day during the month so far. I'm thinking of building an ark. Boomer's ready to round up all the animals two by two. At six in the evening, I stood in front of my window overlooking the street, drinking my last cup of coffee. I watched the mist float in off the Ohio River and silently creep up the street, blanketing the town.

Spring is a favorite time of mine. I especially like this hour of evening when it's pleasant and peaceful. Traffic is almost nonexistent. The street lamps are on, and the mist is creating a halo around the streetlights. It gives the city the appearance of a sepia photograph. I force myself to turn from the window.

This evening, I powered off the coffeemaker, rinsed out the carafe, and put Boomer on his leash. I picked up my briefcase, ready to head home. I stopped short when I heard the door to the outer office open and shut. Footsteps came softly to the door of my private office, and someone knocked. I put my briefcase down and called, "Come in." I undid Boomer's leash and sat behind my desk.

My door opened little by little, and a woman stood in the doorway, a little unsteady on her feet. Her clothes hung on her. She had a belt holding up pants that were bunched around her waist. Her sweater had two buttons fastened in the wrong buttonholes. She stared from corner to corner of the room, with her eyes coming to rest on me. I could see her mouth moving, but she didn't speak a word. The dull cast to her eyes told me what it had cost her to come this far.

I stood up. "Won't you come in?"

She stepped across the threshold and turned her head from side to side, but I don't think she noticed anything in the office. She stood in the middle of the room, found my face again, and never took her gaze off of me.

I moved behind my client's chair and placed my hands on the chair's back. "Please take a seat."

She walked over to my desk and sat in the client's chair, seemingly without a will of her own. I moved behind my desk and sat down. Boomer walked over to her chair, sat beside her, and gazed up at her.

"How may I help you?" I asked.

She slumped in the chair with her eyes closed and dropped her head without speaking. Her claw-like hand reached out and stroked Boomer's head absentmindedly.

"Ma'am, are you all right? Would you like a drink of water or a cola? I could make a fresh pot of coffee."

She raised her head and stared at me with a puzzled look as if she were trying to understand the meaning of my words. "A cola would be welcomed."

I let out the breath I had been holding. At least she could talk. I fixed her a glass with ice and popped the top on a can of cola. After I brought the cola over to the desk and set it down beside her, it was some time before she touched her glass.

Tears threatened to escape from her hazel eyes. She ran her hand through her mousy brown hair, cleared her throat, and licked her lips. I waited, not sure what to do next. I watched the skin of her neck become a blotchy red and saw the color creep up to her face. She put her hands on the edge of my desk and leaned in.

"I didn't have an appointment. I was driving by and looked up. Your light was on, and I glimpsed you standing in the window. Then I saw your sign. It said, 'Confidential Investigations.' I thought it had to be an omen. I took a chance you'd see me. There is nowhere else I can turn.

I need your help. I'm not sure anyone can help me. The police say..."
She spoke so low I had to strain to hear her.

I took out my pad and pencil. "Ma'am, let's start from the
beginning. Er...first, what's your name?"

She poured her cola in the glass and watched it fizz before she
gulped a drink. This appeared to revive her. She sat back in her seat,
sighed, and raised her head. "It's Carol...Carol McIntyre."

"Pleased to meet you. My name is Chance Sunday. Now, how may I
help you?"

"My daughter, Laurel, is missing. It's been over three weeks now
with no word. It's not like her not to call or text me. We used to talk
almost every day."

"I take it you reported her missing to the police. What did they
say?"

"I didn't have to report her missing. They say they haven't been able
to find her either. They want her too, Mr. Sunday. It's not because
she's missing. They think she's an accomplice." Her eyes became larger
as she spoke.

"An accomplice to what, Mrs. McIntyre?"

"To m-murder." She sat up straight in her chair. Her eyes glittered.
"But I assure you, she didn't do it. She's scared, and that's why she ran
away. Please, if you can't help me, I don't know what I'll do. I'm so
worried I can't sleep or eat. I can't go on like this not knowing if she's
alive or...dead."

She slumped in her chair, breathing heavily. Boomer moved in
closer and laid his head on her lap. She put her hand on Boomer's
head. I waited until she looked up again and started breathing more
easily. She took another sip of her cola.

"Ma'am, I'll try my best, but if the police can't find her with all their
resources, I'm not sure what I can do. My services are expensive, and
there is no guarantee."

"I don't care what it costs. I can't go on like this." She kept shaking
her head from side to side. Abruptly, she looked up. "Oh, I can give

you a retainer if you're worried about the money." She started digging through her handbag and fished out her checkbook.

"Ma'am, I get two hundred dollars a day plus expenses. I'm not worried about payment. I just don't want you wasting your money."

She swallowed hard, but she wrote the check. "Here's a check for a thousand dollars. You can bill me for the rest. Oh, she said, and dug through her bag again. "Laurel is twenty years old. I brought a recent photo. I took this at Christmas and had it enlarged. Before I forget, here's a list of her friends. I'll call and tell them they'll be hearing from you. The police have the same information."

I stared at the photo, and something clicked. I'd seen that face somewhere. "That's great, thank you. I'll hold your check until I look into the case. If there's nothing I can do, I'll return it. Now, what kind of trouble is your daughter in, and what does her father think about your consulting me?"

"Her father said to leave it to the police. He's no help. Since we haven't heard from her, he thinks she's...she's dead. He said I could do what I liked. He's her stepfather, and the two don't get along. He adopted her after we married, but somehow, they were always rubbing each other the wrong way from the get-go. She never knew her real father. He died before she was born."

I pushed a box of tissues toward the edge of my desk.

Mrs. McIntyre shook her head, gulped, and grabbed a tissue to stop the tears. "She can't be dead. I just know she can't be. She's all I've got." She stared up at me with those big, sad eyes.

What could I do but agree to help her? Glancing at the picture again, it hit me where I'd seen her daughter's face. "Mrs. McIntyre, if she's innocent, why did she run away? The police would have protected her."

"That's what the detective I talked to said. My daughter is a student at the state college in Pinedale. We managed to pay for her college expenses and give her a little spending money, but money was getting tight. My husband's business is not as profitable as it once was.

"She wanted experience working in a lab, so she took a job in a research lab cleaning up at night. This was right up her alley. It's a small lab, and she plans to be a chemistry teacher when she graduates. Some of the researchers let her help with their experiments from time to time. She felt lucky getting the job and being able to help with her expenses.

"On this Thursday night she was working, let's see, it would have been Thursday four weeks ago this coming Thursday. Most everyone had left for the day, but there were three people still in the lab in the basement working late. Three men came into the lab by the back door and killed everyone in the basement lab—well, everyone else, I guess.

"My daughter's body was not among them. They found her purse, phone, and an open textbook on the table in the lunchroom. She must have been studying for a test on her break when the men entered."

Mrs. McIntyre gulped for air and took another drink of her cola. She grabbed hold of the arms of her chair in a viselike grip. When she had herself under control, she relaxed her grip and started talking again.

"We didn't know what happened. I feared they had kidnapped her. When she was presumed missing, the police put her picture in the newspaper. A man came forward and said she had stowed away in the backseat of his car. He drove cross country from Pinedale to Highway 50 and turned towards Parkersburg.

"He didn't know she was in the back of his car until he stopped for gas at Tucker's Truck Stop. While he was pumping gas, he glanced inside the rear window of his car. He saw something move on the floor. When he opened the door, he found my daughter. She begged him to keep quiet and shut the door. He finished filling his tank and drove away. He pulled over down the road and demanded an explanation."

"Yes, now I remember reading about the man and the hitchhiker in the paper. What was this man doing near the vicinity of the murders?"

"He's a pharmaceutical salesman, and he was at the afterhours clinic maybe half a mile away from the research lab. He left his car unlocked. When he came out, he locked his sample case in the trunk and jumped in his car. He said he never looked in the back. He had his mind on the sale he had made at the clinic."

"Refresh my memory. What was your daughter's explanation for hiding in his car?"

"She said while she was in the lunchroom, the loading bay door to the facility burst open. Three men rushed in like commandos. They headed straight for the basement lab like they knew where they were going. She hid in the cabinet under the sink. When it was quiet, she crawled over to the stairs. That's when she saw a body draped across the stairs lying in a pool of blood. She panicked and ran out the back door.

"The men were still in the parking lot. They saw her when she came outside. She ran through the woods up to the highway, leaving her car in the parking lot. The sheriff impounded her car. One man ran after her, but she lost him in the woods. She made it to the clinic and found the salesman's car unlocked. She climbed in and hid in the back."

"Did he say why he agreed to drive her to Parkersburg? Most people would have told her to get out of the car or called the police."

"Combined with the frightened look on her face, what she said scared him witless, and he had to help her. He pulled back on the road and set a record getting to Parkersburg. When they reached Parkersburg, he turned down Seventh Street. She told him to pull over at Fairview Avenue, and that's the last he saw of her. She promised she would report what she saw when she got to a phone. No one's heard from her since."

She gulped the last of her cola. Sighing, she glanced around the room. I waited for her to get enough energy to finish her story.

"He drove to the next traffic light and got to worrying about her and turned around. He drove back to the Kroger Store and then up Fairview Avenue, but he didn't see her. The police say they believe him. A man came forward and said they saw a man letting a woman out of his car at about the right time of around midnight. He said she walked up Fairview. That's the last anyone has seen her."

"Do you think she could have known who the killers were? Could they have been friends of hers?"

"The detective asked me the same thing. I can't believe any of her friends would do something like this. We've known her friends' families forever. The families are wealthy. There would be no reason to commit a crime like this."

I wasn't going to burst her bubble, but sometimes good kids go bad. I've known the kids of a millionaire to rob a liquor store for the thrill of it. Seemingly nice people would kill someone to see how it felt to take a life. Murder and robbery know no class lines. When I glanced up, she was looking at me.

"I know what you're thinking, but I know my daughter. She wouldn't do anything like this."

I nodded and cleared my throat. There was no need to add to her grief.

"We need to find her first and hear her side of the story. I'm looking over this list and her friend, Davis Howell, lives near Fairview. Did the police question him?"

"Yes, but he said he hadn't seen her. He's a good kid. He's studying to be a lawyer. They've been friends since kindergarten. We used to live next door to him and his parents."

"I'll check with him first. Sometimes people will talk quicker to a stranger than they will the police. He may know something that will help."

"When you looked up and saw my window, were you planning to consult me?"

"I was trying to decide what to do. I must have driven around for two or three hours. When I saw the name on your window, I remembered you were in the paper recently. You found that little girl a neighbor took to another state seven years earlier. I didn't remember your name or that we even had a private eye here in town until Cassie, she's a friend of Laurel's, suggested I call you. She's worried about

Laurel too. I thought private detectives were just in mystery novels, not real life."

She raised a trembling hand to her throat. "Uh...I've been getting phone calls at all hours. The voice is muffled, but it sounds like it's male. He told me to quit asking questions and talking to the police. I'm so scared," Mrs. McIntyre whispered, and wrung her shaking hands.

"Ma'am, if you've got caller ID and an answering machine, just let it go to the answering machine if you don't recognize the number. I hate to say this, but sometimes people get a thrill out of scaring vulnerable people. They might not have anything to do with your daughter."

"I was afraid it might be Laurel, so I answered the phone. All the calls are coming from different numbers."

"If it is Laurel, I'm sure she'll leave a message. If you hear her voice when the answering machine kicks in, you can always pick up."

"Yes, you're right. I'm so worried I don't know what I'm doing half the time. I'll do that from this day forward." She stared at some point on the wall over my right shoulder and bit her lip.

"Ok, Mrs. McIntyre, you've given me enough to go on for now. I'll get started on this first thing tomorrow. I used to be a police officer, and I still have some friends in the department. I'll check to see what they've found and also with the sheriff in Pinedale. They may not want me working on an active case. If not, then I'll return your retainer. I want you to go home and try not to worry. I'll be in touch as soon as I have something." I paused. "Ma'am, there's one other thing I should tell you. If I find your daughter is an accessory in this, I'll have to turn her over to the police."

She nodded and turned her face to me. "I understand. If she's involved in the murders, then she must take her punishment. But, Mr. Sunday, I can't believe she would be. Where would she meet people like that? I just want to know she's alive. She's a good girl. We took her to church every Sunday since she was a baby. She was a member of the church mission team and helped people. I know she wouldn't hurt anyone." She said that as if it explained everything. "You're my last hope."

I stood up, but I could see she was reluctant to stand. I waited and at last she looked up with a dazed expression overtaking her face again. Boomer stood beside her and stared up at her.

"Mrs. McIntyre, you don't look well. I think I should drive you home. Is there someone at home when you get there?"

"Oh, no, no, thank you. I can manage. My home's not far. My car's down in the parking lot behind your building, and my husband will be home. I feel better knowing someone will do something. You've taken a load off my shoulders." She stood up and wobbled a bit. I took her arm to steady her.

I left her long enough to put the leash on Boomer, and then I walked her down the stairs to her car. I followed her in my truck to her home on Clark Avenue. I parked and watched her step out of her car and go in the house. The lights were not on. I don't think her husband was home either. If he was, he was sitting in the dark.

There wasn't much else I could do for now. I turned down Fairview and on to Seventh Street. From Seventh, I made my way out Route 47 toward my home. On the way, I made one stop at the Do Drop Inn Bar and Grill. It's about half a mile from my home and about what you'd expect from a roadside bar. The clientele are locals. If you see anyone in a suit and tie, you know he's coming from his court date.

There are no frills or ferns hanging around. The bar is well worn with scratches and cigarette burns from the time people were allowed to smoke in public places. The place smells of stale beer mixed with the faint aroma of pizza and tonight's special.

I couldn't guess how old the building is. Rough-hewn logs, at least three feet in diameter, form the walls. I don't think you can find logs with three-foot diameters any more. It looks a little rundown. There's one window in front with a flashing neon beer sign. Mounted over the doorway is a twelve-point deer antler. You step into a small alcove and go through a heavily scarred metal door. The parking lot is gravel and filled with trucks sporting gun racks filled with the latest rifles. Sometimes there is the occasional ATV, mainly throughout deer-hunting season. During hunting season, the place looks like an armed camp.

The only light in the main room comes from the lanterns on the tables and a few neon signs on the wall. Homemade plywood booths flank the walls. No cushions. In the middle of the room are seven or eight tables. If you look up at the ceiling's exposed beams, you'll see a stuffed bear leaning lazily against a rafter.

This place used to be my home away from home when I lost my wife and son. The first six months were the hardest I have ever lived through in my life. I sat on a barstool from the time I made it here until closing time, or until I could no longer hold on to the bar. The liquor helped at first to dull my thoughts, but my memory required progressively more and more alcohol to keep all the bad feelings at bay, until even the liquor didn't help.

I could not have gone through those soul-crushing times if it had not been for my friends Charlie, John, and Elsie. The bar owners, John and Elsie Corbin, took care of me during those terrible months. John either took me home when I couldn't hold my head up or called Phil Dixon, my handyman, to come get me.

John is a man who can take care of himself. He always wears a dark T-shirt with camo chinos. His muscular frame demands attention. His pecs are full and well defined. Wide lats add to his perfect V-shaped figure and slender torso. The muscles of his arms give the appearance of granite. He would stand out in any room. He's bald as a door knob with a thick black drooping mustache. His slate-gray eyes miss nothing. Elsie, his wife, serves drinks to the tables while he tends bar and bounces whoever Elsie can't calm down.

When I opened the door of the barroom, everyone in the room raised their hand. I waved back as I made my way to the bar. Elsie came over to take my order. She is about fifty with bleached blonde hair and is still a good-looking woman. She always has a clean, crisp apron on and a colorful silk scarf woven through her hair somehow. I've often wondered how she does it. She must have been a stunner in her younger days. I've never seen her when she wasn't well-dressed and made-up.

She will step fearlessly between two good old boys who have had one drink too many and are itching for a fight. I don't know how she does it, but she calms them down and sends them back to their separate tables. I've never seen her with a hair out of place.

Elsie touched my arm to get my attention. "What'll it be, Chance? The specials are spaghetti or salmon cakes."

"Elsie, you know I can't turn down your spaghetti. I'll have that to go and a beer while I wait."

I didn't have to tell her what brand of beer I wanted. She drew an AmberBock and put it in a frosty mug. I sipped my beer and listened to Willie and Waylon on the old-fashioned jukebox. Before long, she placed a plastic bag filled with Italian goodness in front of me. I drank my last swallow, paid my bill, and stood up to leave.

She kept her hand on the plastic bag. "Chance, I put a salad in there. See you eat every bite. You don't eat enough fruits and vegetables. Oh, and there's a bone in there for Boomer," she said with a smile and shook her finger at me.

"You know I will, Mom. See ya. Boomer thanks you too." She shook her head and grinned. Sometimes I think she believes all us lost souls are her children.

When I climbed into my truck, Boomer stood up and looked expectant. I swear that dog has ESP. "Yes, Mr. Nosy, Elsie put a little something in there for you. You don't get it until we get home."

He let out a pitiful whimper and lay down on his seat with his head resting on his front paws.

I made my way home to my empty, silent log cabin. Maybe I should leave a light on. At least it would look like someone was home as I come up the drive. When I opened the truck door, Boomer jumped out, stared at me, and waited, licking his lips. I reached into the bag and found his bone. He snatched it from my hand and ran off into the woods.

My parents were killed in a fiery crash in the DC area six months before the rest of my family was taken out. The driver received a few scrapes and bruises. When the police found him, he was standing, watching my parents' car burn to cinders. He didn't lift a finger to pull them from the wreckage before it caught on fire. He claimed he was too stunned to do anything.

My parents had built a huge log cabin on some property they owned off Route 47. They planned to retire to the cabin. They also built a smaller cabin where Phil lives. He takes care of the place and me.

When my wife and son were killed, I moved into my parents' cabin. I couldn't stay in the house in Parkersburg I'd once shared with my family. Putting the key in the door of my old house knocked the breath out of me. The house I'd shared with my wife and son is untouched just like they left it. My friends tell me to store my stuff and sell the house, but I can't do that either. Maybe I'll be able to someday, but not today.

Somehow, I survived, but to what end I'm still trying to understand. During my insanity, I couldn't sleep or eat. My depression worried me like a gnat that will not leave you alone. I dreaded the nights worst of all. When I couldn't sleep, I walked the mountain trails in the back of the house until I was too tired to move.

My cabin isn't furnished. My parents were on their way here when they were killed. They planned to furnish the cabin that week. I have a recliner in the living room with a table and a lamp on my left. Boomer's bed is on the right side of my chair. Everything is in front of the fireplace. That's where I sit, read, and sleep.

I furnished one of the bedrooms upstairs with the twin bed and chest of drawers from my youth. I never make it past my recliner. I don't have a TV or a computer. The only entertainment I have is a CD player and radio hooked up to speakers for music and a library full of good reading. At my office I have computers and internet access, but everything in my home is the minimum.

When I think about furnishing the house, I can't seem to find the energy. My kitchen has two barstools, a coffeepot, and two cups. I don't have any dishes or eating utensils. I finished my meal with my plastic dinnerware and sat down to read.

Most nights I read until I fall asleep. Sometimes I read all night. Old memories grab my mind and won't let go some nights, making it impossible to sleep. Being engrossed in a good book keeps my mind from going to the dark side. Once I looked up from my book and noticed it was getting light outside. I looked at my watch and realized I had read all night.

In the mornings, Boomer and I walk down the long gravel drive to the highway for my paper. Out here in the country, the cool, crisp morning air smells clean and refreshes my soul. Walking to get the paper is my exercise for the day. By the time we get back to the house, the coffee has finished dripping. I take my cup of coffee and oatmeal pie out on the patio and sit down to enjoy the quiet of the morning. Boomer settles in beside my chair. It's the same routine every morning. There is something reassuring about routine.

This morning for once it isn't raining, and there isn't a cloud across the sky. Old doom and gloom, the weatherman, said there was a ninety percent chance of rain this evening. I hoped he was wrong for once. I could sit here all morning and listen to the birds singing in the trees. The clear, bright sun is trying to force its way through the canopy of trees leaf by leaf. Sunlight seems to bring every detail of the leaves on the trees into focus.

Suddenly, Boomer's head came up, and he wagged his tail. Phil wandered over to the patio and sat down. Phil is what you would call a loner. He was in Iraq and came home with PTSD. If I had to guess, I would say he's in his late forties. He's tall, maybe six foot five inches. He is clean-shaven and has dark brown hair that he keeps in a GI cut. His dark brown eyes dart around the area before he picks up a section of the newspaper. He is always aware of his surroundings even while resting. I would guess his weight at about one hundred and sixty-five pounds. He looks skinnier than that.

Enemy fire took out his whole platoon and left him the only survivor. He was not expected to make it, but against all odds, he survived after spending six months in a hospital in Germany. Released from the Marines, he felt lost and drifted from place to place. My parents found him begging outside their apartment building on the sidewalk in New York City.

Something about him touched them. He was there every morning when they went to work. My dad talked to him and did some investigating. My parents found out he was a homeless veteran. They told him they would give him a home and a job if he relocated to West Virginia, with the stipulation if they found him drunk that would be the end of his employment. He agreed. West Virginia appeared to fill all his needs. He quit drinking and tried to get his life in order.

He has an ex-wife and a daughter, but neither will speak to him. He writes to his daughter once a week, but she never answers him back. It's like a ritual. Every Friday as regular as clockwork, he writes the letter and mails it. The letters are not returned, so she must receive them. It's possible they find their way into the trash, or maybe she saves them unopened.

I don't know if Phil knows or not, but his daughter has a Facebook page with her picture. One day, I may have to find out why she refuses to communicate with him. I don't know what turned his wife and daughter against him. I only have my suspicions. What I do know is that he is a lonely man, and he is trying to get his life together. He is not the same man who left for Iraq, but then he is not the same man now who returned either.

He can't sleep at night. He patrols the property all night with his rifle as if he were still in the service and on patrol. I guess the booze dulled his senses, but when he came off the drink, he found new problems. Stress gets him agitated and aggressive. He's hard to calm down and dangerous if he has access to a gun. From the way he acts, I would guess when he becomes agitated, he has visions of Iraq and the many atrocities he has seen.

He attends a support group once a week and visits the VA to get his medicine. So far, the medicines are keeping him on an even keel. When I first met him, he did not speak. If he speaks now, it's with as few words as possible. I was afraid he would take off after I told him about my parents. To my surprise, he agreed to stay on. Even though he doesn't talk much, he comes up in the morning, drinks a cup of coffee with me, and reads the paper. We're like an old married couple.

I stood up to go. I always talk to him, but I don't expect an answer. "I'm off to work. Working on a missing person. Are you OK to look after Boomer today? I don't want to take him with me. I'll be waiting in an office most of the day."

He looks up from the paper, smiles, and nods. It must be a good day.

My feelings are a little hurt. Boomer doesn't seem to mind being left behind. He rolled over on his back for Phil to rub his stomach.

"See you later."

Not that anybody cares. I waved goodbye and made my way to my truck. Backing out of the garage, I turned around and headed into town. Next stop is the police station to see what the police have uncovered so far.

Chapter 2

I don't like going to the police station, which is strange considering my profession and previous employment. I had to find out how far the police had come with their investigation of Laurel McIntyre, and if they minded my nosing around. Most policemen dislike private investigators. They either consider us interlopers or shady bottom-feeders. However, I once was a police officer with twenty years on the force. I still had friends in the department, which gave me a small advantage.

Walking into the waiting room brings back memories. Memories I would just as soon forget. Funny how a song or a smell can bring feelings to the forefront you thought you had moved past. The smell of fear, stale whiskey breath, and burnt coffee wafting across the waiting room of the police station reminded me of everything that had happened a year ago. Those memories overwhelm me at times like this. The flashbacks start coming with no way to stop them. Entering the door, I feel as nervous as a criminal caught red-handed.

I walked up to the desk sergeant. He must be new. I didn't recognize him, so I waited for him to notice me. He glanced up at me and back at his computer with a frown on his face. I could have been an annoying fly buzzing around his face.

"What can I do for you?" he asked with his head down.

"I'd like a word with Lieutenant Parks."

"Have a seat. I'll see if he's in."

I found a seat next to a window and looked out.

Waiting is the hardest part of my job. By nature, I'm not a patient person. The desk sergeant left and returned without speaking or looking in my direction. I started to wonder if he had forgotten me. I managed to wait for a half-hour before my mind wandered down forbidden alleys.

* * * *

In that long-ago yesterday, I could still hear Captain Waltham calling me into his office. He introduced me to the head of the narcotics squad from Columbus, Captain Morris. He explained what they needed. I sat there listening to their pitch. Even today their words are like shards of glass jogging sharply through my mind. The scene is so clear in my memory it could have been a few minutes ago.

"The reason we called you into the office is we need your help. You're aware of the drug problem both Ohio and West Virginia are facing. Captain Morris needs someone he can trust and someone who hasn't had his face in the newspapers, someone who isn't known in Columbus. You're a veteran officer with twenty years of service and not likely to lose your head. You did an exemplary job for us in the same style of operation a while back. The only difference is that it was an illegal arms deal coming in from North Carolina then. It's drugs now. A big-time blended operation."

Captain Morris picked up the conversation. "This will be narcotics, illegal arms, insurance fraud, possibly conspiracy, and this is just for starters. There's not much these people aren't into. Our main interest is a meth lab on a large scale with a motorcycle gang running it.

"The kicker is we have no proof. Not even the location of the lab. We know as sure as you're sitting there who's responsible, but not one shred of evidence."

Captain Waltham went back behind his desk and sat. He looked up with a frown and nodded for Captain Morris to continue.

"Everyone who knows anything is too scared to rat them out. The motorcycle gang call themselves 'Soldiers of the Road.' Not only are they supplying Ohio, but they're bringing their product into West Virginia at an alarming rate. As you're aware, Columbus and Parkersburg have made several arrests, but we haven't been able to slow it down." Captain Morris cleared his throat and looked up from what I assumed was my personnel file.

"How big a lab are we talking?"

Captain Morris looked at Captain Waltham before he spoke. "This is not some poor slob cooking meth in his car or a local motel room. No, sir, this is a major lab setup. We're looking at big business. Until recently, they confined their territory to Ohio, but they're getting a foothold in West Virginia.

"Our number-one problem is that we can't identify where they make it or where their distribution points are. They don't sell it on the street. Oh, no, they're too smart for that. This motorcycle gang is at the head of the chain. We've busted the little guy only to find someone else has filled his shoes. No one will talk. Either they're too scared or they don't know anything."

"What about the leader of the motorcycle gang? Since you know who he is, can't you watch him?"

"Yeah, you would think that, wouldn't you? The problem with that is, he has the uncanny ability to know when we've got him under surveillance. We've had him under surveillance time and time again, but it all comes to nothing. We've wasted many a man-hour only to find him riding around in the countryside without a care and eating at Crazy Dave's.

"I'm almost certain he has an informant in the police department. That's why we need someone no one knows. If you take this assignment, you can't tell anyone. Not even a friend."

I nodded and waited for him to continue.

"The one we want is Stonewall Coltrane. They call him Stoney. He's their leader and a psychopath if there ever was one. His right-hand man is Sully. That would be Sullivan Whitehead. He's more a bottom-feeder and the muscle. He follows Stoney around like a whipped pup and does everything he's told to do."

"Wouldn't it be better to get someone from Ohio, who knows the territory? Maybe Cleveland or Toledo. I'd be like a fish out of water."

"Sergeant, we need someone who would not be taken for a police officer. Somebody who can blend in with the gang. I'll not sugarcoat this. It'll be dangerous. We've already tried two undercover officers from Ohio. The first man they beat so badly, he may have brain damage if he wakes up from his coma. They beat him and then pulled him behind one of their bikes.

"A state trooper passing by saw what was going on in the field alongside the highway. When the bikers saw the trooper, they cut the rope and sped away down a wooded path. Before he lost consciousness, our man choked out, 'lab on a farm, motorcycle...Stoney runs it.' After that he lapsed into a coma and has been there ever since. He most likely knows the location, but when and if he wakes up is anybody's guess.

"Our other man is dead. We found him in a ditch on a deserted stretch of highway, shot through the head execution-style. I'm as sure as I can be that we have a leak in the department. I'm taking precautions this time. The only people in on this operation will be myself and your captain."

I couldn't help but grin and look at their expectant faces. "Do you have any suggestions as to how I might join this gang? They don't take to strangers. You don't walk up and ask to join a gang. You have to be invited after you've been vetted, and there's usually an initiation."

"That was a concern, but I think we have that covered this time. The FBI arrested a member of a West Coast gang in Charleston, South Carolina. They caught him trying to board a container ship headed for Canada. They'd been searching for him but on the West Coast. By a twist of fate, a harbor patrol officer recognized him from the flyer. The FBI moved in and arrested him.

"There was a shoot-out at a California bar where his gang hangs out. Someone killed four members of an opposing gang. The FBI believes this guy had a big hand in the killing. Officially, he's wanted for questioning. When he found out the FBI was closing in, he took a walkabout. No one had seen him until the Feds picked him up clear across the country in South Carolina. The FBI agreed to hold him until we have our situation under control.

"When I showed his picture to your captain, he smiled right away. With only a few alterations, you resemble him enough to be his twin brother. You'll need to grow a beard and let your hair grow. Other than that, you're six feet two inches just like him, and, like our perp, you have black hair and blue eyes. Another plus is you used to race motorcycles, so you're familiar with them and can ride." Morris turned his attention back to the papers on his lap.

"Son, you'd be doing your state and Ohio a great service, not to mention the lives that might be saved by getting these people off the street."

A little bit of guilt never hurts. Both men stood up. I took that as my cue to leave.

I stood up and shook hands with Captain Morris.

"Well, son, what do you say?"

"I didn't expect this. I'll have to think about it and talk it over with my wife and son. I'll let you know...tomorrow."

"We'll look forward to hearing from you. There's no denying we need you, but the decision is up to you. There's no question this is a dangerous assignment, but one I—we—feel you're well suited for."

I left the captain's office more than a little stunned. I had to talk it over with Amy. There was no question I wanted to do this. When you do the same thing day in and day out, you want a change even if it is dangerous. Maybe the danger is what attracted me, the adrenalin rush.

When I came home, Amy met me at the door with a smile and a kiss. "Come on in the kitchen. I'm making beef stew. How was your day?"

"Not bad. I drove around and handed out a few tickets for minor infractions. How about you?"

"You know I never do anything exciting. The most thrilling thing in an accountant's life is when we discover money we didn't expect."

I took out a beer from the refrigerator. I guess I was stalling for time. I didn't know how to bring up the subject. Startled, I raised my head and realized Amy was talking to me.

"Chance, I'm talking to you. Do you want to go to Mother's for dinner Saturday?"

"Sorry, I guess I had my mind on something else. Sure, Saturday will be fine."

Her mother never liked me or my work. Under no circumstances was it pleasant visiting her. She never failed to get a few digs in under the guise of a compliment. However, when you're married, I guess compromise is a requirement.

Amy searched my face and took my hand. "Penny for your thoughts."

Usually, I could talk to her about anything, but I didn't know how to tell her about this latest disruption in our lives. I guessed the best way was to blurt it out. I looked into her earnest face and almost lost my nerve.

"The captain made a proposal today. I want to do it, but I want to talk it over with you first. I won't do it if you're not OK with it. We need to consider the pros and cons and what it could do to our family."

"You make this sound ominous. What does he want you to do? Oh, Chance, it's not more undercover work, is it?"

I nodded, and she turned sharply to look out the kitchen window.

I walked over to where she was standing, put my hands on her shoulders, and turned her around.

"Sweetheart, I can guess how you feel about this. He wants me to go undercover in a motorcycle gang. I don't know how long I'll be gone. I won't sugarcoat it. It could be dangerous, but it would mean a promotion. He promised me the next opening in the detective squad is mine."

"Oh, Chance, I remember the last time you went undercover. I never had a good night's sleep until you came home. You were gone for six months. How dangerous are we really talking here?"

"The captain thinks there's a mole in the department in Columbus. There were two undercover officers. One is in the hospital, and one is dead. It involves drugs. Drugs coming into West Virginia. You know I lost my only cousin and best friend in high school to drug overdoses. If there's a chance I can help stop this epidemic, I want to try."

"You know how I feel about this and I know your feelings. You're my heart and soul. I'd be lost without you. I love you, more than I've loved anyone. If anything happened to you, I couldn't bear it. Please don't ask me to say it's all right for you to do this."

"All I'm asking is that you think about it before we decide. This has to be a family decision."

I could see tears forming in the corners of her eyes. I pulled her to me and held her close. She trembled in my arms.

"I'll tell the Captain no in the morning. I don't want to do this to you again. They'll just have to find someone else."

She looked up at me with tears in her eyes. "What do you want to do?"

"You know, I want to do it, but not if you're set against it. I won't do that to you, not again."

Amy took a deep breath and exhaled slowly. "Oh, no, you don't. You're not putting this all on me. I don't know the right thing to tell you. I know your job is dangerous as it is, but this extra risk? Oh, Chance, I don't know. It's scary. The captain promised you a promotion last time, but it never happened."

She raised her head and reached up, running her finger along my jawline.

"If this is what you want, then I won't stand in your way. Please, oh, please, be careful and come back to us in one piece."

We spent most of the night discussing it. In the end, Amy gave me her halfhearted blessing. The next morning, I stopped by the captain's office with a few questions.

I knocked and entered his office.

When he saw me, he grinned and motioned for me to sit down. "Can I get you a cup of coffee?"

"No, thanks, I'm fine." I had to grin. He looked more nervous than I did.

"I figured you'd be here first thing. I'd be surprised if you didn't have a few questions. What's on your mind?"

I tried a little blackmail of my own. "Sir, as you know, I've always wanted to be a detective. When I helped in the West Virginia–North Carolina illegal arms sting, it was with the promise of a promotion to detective. I passed my exam. I don't mean to sound mercenary, but what's in it for me? I'll be risking my life and leaving my family for who knows how long."

The captain cleared his throat and pulled at his right ear before he looked me in the eye.

"We hope it won't be for long. What we want is for you to plant trackers on their delivery trucks and a webcam in their lab."

"Is that all?" I was sure he heard the incredulity in my voice.

"I know, I know, but we have to get an airtight case. We have to get everyone involved off the street. If Morris's guess is right, there are some important people mixed up in this. Just getting the location of the lab is a first step.

"Chance, I'm sorry about the promotion last time, but there hasn't been an opening in the detective squad. There'll be an opening coming up when Jason retires. It's yours if you take this assignment. I'll hold it for you. You have my word."

I said those fateful words, "I mean to hold you to it."

"Does that mean you're accepting the assignment?"

"Y-Yes, sir. When do I start?"

The Captain beamed from ear to ear and pumped my hand.

Ostensibly, the captain loaned me to the Federal Court in Charleston. This provided an excuse for me to be out of the office. I met both captains the next day at my home. We arranged to meet in my garage shortly after midnight. They parked on the next street, walked to the back of my house by the garage, and came through the side door, using a flashlight for security reasons. We watched the street with the lights off in case anyone had followed them.

By flashlight, they went over the dossier the captain had on Julien "Gunner" Levesque. From all reports, he was a French Canadian who lived by his own rules and damned the consequences. His story read more like that of a Wild West outlaw than a modern-day biker gang member. I found it hard not to like this outlaw the more I read about him. He was not a good man, that was plain to see, but I couldn't help admiring someone who did things his way and lived the way he chose.

I let my beard and hair grow for a month. My hair had already been in need of a haircut, so that helped. Captain Morris decided to keep me out of circulation for two months to let my beard and hair grow longer. It seems Levesque had a scraggly beard à la ZZ Top that came down to the middle of his chest. They decided two months would be about right with some cosmetic extensions to my beard.

That would give me time enough to fall into my role as an outlaw biker. I needed time to memorize Levesque's dossier and the facts about his West Coast gang. It was almost two inches thick. There couldn't be any mistakes. Whoever their informant was, he was thorough. If anyone asked questions, my life depended on my answering correctly.

The part that really piqued my interest was Levesque's bike. He had a fully customized 1946 Harley-Davidson 1200 cc Knucklehead Type 74 with a four-speed gear box, hand gear change, and foot clutch. It's a double-cradle frame with pressure lubrication. I always wanted a 74, but no way could I afford one.

I couldn't wait to try it out. It had a 53 HP engine with a single carburetor and overhead valves. The specs didn't say in the report, but it weighed 560 lbs. and had a max speed of 110 MPH. Man-o-man, it was painted candy-apple red. They were going to let me ride the holy grail of bikes. As far as I was concerned, it didn't get any better than this. I felt like a kid at Christmas.

"Chance, we'll have the bike ready next week. We'll deliver it to your home, but it must be after dark. When you're trying it out, it must be after dark as well. We can't take a chance on your being seen with it."

"I've been thinking about that, and I have a better location for the bike. I'll give you directions to my parents' property on Highway 47. It's in the country with the closest neighbor a half-mile away. You can deliver it there, and I'll keep it out there."

"Excellent. We'll do that."

The next several weeks I familiarized myself with the Harley 74 and memorized the dossier on Levesque. My captain came by from time to time and quizzed me on Levesque. I took long rides in the country and immersed myself in this new role of rogue biker.

On the last day of the second month, the wind was gusting and spitting rain in my face. I kissed my wife goodbye. I stopped by my parents' farm to get the bike. The bike started on the first try. I let out the clutch and headed for Interstate 77 and then I70. I took the exit for Highway 62 before Columbus toward Gambier.

Once away from the city and traffic, I rode until I saw the sign for Crazy Dave's Bar-B-Q Pit, up ahead on the right. The weather had chilled me to the bone, and I was glad for a place to seek shelter even if it was Crazy Dave's. A neon sign flashed EATS. I heard the roar of motorcycles long before I reached the hangout. Pulling into the gravel parking lot, I noticed it was more red clay dirt than gravel.

Besides gasoline and oil, I caught a whiff of the heady aroma of wood smoke and barbeque in the air. My mouth watered. I hadn't eaten anything since breakfast. Mostly I wanted a place to warm my stiff arms and legs. Turning my bike around, I pointed it toward the open highway at the far corner of the parking lot, ready for a fast getaway if the situation went south.

Walking toward the bar, I had to fight my way through a mud shower of returning motorcycles in the parking lot. Negotiating mud puddles, I made it to the front door. Standing in the doorway, I let my eyes adjust to the dim light and waited for some of the cigarette smoke cloud to settle. Apparently, the ban on smoking in restaurants and bars did not apply here.

Four men in the middle of the room were shooting pool. Two men leaned against the bar. I strolled across the room to the bar. All action stopped as if something had suspended the room in time. I felt every eye in the room follow me. Bellying up to the bar, I waited for the bartender to come over.

The bartender had to be Crazy Dave from the description Captain Morris had given me. He was six foot six if he was an inch. If I had to guess, I would say he was closer to seven feet. Mercy, the man was built like a refrigerator with a head and stubby arms. There was a pack of Camel cigarettes rolled up in his T-shirt sleeve. His arms revealed a tattoo of a skull and cross bones on the right. On the left, he had barbed wire wrapped around some creature with blood dripping from its fangs. On his neck, there was a spider web with what looked like a black widow spider. He wore a red bandana on his head. He must have been bald since I didn't see a fringe of hair peeping under the bandana.

Dave leaned against the bar and pretended to talk to the two men at the far end of the bar. While he talked to the two men, he watched me out of the corner of his eye. He did not move until I turned around to watch the four pool players in the middle of the room. Wiping the bar vigorously, he made his way down toward me at a snail's pace.

He worked his way almost to me. I turned back to the bar after the pool players quit. In the bar mirror, I saw two men start my way. They stopped before they reached me and turned around. I saw the bartender signal them to go away. While I waited for the bartender to speak, I watched him continued to rub down the bar with his head bent.

When he had almost rubbed the varnish off the bar, he decided to speak. "What'll it be, mister?" he mumbled and continued wiping the bar in front of me with his head down.

"Anything to warm me up. How about a schooner of whatever you have on draft? Do you serve food at the bar? I haven't eaten all day."

He appeared to decide I was no threat and was willing to serve me. "One beer coming right up. What ya want to eat?"

"What do you recommend? I'm assuming you're Crazy Dave, and this is your establishment."

"You'd be right. Pulled pork sandwich is the specialty of the house."

"That suits me. How about French fries and slaw on the side?"

"Coming right up." Crazy Dave yelled through hole in the wall, "Maylene, plate up the special."

Dave pulled 20 ounces of nectar of the gods from the tap with very little head and slid it down the bar to me. I took a drink and wiped my mouth on the back of my hand. I was glad my mother would never find out about this. She was a stickler for using a napkin and manners.

Before I'd drunk half of my beer, a plate of the best pulled pork I had ever tasted was in front of me. The beer-battered seasoned French fries tasted like heaven, and the slaw was creamy with a slight tang. I ate without looking up from my plate until every scrap of food disappeared. I paid my bill and ordered another schooner. After I'd put my money on the bar for the beer, I turned around and scanned the room. By this time, the bar was filling up. From the whispers going around and eyes darting in my direction, the atmosphere was not feeling friendly.

One stout, bowlegged biker strolled up to me. He must have been in his forties, with a nice start on a beer belly. That took nothing away from the muscles he kept flexing. It was hard to tell the color of his greasy hair, hanging in strings around his face. He kept pushing it back and tried to look menacing.

He looked me up and down and sneered. "I've not seen you in here before. You new to the area or are you one o' them Sunday cycle riders?" He threw his cigarette butt down on the sawdust floor at my feet and stubbed it out with the toe of his boot.

I gave him a wide-eyed stare before I spoke. "Don't know what you mean by Sunday rider. I'm more often than not too hung over to ride on Sunday. Not that it should matter to you, but I'm not from around here. Just passing through your fair country. I've been riding for four days and sleeping rough. Is there a motel around here? I could use a little comfort."

He turned on his heels without saying another word and went back to a booth by the side door.

Dave cleared his throat behind me. "No offense, mister, but I couldn't help hearing about you needing a motel. Around here, we don't take to strangers. But in answer to your question, there's a motel about a mile down the road north of here. Keep on the road you're on and turn left at the fork. It's called Dean's Budget Motel. It ain't anything special, but it's clean. Anything else you want for your comfort is up to you to find."

"Thanks, a good night's sleep and a hot shower are all I'm looking for, for now."

I drank the rest of my beer, pushed off from the bar, and started toward the door. Halfway across the room, two men stepped in front of me. I guessed the taller of the two must be Stoney. He was about my height with scraggly, dirty-blond hair and a scar down his right jawline. His face sported a couple of days' beard growth.

He looked me up and down. The picture Captain Morris had was not good and had been taken from a distance, but this man fitted the description of Stoney. The red plaid shirt he wore hung out over dark blue jeans. I could see the bulge of a pistol in the front of his pants. His almost colorless gray, bloodshot eyes bore into me.

The other man was a head shorter and thirty pounds heavier. He had dark brown curly hair and dark brown close-set eyes. He was clean shaven with no noticeable scars. He had to be Sully. I remember the captain saying where you found one, you saw the other. Sully was dressed in a blue denim shirt with a khaki collar and cuffs. His shirt was tucked into faded jeans. I didn't see the bulge of a gun, but he had a hunting knife in a sheath on his belt. The flap was undone for easy access.

It was looking like I would have to fight my way out. I calculated my options, but the way the men were moving behind me made a clean getaway not an option. I watched the other bikers out of the corner of my eye and directed my wide-eyed stare at Stoney. He was the first to look away. I guess that made me the winner.

"That your bike out front? The red one," Stoney said.

"Yeah, what about it?" I tried to put as much quarrel in my voice as I thought a man in my position would.

"It's a 74, ain't it? I always wanted me one of them. They're scarce. Where'd you get it?"

"Santa Claus left it under the tree 'cause I've been a good boy. Now, step out of the way," I said through my teeth.

Stoney and I stood toe to toe by this time. It reminded me of a cockfight we once raided. I watched an antsy Sully as he clenched and unclenched his fists. The tension in the room was palpable.

Stoney smiled and looked around the room, then back at me. "No need to get in an uproar. We didn't mean nothin' by what we said. We been admiring your 74 is all." He continued to stand in front of me.

Sully did the same.

"Are you going to get out of my way or are we going to stand here all night? I'm tired. I don't have time for this foolishness. If you're looking for trouble, you've come to the right place. Let's get it on so I can get a good night's sleep."

"You sure are touchy. We don't want no trouble." Stoney took a step back with his hands up.

Sully did the same.

I sidled between them, keeping both men in my sight with the help of the beer sign mirror next to the door. My first thought was to run, but I forced myself to amble leisurely toward my bike. It was like being thrown in a dangerous animal's cage at the zoo. Any show of nerves or unease would show weakness. After all, I was expected to be a psychopath.

I mounted up and started the engine. Stoney and Sully were in my rearview mirror, standing about halfway between me and the door. I left the parking lot and headed toward the motel. Before I reached the motel, I heard bikes coming behind me. I slipped my gun from the saddlebag into the back of my jeans. They came up alongside me and motioned for me to pull over. I pulled to the side of the road, but I didn't shut off the engine. They pulled alongside, one on either side of me.

I glared at Stoney and then glanced around at Sully. I figured a little crazy was appropriate for the situation. "What do you want?"

"Hey, man, we don't want nothing. We thought we might do you a favor."

"I don't need any favors. I'm tired, and I'm on the trail of a room where I plan to sleep for two days. Now get out of my way."

"You just might need a favor, friend. We ran your plates. The name we got back and the description ain't you. It's your brother-in-law, Dale Macon."

"How'd you run my plates? You the law or something?" I stared at them before I grinned and said, "By the way, my brother-in-law is Tony Gottlieb."

"All right, just checking. We got friends in high or low places, depending on how you look at it."

"If you ain't the law, what do you care?" I tried to come across as angry instead of nervous.

"Look, man, we ain't no cops." Stoney spit on the ground and looked up with a grin.

"What'd you mean by that crack about running my plates if you ain't cops?"

"We got a friend in the police department that keeps us informed. He thinks you're Gunner Levesque. He said the Feds are looking for you."

"What if they are? You plan on doing something about it? Maybe you're looking to collect a reward. You can try to collect, but I wouldn't advise it. I ain't been good at too much in my life, but what I am good at is killing."

"Man, you sure are quick to take offense. We only want to help out a brother soldier of the road. If you go to the motel Dave sent you to, you're libel to get nabbed. The cops cruise that joint every other day at least and run plates."

"Where would you suggest I go?"

"That's why we been asking these questions. My name's Stoney and this here's Sully. That's our gang back at Dave's. We got us a little something going five miles from here on a farm. There's an old Airstream travel trailer there you can use until you're ready to leave. No strings.

"We heard about you from Sully's brother. He said at that shoot-out at the bar in California, you held off five bangers, killed one, and wounded two local Leos before enforcements showed up. He says you escaped in the trunk of a police car, and that's one reason the cops are mad as hatters. They can't prove you were the one doing the shooting, or you were even there."

I took off my helmet and stared at Stoney. "Maybe you can tell me what I had for breakfast yesterday, or you know where my mum went after she left me on the steps of St. Anthony's?"

"You're a stranger, and you stroll into our place. We like to know who we're dealing with. You can't be too be careful these days. We already had two undercover cops sniffing around. We're satisfied who you are."

He held up a picture of what he thought was me on his cell phone. It was Levesque's picture off his driver's license. I think I take a better picture, if I do say so myself.

"Do you want to stay at the farm or not? Don't make no never mind to us. A word of warning. If it turns out you're not who you say you are,

I'll make it my mission to destroy everyone you love. Then I'll destroy you. Are we clear?"

"A word of warning for you as well. You touch anyone in my family, and I'll do the same to you. Just so we're clear." I put as much menace into my voice as I could. Little did I know what would happen down the road.

Stoney spit again. "Back to the how come we stopped you."

"You said no strings. I can leave any time I want. I need a place for two or three days, and then I'm on my way out of the country. It's too hot here."

"That's what we're offering. Our only condition is we'll have to blindfold you in and out of the farm. Sully, here, will put your cycle in the back of his pickup. You need to hand over your cell as well."

"I need my phone. Why should I give it to you? I'm expecting a call from a friend that's helping me get out of the country."

"We'll keep it turned on. If this friend calls, we'll let you know."

"What about my gun? I'm not giving that up."

"We're not asking you to. You want the RV or not?"

"Yeah, I need a place to lie low for a while. I don't have much of a choice, so I guess I'll trust you for now. If you double-cross me, hell will seem like a vacation spot compared to what I'll do to you."

The two men laughed, but the mirth didn't reach their eyes. It was like facing down a couple of rattlesnakes.

I expected them to ask for my cell. I was sure they would check my calls in and out and look for anything suspicious. It was a burner, and it was clean except for one number. The number of my contact in Erie. If they checked, they would find he had a fishing boat and a record for smuggling. That should satisfy them.

I had a second phone in a special pocket inside my boot. I had disabled the GPS, and the phone itself was turned off until I needed it. This would be my only means of communication. To say I was on my own was an understatement. No one knew where I was. I didn't even know.

Sully left and returned a short time later with a black three-quarter-ton pickup with tinted windows. He ran my bike up the ramp and onto the back of his truck. He tied it down, and we stepped inside the cab of his truck. Stoney put a blindfold over my eyes, and we were on our way. When we arrived at the farm, Sully removed the blindfold.

To my surprise, we were definitely on a farm. Not only that, but it was a working dairy farm. A man was bringing the cows in from the pasture to the barn as we drove up. A man and woman came out of the main house walking toward the barn. We stepped out of the truck and went around to the tailgate.

Stoney saw me looking at the couple. "Them two there's Don and Bonnie. It's their farm. Over there's the RV. Help yourself," he said and nodded in the direction of an ancient Airstream RV with a deck in front and a shed on the side.

I nodded at the owners, but either they didn't see, or they ignored me. After letting down the ramps on Sully's truck, I untied my bike and rolled it off the back. The shed beside the RV had just enough room for my bike. I rolled my bike in there and took my saddlebags with me to the trailer. I stepped onto the deck and glanced back at my bike. Sully didn't think I saw him, but I watched him slide around behind the shed and come in from the back. He chained my motorcycle to one of the supports for the shed.

I opened the door to the trailer and stepped in. To my surprise, there was a TV, and canned food in the pantry. The refrigerator was stocked with beer. I found clean sheets and blankets in a closet. I made up my bed, took a beer from the fridge, and sat down to watch TV.

I sat where I could watch Stoney and Sully with Don and Bonnie through the open door. They gave the impression of an argument going on between Stoney and Don. From the hand gestures, I figured I must be the topic of conversation. No doubt they would go over my bike and check my saddlebags first chance they got.

Captain Morris was right. They had a mole in the department. It wouldn't take long to find out who ran my plates. In case they had the place bugged, I couldn't take a chance of using my hidden phone. I searched the usual places for a concealed camera or microphone, but I didn't find one. It didn't mean there wasn't one.

I would have to go for a recon later that night and use my phone when I felt safe. I needed to deploy the camera as soon as possible. I couldn't take a chance on their finding it and me still here. The camera, along with the trackers, was small and hidden in a secret compartment in my saddlebags.

Don came down to the RV around six PM carrying a basket. He was of average height with dark brown thinning hair, graying around the temples. His hooded hazel eyes looked out of his clean-shaven face. His denim shirt and jeans were worn but clean. He knocked and set the basket down on a rail of the deck.

I moved to the door before he stepped off the deck. "Hello. Say, what's this?"

He turned and looked me up and down before he spoke. "Yeah, well, my wife sent down supper. I don't want you coming up to the house. My wife...she's not well. After what's happened, I don't want any more strangers around my farm. Stoney said you're OK, but I can't afford to take chances. There's too much at stake. He thought the last two were OK. Turns out he was dead wrong."

"I don't give a rat's ass about what happened before I came. I don't like being here anymore than you like me here. All I want is a place to rest and to keep a low profile for two or three days. After that, I'll be on my way. No sweat."

"Whatever." Don shrugged and pivoted on the heel of his boot. He strode back to the farmhouse. I watched him go before looking to see what was in the basket. I expected a sandwich at the most. There was fried chicken, potato salad, green beans, and biscuits. I opened the last container to find a blackberry cobbler.

After my big meal, I lay down to rest. I expected to be busy later that night. My alarm was set for three a.m. Closing my eyes, I must have fallen asleep the moment I shut my eyes. When the alarm sounded, I almost jumped off the sofa. It took a minute for me to get my bearings and remember where I was. I took out my cell from the hidden pocket inside my boot and reactivated the GPS.

I put on my moccasins and ripped the seam in my saddlebags to get to the hidden compartment, which concealed a pencil-thin webcam and trackers no bigger than a dime. When I turned my cell on and checked, I noticed the farm had Wi-Fi. I hoped the captain could capture the video when it went into operation.

The webcam was battery operated and from my experience, the battery's life span would not last more than three or four days. It was motion activated, so that might save a little on battery usage. The most likely location for the lab had to be the barn. It had the room, and the odor of cows and milking to hide the aroma of meth. The barn would be my initial stop. Assuming the lab was in the barn and I could get into the lab, I had to place the webcam tonight first thing. I might not get another chance.

* * * *

Looking back to that night while I sat there in the waiting room of the police station, I felt the sweat of nerves coming through my shirt, although the room was cool. Everything rushed at me with clarity. Thinking about it made it hard to catch my breath. My chest was pounding as it had been that night. I stood up and walked around the waiting room. I made myself sit back down. Unfortunately, the trouble with painful memories is they won't leave you in peace. Against my will, I remembered the rest.

47

Chapter 3

Setting a course toward the barn, I'd used the shadows of a shed, a tractor, and the various farm implements to advantage. As luck would have it, there was a full moon. The night was almost as bright as the day. Twenty feet before the barn, I ran out of cover. I scanned the area, looked up at the farmhouse, and took a deep breath before making a dash for the side door of the barn. Flattening myself against the rough wood of the barn, I sidled down to the side door. Someone must have oiled the hinges. The door opened quietly. I cracked the door and listened, but I did not hear anyone inside the barn. I decided to chance it and step inside. I took a deep breath before venturing farther into the barn. The silence of the barn was almost deafening. Apparently, they did not think there was a need for a guard.

Surprised as well as puzzled, I found an immaculate milking room. I thought the lab must be somewhere else as I made my way across the wide expanse of the room. Nothing was out of place. Everything looked to be neat and orderly, ready for the next day's milking. I wondered if I had risked my cover in vain. If the lab wasn't here, where could it be?

Moving around the room, I caught a whiff of something strange to the environment. The smells of fresh milk and cows were strong the minute I stepped inside, but this was something utterly foreign to the environment. An ordinary working farm was the beauty of this operation. Added to the dairy aroma, I picked up another, more pungent smell coming from the far side of the room. The odor was faint at first, but the closer I came to the far wall, the stronger the odor.

I made a rough estimate and decided the milking room took up three-quarters of the barn. Where had they stashed the lab, and how was I going to find it? If it was in the unaccounted-for quarter of the barn space, how was I going to get in the lab?

The moonlight coming through the window reflected off a lone rack on the far wall. It looked out of place as the only piece of equipment against the wall. I examined the rack. Behind the rack of milk cans and assorted odds and ends, I noticed a lock on the wall. On closer inspection, I could see the faint outline of a door. The rack was on rollers and easily slid away from the wall. I picked the lock while holding a small LED light in my mouth. The door did not have a doorknob or handle. I pushed on the door, and it popped open.

Once inside the room, my eyes adjusted to the dark with the help of the moonlight coming through windows high up in the room. As I scanned the room, I saw it had its own ventilation system, water, and electricity from a generator. I blinked my eyes several times. I couldn't believe I had stumbled on to the lab. The lab everyone was trying to find.

Using my LED flashlight, I scanned the room. In one corner, they had twenty-seven various firearms lined up against the wall. There were two kilos of hashish and another three kilos of cocaine on a table. I found a packing box with at least 2,000 prescription pills of the OxyContin variety. Next to the table was a tablet press capable of producing upward of 1,400 tablets a minute. I glanced at an open packing box sitting in the chair beside the table. It contained several zip bags in the box filled with pills. They must have had several thousand pills ready to go. I took pictures with my phone.

It was definitely the lab the FBI, as well as the West Virginia and Ohio police, were trying to find. The stench from cooking meth permeated everything. I found a mask and covered my face to keep from breathing in the toxic fumes in the room. My next problem was finding an inconspicuous place to position the webcam. A ladder leaned against the wall at the far end of the room. I carried the ladder to where I could lean it against the loft railing.

Climbing into the loft, I crawled over to the ventilation system, trying to keep from being seen through the loft windows. It was the perfect spot to place the pencil-thin webcam. The camera was black, and the base of the ventilation system was also black. The camera gave off a soft glow when it was working, but I didn't think the workers would look up from their tasks. The webcam would be hard to see anyway through the gear the lab workers had to wear while in production and packaging. I pointed the camera at the lab table, turned it on, and helped it piggyback off the farm's Wi-Fi with the app on my phone.

I had found what I came to see. I needed to make my way outside as quickly as possible, and with a bit of luck, no one would see me. After replacing the ladder, I relocked the door and pushed the rack into place. After I opened the side door, I stepped back into the cool, clean night air.

On my way back to the trailer, I rounded the last shed and heard someone cough. I stopped in mid-stride and fell back in the shadows. Peering around the corner of the shed, I saw Don standing outside his back door smoking. He finished his cigarette, stamped it out in a bucket of sand by the door, and started walking toward the barn. He reminded me of Phil and his nightly patrol.

I kept in the shadows and slipped behind a hay baler in the nick of time. Don slid the main door back and stepped inside the barn. I took the opportunity to make a hasty retreat to my trailer. When I'd made a dash for the barn, I'd left the trailer door ajar so as to not to make any noise opening and closing it. Once safely back in the trailer, I stayed by the window watching for Don. I hoped I had put everything back like I'd found it.

A short time later, Don came out of the barn by the side door. I scarcely had time to undress before he made his way over to my trailer. His flashlight shone over my bike. He walked over to the bike and examined it using his flashlight. He stood back and continued to stare at my motorcycle before he walked around it. The only article of interest about the bike would have been my saddlebags, but I'd brought them in with me. Don turned and made his way to my trailer. He stepped upon the deck and tried the door to the RV. I'd locked it on my return.

I slid beneath the covers and pretended to be asleep. I watched through my eyelashes and glimpsed Don peering into my bedroom window. He appeared satisfied and moved away while lighting another cigarette. I got up and watched him amble back to his house. I sat down on my bed and drew a long breath. This had been a close call, too close.

After Don returned to his house, I waited for an hour before stepping outside again. I moved behind the trailer and walked across the pasture. In back of the trailer was a giant rock; I'd noticed it earlier. Sitting down behind it, I took out my phone, activated it, and called the captain. He answered on the first ring.

He spoke before I could say anything.

"Chance, I've been waiting on pins and needles. Are you all right? We were getting worried. I have Captain Morris here with me and John Russell of the FBI."

"This is the first chance I've had to call you. Stoney invited me to stay at the farm for a few days. The captain was right. There is an informant in Columbus. I don't know a name, but someone ran my plates. That should be easy enough to check. They have a professional lab set up in an active dairy barn. The farm has Wi-Fi with the name 'Busy Zelda.'

"I deployed the webcam and piggybacked it off their Wi-Fi. That will be more reliable than my cell phone. They did not have the guest user password-protected. It's also riskier to do it this way, but I thought it worth the risk. Once people set their router up, they rarely check it again unless something is wrong with the device.

"I have no idea where I am, except I'm about five miles northeast of Crazy Dave's. They blindfolded me to bring me here. I have the first names of the dairy farm owners. Stoney called them Don and Bonnie. See if you can pick up my cell transmission. I texted you the webcam's IP address. Did you get it?"

"Yeah, we did. Hold on. We're checking it now."

"With GPS, you should be able to ping me. I can't keep my phone on for long. I don't know what their security measures are. These people are nobody's fools. I have to get back to my trailer. I took pictures in the lab, which I've emailed to you."

"Hold on, we're getting something now. The FBI came to my house and set up the software on my laptop. Captain Morris is checking my computer as we speak. Just a sec, let me take a look. OK, OK, we've got you. We're trying to find the webcam."

"It's dark in there, but the webcam picks up in night conditions," I said.

"Well, I'll be a son of a gun. We got it. Coming in clear. Russell will notify the FBI, and we'll get ready to raid. We want to catch them in full production at the time of the raid. We need to catch all parties involved.

"Another problem we have is, we don't want to show our hand until we put eyes on their distribution points. We will coordinate everything through the FBI because of the mole in the department. Where there's one mole, they could have another. We can't take any chances.

"You've done good, son, but you need to get out as soon as possible. The longer you stay, the more dangerous for you."

"I can't leave too soon and take a chance on them getting suspicious. I still need to find out a little more about the operation, and then I'll leave. I can't keep this phone on any longer than necessary. The farmer is already suspicious. The next time I call, I'll be on my way out of here. Tell Morris about the mole. I'll put trackers on the distribution vehicles if I get a chance. 'Til next time." I disabled the GPS again and turned my phone off before hiding it in my boot.

At the trailer, I slept sporadically until daybreak. It was overcast, and my head ached. It felt like an anvil sat on top of my forehead. I staggered to the kitchen and made a pot of coffee. Cool mornings were what I enjoyed the most.

I took my cup out on the deck and watched the sun breaking through the clouds. The clouds were backlit by the sun, giving them a halo effect. I watched the clouds turn colors as I sat sipping my coffee. Every time I see clouds, I think of the painter Bob Ross. I still watch him on DVD. I have his entire PBS series.

The old adage kept running through my mind. "Red sky at night, sailors' delight. Red sky in morning, sailors take warning." I should have taken heed. This was indeed an omen. I had never seen the morning clouds turn such a deep crimson color with purple edges.

I looked up and saw the lady of the house coming my way with another basket. She looked to be in her late forties. She was painfully thin with pale skin and fine, light brown hair. Her husband said she had been sick. She had no eyebrows or eyelashes, and what hair she had was graying and thin. It was not hard to recognize the ravages of cancer and chemotherapy.

She walked up on the deck and handed me a basket. "I saw you come out on the deck, Mr. Levesque. I figured you might be hungry, so I made your breakfast. It's just eggs, bacon, and toast. I put some of my homemade apple jelly in there."

"Thanks. Wait a second and I'll get your basket from last night." I went into the kitchen and grabbed the basket.

She took the basket and turned to leave. I needed to gain her trust and find out what she knew.

If I could get her talking, I might find out more from her than nosing around on my own. "Ma'am, you can call me Gunner. That's what most people call me. I'm sorry, but no one told me your name."

"My husband said not to have anything to do with you or tell you our names. I can't see any harm in it. My name's Bonnie and my husband is Don."

"I appreciate the food. It's been a long time since I had a good home-cooked meal. Thanks for supper last night. Won't you sit down a while? I'll eat this before it gets cold, and you can take both baskets back."

I kept my head down and pretended to make small talk. "Your husband not here today?"

In between bites, I looked up and watched. I could tell she didn't want to go against her husband's wishes, but she wanted to talk. She looked back at the house and then at me. She sat down and let out a sigh. I could see a certain sadness in her eyes and something more. Maybe desperation as well.

"I believe I will sit. It's pleasant here on the deck. We used to have a full-time hired hand. This is where he stayed. His name was George, but everyone called him Pop. He died before I got sick. We can't afford a hired hand now or chance it is more to the point. Don's gone into Columbus for supplies."

"It must get lonesome out here for you."

"Sometimes, but generally I like the peace and quiet. When I was well, we used to take vacation trips to Wyoming and Montana during summer break. Did you know you could ride for three days on horseback across Wyoming and not come across another person? I enjoyed those trips and the solitude with just me and Don. We had no worries then. Not like today." Her eyes misted as she stared into space. She looked back at me and shook her head.

"Every now and then, you want to talk to someone even if it is only small talk. When it was just me and Don, we could talk about anything. Nowadays, it seems all he can talk about is our situation." She looked back at the barn and sighed. "It's peaceful now, but it'll get busy here in the next couple of days. I suppose you'll be staying for a few days."

"Yes, Ma'am. I have to get back on the road pretty soon. I'm thinking when I get to where I'm going, I might set up an operation such as this. How'd Don and Stoney meet? From what I've seen, they're from different worlds. It isn't likely their paths would have crossed."

"I wish their paths had never crossed, but they did that fateful day. It was in the hospital, of all places. We found out I had stage four colon cancer, and I had to be operated on. After that, it meant chemo and radiation. Sully, Stoney's friend, had been gutshot. With both of us being operated on at the same time, they met in the waiting room. I think it would have been better if I had died."

She closed her eyes tightly. When she opened them, one tear escaped and ran down her cheek. She turned her head and wiped the solitary tear away with her hand and watched the clouds gather before she turned around.

"My husband used to teach chemistry at the university, but they had cutbacks. He didn't have tenure. It's the same old story. Last in is the first out. We tried to keep paying our health insurance, but it was getting to be too much. We had a $5,000 deductible and insurance only paid 80 percent, so we were left with the $5,000 plus the 20 percent, which amounted to more than $80,000 and growing. The hospital lets you make payments, but a debt that large takes a lifetime to pay off. Even making minimum payments became difficult for us."

"You had the dairy. That must have been income for you."

"Yes, but we needed improvements to the barn. The equipment was worn out and broke down all the time. The herd was tired with mostly old cows. When they had calves, we had to sell them just to keep our heads above water. The bills kept piling up. We had two men working part-time for us, and it was all we could do to pay them.

"Don was worried about me, and he talked to anyone willing to listen. Stoney saw an opportunity for both of them to benefit. In a moment of weakness, Don agreed to this arrangement. He believed it was the only way out of our predicament. A way to pay the bills, and a way to see I had the best medical care. He can't get out of it now."

"I understand about the lab, but what happens after that? It must be hard, not to mention dangerous, to get the product to buyers."

"You ask a lot of questions." She looked at me through narrowed eyes and stood up to leave.

"Yeah, I guess I do, but I want to start an operation like this when I get to where I'm going. Stoney musta told you I'm OK. From what I heard when Stoney and Sully were talking, they have the lab right here on the farm. Sweet."

She sat back down again. "I don't guess there's any harm in telling you a few things. I don't know everything. Don tries to keep as much from me as possible. He's been extremely good to me. He really loves me, you know. Some men would have left at the first talk of cancer."

I nodded that I understood. She smiled sadly.

"I have to keep away and not talk to any of my old friends. The only people I can talk to are bikers, but Don makes me stay in the house when they come. I know you wouldn't be here if you weren't hiding from the law. I'm not stupid. The law must want you, so I guess it's OK to talk."

"Yes, ma'am. I'm trying to leave the country as soon as I can."

"As far as I know from listening to them talk, this is how it goes. This delivery truck comes and picks up the product. It says Phillips A-1 Commercial Food Delivery on the side. The truck delivers to these little mom-and-pop stores. I think he most likely delivers produce to the stores and what they make here.

"Then someone comes to the storeroom at these stores, picks up their supply, and leaves the cash in a lockbox. There's a metal box with a pull-down slot like they have at the bank for after-hours deposits. He walks out of the store with his supply in plastic grocery bags like any other customer. After that someone from Stoney's gang picks up the money and gives us our share."

"Sounds like you got a sweet operation here. You ever been raided?"

"No, not raided. We have had a couple of people nosing around, but Stoney took care of them."

"How'd he do that? What happened to them?" I kept my head down and finished my breakfast.

"You ask a lot of questions for a stranger. I don't ask questions, mister, 'cause I don't want to know the answers. I feel responsible. Sometimes I can't sleep at night for thinking about it. I wish it could be over, but I can't see a way out of this hole. Some days I want to jump in that hole and pull it in after me. I advise you to steer clear of an operation like this one. The hole you dig for yourself gets deeper with each day."

I felt sorry for the frown on her face. She looked down at her hands before taking a ragged breath, then rubbed them together like she was trying to wash away the guilt. Standing up, she hit her hand on the table. She bit her lip and stumbled down the steps, taking the supper basket with her. Almost as an afterthought, she turned at the bottom of the steps and looked up at me.

"Oh, before I forget. I meant to tell you, you'll have to fix your lunch, but I'll be back in time to fix supper. I have to go see my oncologist today."

"Not a problem. There's a well-stocked pantry here. I can do for myself."

"I'd better be going now. It takes me a while to get ready."

I reached over the railing and handed her my breakfast basket. Watching her slowly limp away with hunched shoulders, I felt sorrow wash over me for what was to come and my part in it. I hoped it would give her relief from her guilt. More than likely, it would only add to her burden. At times like this, I remember my grandfather's saying "poor people have poor ways." He understood the human condition more than I ever would.

I sat on my patio the rest of the day and watched. After the evening milking, a white van pulled up and ten men filed out. I sauntered over to the van and saw Stoney get out of the driver's side. I had a cup of coffee in my hand. I leaned against the side of the van and drank my coffee while I placed a tracker under the fender. Another tracker had to be dropped on the delivery van.

I stood up and strolled behind the men into the barn. Before I made it to the door of the lab, Sully stepped in my path and barred the way. Stoney came up behind me. Sully shoved me back a step, poking me in the chest as he spoke. I swatted his finger away with my free hand.

"Stoney, he can't go in there, can he? He can't go waltzing around anywhere he pleases. You know what happened last time. I can't do my job and watch him too."

"It's all right, Sully, I'll take care of it." He waved at Sully to go on in. He turned his attention to me. I could see the danger in those pale eyes as they bored into me. "Why are you nosing around? This wasn't part of the deal when we offered you a place to stay," He moved in closer with his fist clenched ready to do battle.

We were almost nose to nose. I could smell what he had to eat for supper on his breath.

"I'm not nosing around. I saw men get out of the van and wandered over. Anyone with a nose can tell you're cooking meth. When I get to my base in Canada, I'll need an income source. I thought I'd glance over your operation and get an idea of what I needed to do. But if that makes you nervous, I'll go on back to my trailer." I took a step backward with my hands up, almost tripping over Sully's big feet, and grinned.

"I don't let anyone in here that I haven't known since they were babies. This is the sweetest operation I've ever had and ain't nobody gonna mess it up for me. You turn around and mosey on out of here. If I catch you up here again, I'll show you what I do to Nosy Rosies."

"Look, man, I didn't mean no harm." I saluted him and went through the barn door as Don was coming in.

I heard Sully say, "I don't trust that guy. There's something not right about him."

"We had him checked out by our friend on the force. The police don't make mistakes. Everything about him right down to his bike checks out. No informant would have such a sweet ride as that 74. Relax, no need to get uptight."

I heard him chuckle.

"Can't say I blame him nosing around. The operation we got going is perfect."

I could feel several sets of eyes boring into my back all the way to my trailer. I entered and closed the door. When they were busy inside the barn, I walked behind the trailer. I took out my phone and texted the captain about the operation. I turned my phone off the second I sent the transmission. There was nothing left to do but go back and sit on the deck. All I did the rest of the day was drink coffee and watch.

I sat on the deck until after dark settled in, then went back in the trailer and lay down. My alarm sounded at three a.m.. From my trailer, I could see a light still on in the barn. The first group left shortly after four.

Two farmhands came around five and did the morning milking. I wondered if they had an inkling about what was going on, or were they in on it as well? They'd have to be clueless not to guess something was not right. When they left, a van pulled up and Don came out of the house. He followed the delivery driver into the barn.

I strolled over to the van and sat on the bumper. I slipped a tracker behind the delivery van's license plate and continued to sip my coffee. Don and the deliveryman came out carrying boxes marked 'produce.' I saw a frown cross Don's face. They set their boxes down and looked at each other and then at me.

Don grimaced, cleared his throat, and walked over to where I sat. "What are you doing here? Get on back to the trailer. Stoney told you not to wander around. I think you've been here long enough."

I stood up and tried to act as innocent as possible. "You said not to come up to your house. I was waiting to talk to you. I don't know how to contact Stoney. Tell him I'm ready to go." I turned and strolled back to my trailer.

Stoney arrived in early afternoon with Sully and loaded my bike. They blindfolded me again and took me out to I70. I unloaded my bike and started it up. I looked at Stoney and waited. He stared back at me but didn't say anything.

"Stoney, aren't you forgetting something?" I held out my hand.

"I don't think...Oh, yeah, here's your cell. Your friend called. He said to keep low and meet him in New Boston. He said you'd know the place. He said it's a go for tomorrow night."

"Thanks, I'll be on my way. I won't forget this. If you're ever in BC, look me up." I waved goodbye and let out the clutch.

I was on the road and away in thirty seconds. Watching Stoney fade from view in my rearview mirror released some of the tension in my shoulders. I kept my eyes on both men until I was out of their sight. New Boston was the code word for my rendezvous. I went up Interstate 70 and turned onto I 77 toward Cleveland like a good fugitive, in case they followed me. If everything worked out, I would turn on to I 271 past Akron and meet Morris at the next rest area. I sent the captain a text to let him know I was on my way there.

I saw a rest area up ahead. It had a sign that said closed for maintenance. In the parking area, a trailer had New Boston Construction written across the side. It looked like any other parked tractor trailer in a work area. I pulled in and walked up to the trailer door and knocked. The door came open, and a ramp slid out. I stowed my bike inside. Captain Morris came forward and shook my hand.

"Well done, Sunday, well done. The webcam came in very clear, and your trackers are working like a charm. We're coordinating the addresses. It's just like the lady told you. These are all mom-and-pop stores. The FBI is setting up surveillance at each. We'll be able to watch their operation as it unfolds and make a clean sweep of the whole gang, including local pushers. We knew it was far-reaching, but this beats anything we expected."

"Excellent. Glad I could be a part of your operation. Uh, Captain, could I talk to you in private?"

"Sure, come over here. There's a small office."

We entered the office and sat. The office was not big enough for more than two chairs and a card table. I sat and wondered how to begin.

"What's on your mind?"

"Sir, the woman at the farm, Bonnie, can she be left out of this? She's sick with cancer, and she did not participate in the production or sale of the drugs. She has no control over what her husband is doing. And to tell you the truth, I feel sorry for him. He made a bad decision in a dreadful circumstance. Any one of us might have done the same. He was worried about his sick wife with no way to pay the mounting medical bills."

"We can't let him off scot-free. He's the reason the gang is prospering."

"I know, I know, but couldn't you offer him a deal for his testimony against the gang and just leave her out of all this?"

"I'll talk to the DA and see what we can do, but I can't promise anything."

"That's all I ask. Maybe I'm going soft, but you didn't meet these people. I did. They're good people down deep. They were desperate when Stoney came along and dangled a way out in front of them."

"Like I said, I'll talk to the DA. Your part's done. I have an unmarked patrol car waiting to take you home."

"Thanks; will I have to testify?"

"I can't make any promises at this point. As of now, it looks like we have enough to charge them without your testimony. We'll list you as an informant and keep your name off the record. I know he threatened your family. I have no doubt he will make good on his threat if he finds out your identity. The trouble with these gangs is they have connections inside and outside of prison. I don't blame you for being cautious. Try not to worry. We'll provide your family with protection until the trial is over."

"Thanks, sir." I stood up to leave.

He came around the desk and shook my hand. "Sunday, go on home. You deserve a rest. Your captain said to take the rest of the week off."

The unmarked patrol car let me out at my home as Joyce dropped my son, Jesse, off from school. A short time later, Amy arrived home from work. I shaved and cleaned up before going to my barber for a haircut. To celebrate my safe return, we went to dinner at our favorite Italian restaurant on Seventh Street. We ordered the family favorite, seafood spaghetti with Alfredo sauce.

The days turned into a month while I waited for news of my promotion to detective. Jason decided to stay on a little longer and finish a case. The FBI closed in and arrested the gang along with their associates with the first two weeks after my return to Parkersburg. Their dragnet snared ordinary citizens, including a well-known millionaire CEO thrown in for good measure.

They made fifty raids, arrested seventy-two people, and confiscated 20 kilos of marijuana, 7.5 pounds of meth, and 2,000 prescription pills, along with a boat and twenty assorted vehicles. As icing on the cake, they found evidence of insurance fraud. This was just at first glance; they now had access to the gang members' bank accounts and books. Crazy Dave also came under close scrutiny, but so far, they had nothing on him.

In the middle of all of this, I received word that both my parents had been killed in Reston, Virginia, in a car accident. I had to fly to Reston to take care of funeral arrangements. I brought them home to West Virginia. I can still remember standing under the tent at the cemetery and listening to the rain beat on the roof. My feeling is that when a person dies, it should rain. A cheerful, sunny day seems disrespectful somehow. My parents had not lived in Parkersburg for more than thirty years. Few people remembered or knew them anymore. There were not many old friends at the funeral and only a handful of flowers.

When I glanced around the cemetery, I was alone. Amy and Jesse were in the limo trying to stay warm, waiting on me. The next thing I remember was the men filling in the grave. I still remember the feel of Amy's warm hand when she put her hand in mine and stood beside me after they had filled in the grave. After a period of time when we were both getting cold, she took my hand and forced me to come with her to the limo. I don't remember much about the next couple of months.

After the funeral I left for New York to close up their apartment and take care of whatever loose ends were left. There was so much to do I didn't have time to grieve. My wife helped me, or I would never have made it through everything. Nothing seemed real. Both my parents gone in a heartbeat.

The will was probated, and I sold my parents' condo. They left me financially secure. I would not have to work if I didn't want to. Their lawyer referred me to a financial planner, and he handles everything. The money accumulates, but I haven't touched it. I know it's silly, but I can't think about it without feeling depressed.

Their housekeeper helped to dispose of their furniture. I kept a few pieces that reminded me of my childhood, like my father's ancient beat-up rolltop desk. I also kept a Tiffany lamp I remembered sitting on his desk when I was a child. They still had my old bedroom furniture in the spare bedroom. I kept that. Everything that didn't sell is in storage.

The next time the other shoe dropped, I was at a convenience-store robbery. The clerk had been pistol-whipped and left in a pool of blood, but he would survive. I can still see the captain as he pulled up to where I sat filling out a report on the robbery in my cruiser. I waved and finished my report. The captain strolled over to my car and leaned against the rear window. He had a grave look, which made me a little anxious. He stood without saying anything and looked uneasy himself.

I turned around in my seat. "Captain, you're out early. Is something wrong?"

"Chance, what time did you get here?"

"The robbery took place at 2:05 a.m., and I arrived at 2:15. Dotson was nearby and arrived a short time before me. Rescue worked on the store clerk awhile before the ambulance took the clerk to the hospital at 2:30, and the crime lab arrived at about 2:20. They were here until thirty minutes ago. What's this about?"

"Chance, is there someone who can vouch for you between 2:20 and 5 a.m.?"

"I guess you can ask the crime lab or Dotson. Someone must have seen me nearby. I helped them bring in their equipment. I don't understand. Did someone say I wasn't here?"

"No, I need to make sure you have an alibi."

"An alibi?. Why do I need an alibi? I didn't rob the store."

"I know, I know. There's no easy way to say this, son. I don't mean it to sound harsh, but I don't know how else to say it. Chance, your wife and son were killed around 5:30 this morning in Marietta. I wanted to make sure you had nothing to do with it. The husband is always the first suspect. Since it's one of our own involved, the state police will be investigating."

"Wait...my wife...my wife, Amy, and, and...Jesse? No, no! This can't be! What were they doing in Marietta? I don't understand. Was it a car wreck?"

"No, they were killed execution-style and dumped by the side of the road in Boaz. A man out walking his dog saw two men dump the bodies out of a white van and speed away. He called the police."

The stark description didn't sink in until sometime later.

"Captain, Joyce was carpooling this week and taking the boys to and from school."

"That was my first thought. I called Joyce, and she said Amy called this morning at around five and said someone had called her from Memorial Hospital. They said you'd been hurt. She said she would take Jesse with her and drop him off at school later herself.

"I can't tell you how sorry I am, Chance. There are no words. If there's anything I can do, just say the word." The captain hung his head. He couldn't look me in the eye.

"Who did this? What reason could anyone have to kill two innocent people?" Before the words were out of my mouth, I knew what he was going to tell me.

"We're still trying to find that out. We found Amy's car in the hospital parking lot with her purse on the floor and the driver's side door open. Security footage shows a white van pulling up beside her car. We're not able to see who is in the van or the license plate, but it looks like men. They have on dark clothes with stocking masks. When the van pulls away, there is no sign of Amy or Jesse. We found bullet holes in the front seat. The van left at the lower end of the parking lot where there are no cameras. The dog walker confirmed it was a white van."

"A white van! You know who has a white van. You said only you and Captain Morris would know my identity. You promised me...you promised to protect my family. You're sorry. Is that all you can say? Why was no one protecting them?"

* * * *

Thinking about it here in the police station still caused my insides to tighten. I found it hard to breathe, and my throat felt like it could choke me. After what the captain told me, I remembered leaning back and closing my eyes. I couldn't process his words. The tears streamed down unchecked. When I had my emotions under control, I opened my eyes and stared at the him. He couldn't look me in the eye.

Chapter 4

Every time I come to the police station bits and pieces of what happened that awful day keep nagging at me.

I remembered the Capitan said, "Chance, they're all locked up. The judge refused bail. I agree with you that they're the most likely suspects, but I don't see how they could have done it. There are thousands of white vans around this area. The gang aren't allowed visitors except their attorneys, and they're isolated from the general population. There's no way they could have put the word out. This has to be a coincidence or someone else with a grudge against you or your family.

"When we had them locked up, we thought the danger had passed. I'm sorry. I pulled the protection detail."

At this point, the captain's phone rang. "Waltham speaking."

He listened and grew more agitated with each second.

"What fool did that? ... I see."

He hung up and looked up at the sky before he kicked my front tire.

"I don't know how to tell you this, but Stoney is out on bail. Some fool judge in night court agreed to release him so he could take care of his invalid mother until the trial. He had an ankle monitor on. Columbus found it an hour ago in his mother's bedroom. No Stoney."

"Bloody hell! How did he know my name and where my family lived? He must have been the one who called our home number if Amy said someone called her. Our landline is unlisted and in my wife's maiden name. Her cell phone is in the dog's name. I thought we took every precaution.

"You've got another bloody mole. You swore you would not put my name in the report. You swore."

"We're still trying to find out what happened. I didn't see your name in any of our reports. It must have been word of mouth. Someone could have dropped your name not realizing the danger. Someone must have wondered why we were providing your family with protection, and why you've been gone for over two months.

"Chance, go home and let us handle this. Columbus is looking for Stoney and the white van as we speak."

"You've done a bang-up job so far," I said as I started up my cruiser and charged out of the parking lot.

It's lucky there was no traffic. I didn't look before charging into the street. I'm not sure I even knew I was driving.

No way could I go home after the captain gave me the news. I went to the nearest motel and stayed there. Since I couldn't bear to go to my house for my clothes, I went to a department store and purchased new clothes. I couldn't eat or sleep. All I did was pace the motel room or haunt Point Park after dark.

Charlie searched the town for me. He found me and made me come home with him. Somehow, I made the funeral arrangements with Charlie's and Joyce's help. I can't remember those days before the funeral. My mind was in a fog. I couldn't think. Charlie said all I did was pace or stare into space. I didn't start drinking until after the funeral.

The funeral for Amy and Jesse was in all aspects different from the one for my parents. It was held in the United Methodist Church a block from our house. Flowers covered the altar and spilled around the walls inside the church. The church was packed with mourners. Amy's mother refused to sit beside me. I tried to talk to my mother-in-law, but she turned away in a huff. As I started to go back to my seat, I felt a slap on my arm. I turned and stared into her hard, glittery eyes.

She wagged an accusing finger at me. "This is all your fault. You couldn't get an ordinary job like everyone else. No, you had to be a police officer. Now some of the lowlifes you associate with have killed my baby and grandbaby. I'll never forgive you. Never." With those last words, she turned and stomped back to her pew on the other side of the church. I stood numbly looking after her.

Joyce took my arm and led me back to my seat. Joyce and Charlie sat on either side of me. I felt Amy's mother's cold eyes bore into me throughout the service. I don't think she could have blamed me any more than I blamed myself.

Outside the church, I stood around with several of our neighbors. The force of my mother-in-law's anger parted the surrounding people. They moved aside for her without her saying a word. She walked up to me with pursed lips. She opened her mouth to say something, but the words didn't come.

"Mrs. Brooks, I'm sorry for everything that's happened. If I could change the course of events, I would. I loved Amy and Jesse more than life itself. If I could trade my life for theirs, I would without a second's thought. I know you're hurting, but so am I."

"You know nothing. It's just an empty gesture to say you'd trade your life for theirs. Well, you can't trade your life, can you? "You...you couldn't even bury them here in town, no, not you. Amy would have wanted to be buried next to her father. You've gotten your way in everything. Not once have you considered my feelings. You're still going to take them to that godforsaken cemetery out on 47. Well, I'll not visit it." She spat on the ground at my feet, turned, and walked away.

I called after her, but she never turned around. I haven't talked to her or seen her since.

With the help of the funeral home people and Charlie, I made it to the cemetery. I buried the rest of my family next to my parents on Highway 47 at the Community Church. I tried to think of a way to say goodbye, but no words came. I felt numb. The light had gone out of my life. Charlie took me home with him. Before going to his house, we stopped by my house, and he collected my clothes. I couldn't go inside.

The next morning Charlie found me sitting on their deck. He patted me on the back and took a seat across from me. "Why don't you stay with us for a while? There's no one at your house or your parent's place except that half crazy handyman. You need to stay here with us where we can see you eat and know you have someone to talk to. I'm worried about you. You've had two emotional blows within six months of each other. That's enough to throw anyone for a loop."

I tried to smile and reassure him. "Thanks, Charlie, for all you and Joyce have done. Don't worry, I'm not going to do anything crazy. I need time by myself to get my head straight. And Phil's not crazy. He's a tormented soul like the rest of us. My parents trusted him, and I do too."

I packed what few belongings I had with me and threw them in my truck. Stepping into my truck, I took a deep breath and turned the key. Pulling out on the street, I waved goodbye to my friends out of my truck window. Charlie put his arm around Joyce where they stood staring after me. I knew they meant well, but I had to leave. I felt suffocated there. Everyone walked around on eggshells, not sure what to say to me. Every time I saw their son, he reminded me of Jesse and all I had lost.

I thought if I could get a little sleep, I would be fine. As I drove up the drive, I saw Phil with his rifle moving through the woods. I put my truck in the garage and walked from the garage to the kitchen with my suitcase of beer for the refrigerator. I took one and went outside to sit on the patio. Phil made his way around to where I sat.

"Howdy, Mr. Sunday."

"Hey, Phil. You can call me Chance. I guess I'll be staying here now."

"Do you want me to move out of my cabin?"

"No, no. My parents wanted you here. Nothing has changed that way. Would you like a beer?"

"No, thank you. I'm a whisky man. I keep it to two glasses a night. I promised your mother. Mighty nice lady." Phil saluted and started down the trail back to his cabin.

Boomer had been staying here since that fateful day. He sat and stared at me like he expected me to say something. I sensed he wanted my permission to follow Phil. He liked Phil and followed him around like he had bones in his pocket.

"It's OK, boy. Go with Phil. I guess I'm not very good company just now."

I watched Phil disappear through the foliage with Boomer by his side. I wondered if in time, I would be a recluse as well. In my line of work, I saw people become strange with the lack of companionship. I didn't care if it happened to me or not. If I were out of my mind, I wouldn't have to think.

I had two more beers before I went inside. I found an outdoor chaise in the garage and set it in front of the fireplace. The next morning, I realized I should have closed the shutters. Molten rays of sunshine shone through the curtainless windows, waking me up. The sharp rays struck me across the eyes without mercy.

My head hurt, and my stomach turned as I made my way to the kitchen. I reached into the fridge for a beer. I wasn't sure how many I'd drunk the previous night, but the next morning, there were only six left in the fridge.

Phil came in and handed me a thermos of coffee without saying a word.

"Thanks. Rough night."

I raised my beer can, and he nodded.

"I'm having the hair of the dog that bit me right now. When my stomach settles, this coffee will be much appreciated."

He turned to leave.

I called him back. "I've always been curious. How did you meet my parents? It was in New York, wasn't it? They never said."

Phil nodded and left.

I guessed that would be a story for another day.

Columbus kept searching for Stoney, but he was still missing and presumed armed and dangerous. It was all I could do to keep working as usual and not head for Columbus. My head knew I wouldn't have a clue where to look for him, but my heart wanted to find him and make him pay.

Matters came to a head on a Friday night. I was working late, and I received a call about a domestic dispute in the parking lot of an apartment complex. The caller asked for me personally. Sometimes people will surrender to someone they know, so I thought nothing about the request.

As I arrived at the parking lot, I saw a free-for-all between a young woman who was noticeably drunk and flailing her arms at a man trying to hold her at arm's length. I came to a stop and jumped out of my cruiser. I blew my whistle with the hope of distracting them long enough to stop the fight.

The streetlight was broken, and I could not get a good look at the man's face. The man belted the woman. She swayed and collapsed in a heap at my feet before I could catch her. The man ran off toward the street side of the apartments.

I stopped long enough to make sure the woman was all right. I called an ambulance and requested backup. By this time, a crowd was gathering. A friend of the woman agreed to wait with her until the ambulance came.

I ran toward the direction the man had gone and called in his description. "I'm in pursuit of a man of average height. Long, dark hair pulled back in a ponytail. Last seen wearing jeans and a dark T-shirt, running toward Summit Street."

"Copy that. Backup is on the way."

I heard running footsteps and hurried in that direction. I passed behind the apartment complex and came out on Summit, which is mostly family homes. By this time, backup had arrived. They went left in their cruiser, and I went right on foot. Summit runs down to the river, and I kept moving that way. I could still hear running footsteps echoing off the pavement. It was hard to tell in which direction the footsteps were going.

"Clint, I think he's headed toward the river. I hear someone running in that direction," I reported over my radio.

"Roger that, I think you're right. We're headed back in your direction."

I arrived at the river and walked along the riverbank. Up ahead, I saw a man with a ponytail trying to get in a boat. I ran in his direction and made it to him before he had the boat started. I pulled my revolver.

"That's far enough. Step ashore, identify yourself, and put your hands behind your head."

He turned around and grinned at me. He stepped out of the boat with his hands raised.

I was getting an uneasy feeling. I took out my handcuffs. "Put your hands behind your head slow and easy."

"I don't think so." He stood there grinning at me.

I was beginning to wonder if he was on something or if this was a set up. I moved toward him. Before I reached him, I saw someone out of the corner of my eye. He stepped out of the bushes with a sawed-off shotgun pointed in my direction. As I turned to face him, he laughed when he saw the disbelief in my eyes.

"Guess you never expected to see me in Parkersburg, uh, Gunner, or should I call you Chance. Yeah, I know your name and everything about you, cop."

I still had my revolver in my hand. Slowly, I turned toward Stoney. "You might as well give yourself up. The police in two states and the FBI are looking for you. It's just a matter of time."

"Whatever. Anyway, I told you what I'd do if you crossed me. I've done what I came to do, I don't care what they do to me now. You messed up my whole operation."

"Yeah, well, that was my job. You messed up my life, so I guess we're even."

"Not as even as you might think. I told you what I'd do to everyone you cared about. Who do you think had your parents killed? See, I made it my business to know everything about you. Then, obviously, there was the icing on the cake, your wife and son. She was a right pretty little piece, but it had to be done. I always make good on my word."

My rage came from somewhere deep inside and almost choked me. I don't remember seeing anything but his hard eyes. My entire world stood still and out of focus. The man I had been chasing jumped in the boat and took off. Stoney raised his shotgun. I fell to the left and fired as the blast from the shotgun blast flew past me. My shot hit his shotgun and knocked it out of his hand.

Stoney came at me with a knife. We rolled over the ground with him trying to stab me and me trying not to be stabbed. He was on top of me, aiming for my throat. I held on to his wrist with the blade of the knife only an inch from my throat. He was strong as an ox. My strength was ebbing.

To my left, I saw a flat, round river rock. With my last ounce of strength, I held his hand with the knife and reached for the rock. I hit him on the side of his head. He went limp on top of me. His knife grazed my shoulder and stuck in the ground.

I threw him off with the smell of his unwashed sweat in my nostrils. I still had the rock in my hand, unable to let it go. Standing up, a little unsteady on my feet, I bent over him with hatred in my heart. My arm was raised, ready to hit him again, when Clint came through the bushes. He grabbed my hand and held me back.

"Chance, you can't do that. Step away and take a breath. Not that I blame you or not that I wouldn't do the same in your situation. I know you, and you're not that kind of a man. Amy wouldn't want you to do this either. Step away and think about this. He's not worth ruining the rest of your life."

"Don't you understand? My life is already in ruins. He admitted it. He's proud of what he did to my parents, Amy, and Jesse. They're all dead because of him. He bragged about it. I don't see why I shouldn't save the state the cost of a trial." I collapsed to my knees and dropped the rock.

Clint pulled me to my feet and back from the river and Stoney. I sat on a wooden bench with my head in my hands until the ambulance came and carted Stoney away. Clint took me back to the station in his cruiser. Charlie drove me home. My drinking became worse. Nothing helped or eased my mind. I remember very little of what happened in those days of despair.

The day of the trial came. They tried Stoney with his gang and found them guilty of an armload of charges. I didn't attend the first trial. Stoney was tried in a separate trial along with Sully's brother for the murder of my family. Charlie wanted me to stay home, but I had to go to that trial. I took time off work and sat on the front row each day. My eyes bore a hole in the back of Stoney's head. Every so often, he turned around and grinned at me. The trial lasted a week. The jury deliberated four hours and came back with a guilty verdict.

I stood up to go. As I raised my head, I found Stoney staring at me with a smirk on his face. I couldn't take my eyes off of him. My hands gripped the rail dividing the audience from the prisoner. He took a step toward me. At first, I didn't hear him. I leaned in, and he spoke low enough so only I could hear.

"I told you what I'd do. Don't get too comfortable, you SOB. I'm coming for you. I'll see you in hell."

"It'd be a pleasure to send you there first. I don't know how you will make good your promise in jail but bring it on. I also told you what I would do if you messed with my family." He grinned and thumbed his nose at me.

It was like waving a cape in front of a bull. I jumped over the railing and threw myself at Stoney. I felt my hands go around his neck. Two officers pulled me off of him. They had to pry my hands from his throat. While two of the bailiffs held me, Stoney stood up sputtering and coughing.

Stoney broke away from his jailers and made a run at me. One of them stopped him before he reached me. After the jailers dragged him away, I could hear his laughter echoing down the hall, even after he disappeared behind closed doors. The day for sentencing came, but the judged barred me from the courtroom.

* * * *

To this day, I can't help wondering why I accepted the assignment. I am not an ambitious man, but I wanted to be a detective. Once begun, everything was like a snowball rolling down hill picking up speed and getting bigger. I get a headache just thinking about it.

If I didn't have to see Charlie about this missing person, I would run from the waiting room. I stood up, took a deep breath of police fumes, walked around the room, and sat back down again. Where the devil was Charlie? I'll give him five minutes more, and then I'd have to leave. The memories kept rushing at me like a bad trip.

* * * *

My depression spiraled out of control after the trial. I couldn't process my grief, so I drank from the time I left work until I passed out at night. The woman from the dairy farm, Bonnie, died during the trial. Her husband entered the witness protection program. Stoney and his crew were sentenced to life without parole at Mount Olive Correctional Complex.

Everyone around me had died, but I lived on. I didn't care if I lived or died, but I couldn't put an end to my life. I took reckless chances during the performance of my duties, hoping someone else would do it for me, but I continued on. Amy would have thought suicide was the coward's way out. I couldn't disappoint her in death as I had in life, although she wouldn't know. That doesn't mean I didn't think about it often enough. If not for my dog, Boomer, I don't know what I would have done. Since I had a hard time coping with my life, maybe that's why I could relate to Phil.

Matters reached the breaking point one sunny morning. A citizen reported to my captain he found me asleep in my patrol car with a beer bottle between my legs. That's when the captain called me into his office and told me I had a choice. I could take retirement since I had in my twenty years of service, or he would fire me. I took retirement.

The hardest part to take about my family's death is that I blame myself. I did then, and I still do now. Working undercover, I wormed my way into a motorcycle gang and helped take down their operation, which was almost foolproof. Somehow though, I did not have the satisfaction of a job well done.

Amy didn't want me to take the assignment, but she'd refused to stand in my way. I lost my wife and son; my parents, my job, all vanished. I lost everything that meant anything because of my decision. I must live with the bad choice I made.

Charlie insisted I needed an occupation. He refused to let me drift along on the sea of self-pity and booze. He filled out the form for a private detective license for me and mailed it. The captain wrote a letter of recommendation. Before I knew what had happened, I received my license. Charlie found my office for me. At first, I didn't care one way or the other. I paid the rent for the office, but that was all. Charlie kept pushing me until I took an interest in the office and furnished it.

I started fixing the office up at a slow pace When I saw where I had made progress, something took hold of me. I told myself I could waste my time in the office as well as at home. Everyone would be happy. Then the funniest thing happened. I started to get clients. I have to thank Charlie for my new lease on life. Some of their stories were as sad as mine and helping people gave me a purpose. I'd never realized it before this, but I needed a purpose, a reason to live, and helping people gave me that reason. Helping my clients feels good and gives me a reason to get up in the mornings.

* * * *

Coming back to the moment, I stared around the room. It had filled up since I took my little journey through the past. I went to the restroom to splash water on my face. The man ahead of me walked out a little unsteadily. I happened to look in the trash can and saw where someone had discarded one of those small bottles of liquor. I remembered the janitor telling me how many times he had unstopped the toilet in the waiting room. He'd found those little bottles of liquor where someone had tried to flush them, along with baggies of pills and weed. Why anyone would bring something like that into a police station was beyond me.

A different man was behind the desk now. He at last motioned for me to come forward. "Who did you say you wanted to speak to?"

"Would you tell Lieutenant Parks I would like to speak to him? My name is Chance Sunday."

"What is this concerning?"

"A missing person."

He nodded and dialed. Soon Charlie came through the door with a smile on his face. We shook hands, and he took me back to his office.

"Have a seat, Chance. I've been meaning to get out to see you. You know how that goes. Wes said you're working on a missing person. There is no one better than you at finding missing persons. Who is it?"

"Her name is Laurel McIntyre. Her mother hired me to find her. I wanted to check with you in case you didn't want me working on an open case."

Swiftly, the atmosphere became tense. I watched the smile disappear from his face.

"Chance, I don't know what I can tell you." He turned to his keyboard and pounded, using the good-old hunt-and-peck system. I watched him scan the file.

"I can't let you look at this since it's an ongoing investigation. What I can tell you is that we've hit a dead end. She seems to have disappeared from the face of the earth. Her digital footprint ended with her disappearance. No ATM or credit card activity. No social media either. Her friends claim to have not heard from her. Any more than that and I'll have to check with the captain. I'll be right back." He adjusted his monitor in my direction.

I didn't have any trouble reading the report. I quickly scribbled the names and addresses of the pharmaceutical salesman and a doctor at the research lab, as well as the people they had questioned so far. I heard him talking and slid back in my chair after putting my notebook away.

Charlie walked behind his desk and sat. He looked at me with a worried look.

"I checked with the captain, and he said to go ahead. He said if you get any leads give them to us and let us handle it."

"Good, glad there won't be a conflict with my working on an open case."

"We appreciate any help you can give us, but Chance, you ought to let this one pass. We can't find anything to connect Laurel McIntyre to the killings, but my gut says she's involved in some way. Someone had to let those men in. The lab had a security lock. You had to know the password to punch in the keypad. The door was not breached. The men knew exactly where they were going.

"And there's another point to consider. They may have been cooking meth in the basement. The other employees say not, but the smell was strong. They say they were researching an antidote to meth overdose."

"Well, I just started the case, so I don't have an opinion yet. I told her mother I'd look into it before deciding if I could help. She could be innocent like she told the salesman. Her mother thinks she was scared, and that's the reason she ran. If I decide to take the case, and I find her, I'll let you know." I paused for a moment. "The sheriff in Pinedale is also looking for her."

Charlie nodded.

"Will you let him know I'm looking into it? I don't want any trouble with the locals if I can help it." I stood up and shook his hand. "Come out any time, Charlie. So long." I turned to go. Halfway through the door, like Columbo, I turned. "Oh, by the way, what did you think of the drug salesman? Could he have been in it with her or the three men?"

"Anything's possible, but we checked him out. He has a clean record. He came forward right away when the story appeared in the paper. I talked to him, and it was easy to see that he was still scared. It took nerve for him to come forward. He said he was afraid for his family and himself."

"I see. It can't hurt to question him again. Maybe he'll remember something new. Thanks."

Charlie shrugged, and I waved goodbye. I left the police station and walked over to my truck. The situation did not look too good for Laurel. She was a chemistry student at the college. She knew the smell of a meth lab. To say the perfect place to have a meth lab is in a drug research facility is an understatement.

Since it was Saturday, I decided to swing by Laurel's friend, Davis Howell, and see what he had to say. He should not have any classes today. I turned down Seventh Street and followed it to Fairview Drive and turned on Hemlock.

Chapter 5

Three houses up on the left past the curve in the street, I found Davis Howell washing his red Mustang convertible. He stood up, dried his hands, and reached for his glasses. He stood by his car and watched me pull into the drive.

A few inches over six feet, he was a good-looking kid with curly blond hair and blue eyes. He had on cutoffs and no shirt, and he was in his bare feet. He continued to watch me without moving from his position by his car.

I slid out of my truck and walked over to where he stood. "Are you Davis Howell?"

"Yeah, you must be the private investigator Mrs. McIntyre told us about."

I nodded and flipped my identification.

He reached down for a can of car wax and a piece of cloth. He straightened up and unscrewed the lid on the wax before he spoke again. "Mrs. McIntyre said you were coming to see me, but I have nothing to add. I told the police everything I know. I've thought about it, and I don't know what else I could tell you."

He looked away with a frown. Not a good beginning. Dipping into the can, he applied wax to the hood of his car.

"My name is Chance Sunday, and I am a private investigator. That means I'm not privy to what you told the police. I'd like to ask you a few questions if you don't mind. I'm not the police. You don't have to answer any of my questions, but I need your help if I'm to find your friend."

He crossed his arms over his chest and leaned against his car. "Ask away, but I don't know how much help I can be. The police asked all kinds of questions."

"Mrs. McIntyre said you've been friends with Laurel since preschool. I'm hoping you might know about a friend or a place she might go when she's scared."

He shook his head no.

"Did you see Laurel that night?"

"Like I told the police, I hadn't seen her. Just because I live in the vicinity where she was last seen doesn't mean she came here. My parents would kill me if they found this mess involved me in any way."

"I appreciate your situation. Keeping that in mind, I figure you told the police as little as possible. I'm asking for your help. Her mother's ready for a nervous breakdown. I find it hard to believe she would come all this way and not stop at her best friend's for help. I'll ask again, did you see Laurel that night?"

He looked down and shifted his weight from one leg to the other. He raised his head and swallowed hard. Not everyone is a born liar.

"I told the police no. If you repeat this, I'll deny it. I'm between the proverbial rock and a hard place. I want to help Laurel, but I don't want to get involved. My folks can't know anything about what I'm about to tell you. Understand?"

I nodded.

"My father is a bank president. He would not tolerate any hint of a scandal." He shook his head and sighed. "She came here that night; she looked so scared. I couldn't turn her away.

"My parents made me an apartment in the basement of their home. They were out of town at a financial conference. I was sitting half-asleep in front of the TV when I heard a knock. It must have been about twelve-thirty. I let her in and didn't ask any questions. She said she just needed a place to crash for the night. I gave her my bed, and I slept on the couch.

"The next morning, she was gone before I woke. I'm a sound sleeper, so I didn't hear her leave. I haven't heard from her since. I don't know what spooked her. The next morning, I heard what had happened on the radio. When they said the name of the lab, I knew it was where Laurel worked. I swear I don't know where she is now. I'm only telling you because I hope you can help her."

"Did she often come by your apartment?"

"No, not anymore. We used to be close, but situations change. It's been six months since I'd seen her. Since high school, we've gone to different colleges. I haven't seen much of her. She might have been more in touch with Susie, uh, Susie Sharp. They were best friends, and I think they kept in touch."

"Do you think she could have been involved in this business at the research lab?"

"Honestly, I don't know. If you'd asked me that a year ago, I would have said no way. Last time I saw Laurel was at Thanksgiving. We talked for a while, but she didn't seem like the same Laurel. She had a problem at work that all four of us discussed. It was a case of should I or shouldn't I tell what I stumbled across.

"Something else was worrying her. It wasn't just her problem at work. She was on edge. Her color wasn't good, and she'd lost weight. I asked her if something else was wrong, but she shook her head and walked away."

"Can you think of anyone or any place she might go where she'd feel safe?"

"Sorry, like I said, we kind of drifted apart. As far as I know, Susie Sharp is the only one she kept in touch with. She would know if anyone does."

"Do you think they're on the kind of terms where she would know what else was troubling her?"

"If anyone does, it would be her. Other than Susie, I have no idea. "

"Thanks. Here's my card. If you think of anything that might help, or you hear from her, give me a call. Oh, before I go, I have one other question. Just routine. Where were you between ten and midnight that night?"

He nodded and stared at my card before putting it in the console of his car. I had the impression he was stalling long enough to come up with an answer.

"Huh, oh, I was here all night, alone. I didn't feel well."

"Great, thanks. I'll probably be talking to you again."

I hoped Saturday would be a good time to catch the salesman at home. He had a Coolville address, a small village within twenty miles of Parkersburg. I turned on State Route 144 and made my way to his address past an old cemetery on the right. His house was the next one on the left. It was cedar and stone and sat atop a hill with a circle drive. I drove around to his garage and parked.

When I stepped out of my truck, I heard voices coming from the far side of the house. I made my way there and waved at the man. The woman saw me first and nudged him in my direction. He was of average height with lank brown hair and a pale complexion. He had stooped shoulders and a spreading middle from too much time in the car or behind a desk and not enough exercise. I saw two children, a girl and a boy. They were playing croquette with him and a woman. I assumed she was his wife. He walked over to where I stood at the corner of his house.

As he came nearer, I held out my hand. "Nice family."

He didn't shake my hand.

Nodding, he looked back at his family and then at me. His hands started to tremble. "If you're selling something, I'm not buying."

I took out my ID.

He took it and scanned it before giving it back.

"Mr. Grover, as my license says, my name is Chance Sunday. I'm a private investigator trying to locate Laurel McIntyre. As I understand it, you were the last person to see her the night of the tragedy in Pinedale."

He looked back at his family and rubbed his hands on his pants. He nodded and swallowed hard. "Yeah, that was me. That's a night I'll never forget. What are you here for? I thought they would have found her by now. I told the police everything I know. I only gave her a lift.

There's nothing more I can tell you." He held his hands to keep them from shaking. He rubbed them together and looked back at his wife before turning around to me.

"Yes, I read what you told the police, but they are out of options. No one has heard from her since that night. Since you talked to the police, I thought you might have remembered something that would help. Did she say anything that would give a clue as to where she was going? A name or an address?"

"Look, I don't want to get mixed up in this any more than I already am. We didn't talk. I did a stupid thing by giving her a ride. I didn't know what else to do. I couldn't leave her by the side of the road late at night. The people who did this are dangerous. I've got a wife and two kids to think of. Now, please go."

I watched beads of sweat form on his brow.

"Sir, no one realizes your concern more than me, but a young woman's life is at stake. Her mother is worried sick. Please tell me your story again, and I promise I'll tell no one I talked to you."

He started walking toward the garage, and I fell in step with him

"It's just like they said in the papers. I'd made a very good sale at the after-hours clinic, and I didn't have a care in the world. When I made it to my car, I locked my case in the trunk and jumped in my car. I turned the radio up loud and headed home. When I saw the Tucker's Truck Stop sign up ahead, I remembered I needed gas. While I was filling up my tank, I happened to notice something moving in the back of my car.

"I opened the door and there she was. She was white as a sheet and begged me to close the door. I was too stunned to think, so, I closed it. She was so scared, she was shaking. No way could she fake that. You can imagine my predicament. I didn't know what to do.

"After I closed the door, I finished filling up my tank. I got back in my car and drove a short way down the highway before pulling over. My intention was to make her get out, but after she told me her story, I couldn't. I don't know what I was thinking. In the end, I agreed to take her to Parkersburg.

"No way could I leave a young girl by the side of the road in the middle of nowhere at night. In the light of day as I look back, I was afraid those people might have followed her, and we were both in danger. This was no time to argue. I wanted away from there as fast as possible."

"Did she act as if she knew the men who broke in the lab?"

"The police asked me the same question. I've thought about it, and I don't think she did. She sure was scared. She stayed on the floor in the back of my car until we reached Parkersburg. When she asked me to pull over at the Kroger store, I asked her if I couldn't take her some place safe. She said it would be better if I left as quickly as possible. I told her to call the police when she got some place safe. She said she would, but she didn't."

"Did you ever do business with the research lab where she worked or know any of the people who were killed?"

"No, I sell drugs that are in production and approved. I make the rounds of clinics or doctors' offices and give out samples and take orders. That's all I do, nothing illegal."

"Were there any rumors about the lab? I'm trying to figure out what the thieves were after. On the surface it looks like a senseless crime. From all accounts, they only had a small amount of meth for their experiments."

Mr. Grover looked sheepish and put his hands in his pockets and took them out again. "Well...you hear rumors. I don't know if any of it's true. I would not like this repeated, but there were rumors going around. Labs don't make money unless they have a breakthrough or come up with a promising treatment.

"They had neither, yet out of the blue, they were buying new, very expensive equipment. I thought they might have shown progress in whatever they were working on and received more funding. However, there was nothing in the trade journals to suggest they were on to anything. There was a lot of talk at the office, but no one knew anything for sure. As far as I know, it was all water fountain gossip. It does make you wonder though."

"I see. That's interesting. Thank you for your time. Here's my card. If you think of anything, no matter how trivial you think it is, please call me. Laurel's life is at stake, and her family is beside themselves with worry."

"I've racked my brain ever since it happened. I can't think of anything else. I guess I was too scared at the time."

Waving goodbye to Grover, I went back around the garage.

Mr. Grover stood by the corner of his house until I got into my truck. I saw him tear up my card and throw it in the trash. He watched me go down his drive before he turned back to his family. I headed for the highway and Parkersburg. Alfred Street was on my way home, and I needed to talk to Laurel's friend Susie.

The address on Alfred Street was an apartment in an old converted three-story house. The building was perched upon the side of a steep hill. I parked across the street, climbed the almost vertical stairs from the street, and stepped up on the wooden plank porch. The first thing I noticed was the smell of last night's cooking and rotting garbage. The outside of the porch had green mold growing over the lattice around the porch and up the columns.

Flies buzzed around the open screened doorway. I entered through the screen door into the hallway. I heard running footsteps, and two young boys with water pistols ran past me through the open door. A toilet flushed somewhere in the building. Next, I heard a woman yell at someone to put their beer cans in the trash.

The number on the mailbox indicated Susie lived upstairs. The carpet was worn on the steps, and there was a strange pungent odor permeating the hallway. I climbed three flights of stairs to apartment 2C and knocked on the door. I heard the shuffling of feet on a bare wood floor and a groan. I knocked again and waited. The chains on the door rattled, and the door hinges squeaked as she opened the door a crack.

One bloodshot blue eye stared up at me. A strand of blonde hair fell across her eye. She blew it out of the way and cleared her throat.

She sniffed and asked, "What d'ya want?"

"Are you Susan Sharp?"

"I might be. Who are you?"

"Mrs. McIntyre called you. My name's Chance Sunday. I'm trying to find your friend Laurel. May I come in?" I flipped my identification for her to see.

Without saying a word, she sighed and closed the door. The chains rattled again, and the door came open. She turned and walked back into her apartment without speaking. I stepped into her living room uninvited.

Clothes were strewn over the couch, and underclothes were in a pile on the floor. I looked around at the apartment with its peeling plastered walls. There were water stains in the corner where the ceiling met the wall. The wallpaper border was coming loose in several places.

Susie had on a sheer gown that left nothing to the imagination. She picked a bundle of clothes off the floor and searched through them. Grabbing a rumpled lump, she shook it out and shrugged into a white terry cloth bathrobe with a pattern of big pink flowers. Running her fingers through her hair, she collapsed in the nearest chair. She did not ask me to take a seat so I continued to stand.

"Sorry, I'm not presentable. Tied one on last night. My head's killing me. Would you like some coffee? I don't have tea. Never drink the stuff. Too weak for me."

"No, thanks. I just want a little information about your friend Laurel."

"Look, mister, I can't think straight. I need a cup of coffee."

Here again, it sounded like she was stalling for time to think of some answers. It's good to have loyal friends, but I don't think her friends realized the seriousness of Laurel's predicament.

She stood up and staggered toward the kitchenette, holding on to the furniture as she went. She might have been cute at one time, but she had let herself go. She did show a certain sensuality in the way she swayed her hips. Her robe came open, and she didn't bother to retie her belt. She didn't mind flaunting her assets.

Susie made it to the kitchen, found the coffee, and filled the carafe with water. She sloshed the water in the coffeemaker, added coffee to the filter, and turned the coffeemaker on. Reaching into a cabinet, she came out with a bottle of what I hoped was aspirin. She took several with a shaking hand. I heard the coffeemaker come to life. I moved a mound of clothes off the couch and sat down. She stumbled back into the living room, collapsed into the nearest chair, and closed her eyes as if she might fall asleep where she sat.

I cleared my throat to get her attention. "As you know, I'm trying to find your friend Laurel. Do you have any idea where she might be?"

She opened her eyes and looked up at me. "Like I told the police, I haven't seen her."

"I know what you told the police. I think it's admirable that you want to protect your friend. Laurel's mother is worried to death. She's on her last nerve.

"Susie, you were her best friend. The least you can tell me is if she had a boyfriend or if there's a place, she would go to feel safe. She could be in great danger, and I need to find her."

"I told the police everything I know. How many times do I have to say it? I haven't seen her."

"You want me to believe you're her best friend and she didn't tell you if she had a boyfriend? I'm not buying it. What about it? Did she have a boyfriend?"

"I told you I don't know." She looked down at her feet and shook her head. "She might have had a boyfriend, but I don't know his name. She never told me. It was some kind of a secret, I guess. She just smiled when she talked about him. That's all I know. Please leave me alone."

"I can't do that. I have to find your friend. You're not being very helpful. Let me tell you what I think. I believe Laurel came over here. She needed help, and who better to turn to than her best friend? If you know where she is, you need to tell me. If those men find Laurel, they will not hesitate to kill her or you if you're in the way. Her information was in the paper when she went missing. All they have to do is ask around to find out who her friends are."

She bit her nails and stared across the room. "Look, I don't know anything."

I raised my voice a little and put an edge to it. "Call me crazy, but I don't believe you. She would have come to you first and asked for help. Early the next day after the trouble at the lab, she left Davis's apartment and went somewhere. She didn't go home. She came to see you, didn't she?"

Susie put her hands over her eyes and leaned back in her chair. She opened her eyes and looked at me. "I told you no. I told the police no. I don't know anything." She had her fingernails bitten down to the quick. She lowered her head and continued to chew on her fingernails.

"If the police find out you lied, you could be in trouble yourself. There's obstruction of justice, aiding and abetting, and an accomplice after the fact for starters. If Laurel is guilty of helping those men, well, you're going to jail along with Laurel."

"Stop it, stop it," she yelled, and put her trembling hands over her ears. "You're scaring me. I have to think. I don't know what to do."

"Of course, I'm scaring you. This is scary. Both of you girls are in trouble up to your eyelashes. Now tell me where I can find Laurel. I need to get her to safety and do my best to get this mess straightened out."

I waited. She fumbled with the sash of her robe, weaving it through her fingers. Everything was suddenly quiet. The coffeemaker beeped at the end of its cycle and sounded like a gong in the quiet of the apartment. Susie stood up a little unsteadily and stumbled into the kitchen. She tried to pour herself a cup. Her trembling hands spilled most of it.

I followed her into the kitchen. Taking the coffeepot from her before she spilled it all, I poured her a cup. She dumped at least three teaspoons of sugar into the cup. It was a fight with the ants to see how much sugar made it in the cup. Both hands wrapped around the cup as she moved it to her mouth. She gulped the steaming liquid without noticing how hot it was. I poured her another cup. She took it into the living room with me following her. There was a little more color in her cheeks.

"I don't want to get into trouble. Laurel's my friend. I had to help my friend. That's all I did. She said she was in trouble. I didn't know what had happened until I heard it on the evening news. I wouldn't be telling you this now, but I know she needs help. You have to help her. Everything is such a mess. I didn't know what else to do. Please don't tell Laurel I ratted her out."

She took a deep breath and stared down at a spot on the floor. "Look, Mr. Sunday, you don't have to tell the police about me, do you?" She peered up at me from under her lashes.

"Just tell me where to find her, and I'll try to keep your name out of this if I can."

She sighed and drank the last of her coffee. She set the mug down in the nest of water rings on the side table. "OK. I guess I have no choice. My father has a hunting cabin off Morgan's Run on the way to Elizabeth. It's on the Kanawha River. I took her there. She has a burner phone, but there's no cell signal or phone in the cabin. She has to walk a ways to find a signal. I take her groceries and leave them in a certain spot. There's no electric. The cabin is heated with a wood stove, and the cooking stove and refrigerator use propane. No one would know to look for her there. I figured she'd be safe until she could decide what to do."

"I hope you're right. Get a piece of paper and draw me a map, so I can find her. Are you sure no one followed you there?"

"I'm extra careful. I don't go to the cabin. We decided on a drop-off point to be safe. I go at night and pull over with my lights off and wait. If no one comes down the road for at least fifteen minutes, I get out and leave the groceries. Laurel leaves me a note of what she needs for next time."

"I see. Did she say anything about what happened?"

"No, she said something terrible happened and her life was in danger. She begged me not to tell anyone where she was. She said she had to have time to decide what to do."

"Laurel's lucky to have such a good friend."

Susie handed me the map. I folded it and put it in my pocket.

"I need to ask you one more question, just routine. Where were you between ten and midnight when all this happened?"

Her eyes were wide with fright. "Why are you asking me? I had nothing to do with it."

"I'm not saying you did, but I would be a poor investigator if I didn't ask."

"Yeah, sure, I was here, all night. I wasn't feeling well."

"Now, that wasn't so hard. Thanks. I'll probably be seeing you again."

I made my way to the door and watched her stumble into the kitchen once more before I closed the door. It's unusual for two young people to be home all night with no company. I'll definitely need to check up on those two.

I stopped at the corner gas station and filled up my truck. As I filled the tank, I watched for any cars that might be tailing me. I thought I had seen a black Tahoe with heavily tinted windows behind me when I'd left Davis's house and again at Susie's. There was one parked across the street with a mud-smudged license plate.

I went by my office first before heading to Elizabeth. In my office, the front window overlooks Sixth Street. I stood at my window drinking a cup of coffee and scanned the area. I saw the same black Tahoe in the next block. Before I headed out, I walked across the street and made my way to where the Tahoe was parked. When I got closer, someone fired up the engine and peeled out of the parking space.

I went back to my truck and headed for the Do Drop Inn. All the way there, I saw a black Tahoe three cars to the rear. As I turned in at the bar, the Tahoe flew past. I tried to see the license plate, but it was still smudged. The tinted windows made it impossible to see the driver. I had an uneasy feeling as I stepped through the door of the bar.

Elsie came over when she saw me. "Chance, dinner's not ready. Can I get you a beer or some lunch?"

"No, thanks, it's a little early. I've run into a spot of trouble. I'm being followed. Is it OK if I borrow your ATV? Tell John I'll have Phil bring it back either tonight or in the morning."

"No problem, you know where it is." She handed me the keys.

I left by the back door and walked up through the woods to a shed. Firing up the ATV, I made my way the half mile through the woods to my house. I walked down to Phil's cabin. Peering in through the window, I saw him asleep on his sofa with his pistol lying across his chest. Not a good idea to wake him up when he has a pistol in his hand. I slid him a note under his door to take the ATV back.

I have a second vehicle, a Jeep Wrangler, which belonged to my father. He always left it at the cabin to use when they came for a visit. I rarely drive it, but it was my best option today. I fired it up and backed out of the garage. Rolling down the drive at a snail's pace, I looked up and down the road, but there was no Tahoe in sight.

I turned left. I knew another way to get to Elizabeth that didn't involve going past the Do Drop Inn. The road is longer and more winding, but it gets you there just the same. Before I headed there, I had to make one more stop to speak to Dr. Leatherwood, one of the research scientists.

I detoured to Pinedale and plugged her address into my GPS. Pinedale is a small town with one traffic light. There's a bank, a United Methodist Church, a hardware store, a small cafe, and not much else. If the college wasn't there, there would not be many reasons to visit. The courthouse sits upon a hill on the right overlooking the town.

Across a ravine to the left sits the college. It is a fine small college. Many of my friends graduated from there. My next-door neighbors in town, a middle school principal and his wife, both graduated from the college.

I found Dr. Leatherwood's house on a tree-lined avenue outside of town. It was a red-brick ranch-style house on a corner lot. I rang the door bell. A short, rotund lady of about forty answered a short time later. She was wearing sweats and a T-shirt, and had her red hair pulled back in a ponytail. She had a duster in her hand that she held as if she might have to use it.

"May I speak to Dr. Leatherwood?"

"You've got her. If you're selling something, you've come to the wrong address." She started to close the door.

"Ma'am, my name is Chance Sunday. I'm a private investigator hired by Laurel McIntyre's mother to find her daughter. May I have a few minutes of your time?" I held up my license for her to read.

Her green eyes raked me over before she stepped aside and motioned me into the living room with her duster. It was a pleasant room with a comfortable overstuffed sofa and chair. The coffee table looked like one of those old railroad trolleys with polished wood and metal accents. A Christmas cactus sat in the middle of the coffee table.

She asked me to sit and sat down after I did. Calmly holding her hands tightly in her lap, she sat across from me very still without speaking.

Before I met her, I imagined the doctor would look like my fifth-grade teacher, Mrs. Roper, who always wore severely cut suits and never smiled. With her glasses perched on the end of her nose, she could stare down her nose at you when she talked to you. I still remember shaking in my boots when she gave me the stare.

To my surprise, Dr. Leatherwood looked like someone's mom. Although she was giving me the silent treatment, I didn't think she would send me to the principal's office today.

She cleared her throat and stood. "Would you like a cup of coffee?"

"No, ma'am, I'm fine. I'll try not to take up too much of your time. As you know, Laurel is missing, and from the police report, you may have been one of the last people to talk to her."

She sat back in her chair and gave me a long, hard stare. She must have decided I was no threat. She nodded and cleared her throat. "Yes, I remember noticing her in the lunchroom bagging the trash that...that night it all happened." She drew in her breath before continuing. "It was not her usual night to work. I said as much. She said she was going home for a long weekend. I said see you next week and waved goodbye."

"Were you and the others on friendly terms with her?"

"I would say we were. She had an inquiring mind. Our research interested her. She asked intelligent questions. We let her help us out from time to time when we needed an extra hand. She showed promise as a researcher. I talked to her about going into research instead of teaching. She said she was considering it."

"That night, what time did you leave?"

"Let's see, I believe I left around seven-thirty. I had been there since five-thirty in the morning. My tests went south. It had been a long, frustrating day. The computer system went down, and there was something wrong with my calculations. I'm afraid I didn't notice much. I just wanted to go home and sleep."

"Did you notice anyone in the parking lot when you left?"

"I can't say for sure. As I said, I was tired and frustrated. I had my mind on my research as I left the building. Sorry to say, I didn't look around when I got inside my car. Although I think I would have noticed if there had been a strange car in the parking lot."

I nodded and made notes.

"Do you remember if Laurel had been on edge or out of sorts recently?"

"You can stop right there. Laurel was a fine, intelligent young woman. You cannot convince me she was in on this atrocity. No way.

However, I have to say, she did seem out of sorts. Not her usual happy self. I put it down to final exams or man troubles. Nothing more."

"I hope you understand I have to ask these questions. Please don't be offended. I have to go where my nose takes me."

She nodded and crossed her arms giving the impression; she had said all she wanted to say.

"Someone suggested there was something going on at the lab besides the research. An influx of money not related to the research for fancy new equipment. Do you know anything about that?"

"First off, let me say my only concern is my work. Mr. Leslie paid me a salary. He handled the business end of the lab."

"Did he discuss with any of you about his research into meth addiction and an overdose antidote?"

"No, scientists are typically closed mouth until they have a break through."

"Was there more money than usual?"

"I wondered when someone would tumble to that. Yes, yes, there was. Although Mr. Leslie handled the business end, it was obvious new money was coming in. We operated on a shoestring most of the time. Sometimes I bought supplies for my experiments out of my own pocket. We were never paid on time. It makes it hard to budget your finances. Then, he started paying us on time. We all received a raise and new equipment. When we put through a request for supplies, they were delivered right away. Previously, you had to wait a long time to get your requisition approved and delivered."

"None of you questioned this?"

"As far as I know, no one did. Like I said, our only concern is our experiments. We were happy to have supplies we didn't have to buy out of our own pocket. I didn't question the windfall. I assumed Mr. Leslie had received new funding, and was getting close to announcing something important.

"He told us his research was looking promising. Now, there's no one left to complete it. I'm not even sure if I still have a job at the lab.

Everything is on hold until his will is probated, and an audit can be carried out. None of the researchers could buy the business as far as I know. I'm sorry, I can't help you."

"If no one buys the lab, what will you do?"

"I get offers from time to time. I have friends in some of the big labs, but I prefer a small lab. I'll have to do what I have to do. It will mean leaving Pinedale, and I would hate to do that." She shook her head and looked at me.

There was an awkward pause.

Taking this as my cue, I stood up. "Thank you for your time. I'll leave my card, and if you think of anything that might help, no matter how insignificant, give me a call."

She picked up my card and placed it in a bowl on the coffee table. "Yes, I'll do that. I hope you find Laurel. I like her. I would hate anything to happen to her. She had promise."

I waved goodbye and slid behind the wheel of my Jeep once again. This time I headed for Elizabeth. I hoped Susie wasn't sending me on a wild goose chase, and I would find Laurel safe and sound. So many questions needed answering, and only Laurel could give an explanation for most of them.

Once in Elizabeth, I took Elizabeth Pike to Morgan's Run. According to Susie's map, I turn on a gravel road beside a huge crooked pine leaning on a massive boulder. If I reach the Muddy Bottom Public Golf Course, I've gone too far. I found the tree and the boulder and followed the drive toward the Little Kanawha River. The drive was not much more than two ruts. When I came to a clearing, there sat the little cabin.

The cabin was made of logs. The logs were weathered to a silvery gray and looked hand hewn. There was a porch all the way around the house as far as I could see with a cedar shingle roof. The fireplace and foundation were made of native stone. Azaleas and arborvitae surrounded the porch. A stone walk led up to the porch and front door.

I sat in my car and watched the place. It didn't look like anyone was home. I decided to investigate and stepped out of my car. As I walked toward the cabin, something happened. All I remember hearing is a deafening bang and having a sense of flying through the air. The next thing I knew, I woke up in a hospital with an aching head.

Chapter 6

As I came fully awake in my hospital bed, it seemed my whole body was hurting. My face felt sore and hot. Gingerly, I opened my eyes. Everything was out of focus. Gradually, the more I opened and closed my eyes, the clearer the room became. From what I could see of the room, I was in a hospital. I couldn't remember what happened. Panic set in; I was afraid to move. My eyes roamed around the room and came to rest on my friend Charlie dozing in the visitor's chair.

I let out the breath I'd been holding and tried to speak, but all I could manage was a croak. I tried to clear my throat and realized I had a tube down my throat. Fear made me try to move and struggle to sit up.

Charlie rushed to my side and put his hands on my shoulders, holding me down. "Chance, be still. Don't move. You're connected to all kinds of tubes. I'll call the nurse. Calm down. Welcome back to the land of the living. Everything's all right."

I saw him press the call button. When I calmed down, I found I could move my legs. I flexed my toes, and they worked. Relief rolled over me, and I exhaled slowly and inhaled to the count of five. I could move my hands and arms even if they were sore and connected to IVs.

The nurse came in and looked at my monitors. She wrote on my chart, nodded, and left the room. A short time later, someone I assumed was a doctor came in pushing a laptop on a mobile station.

He was slightly below average in height and had a bald streak across the top of his head with a little sprig of hair in the middle. His white coat was crisp without a wrinkle as if he had just put it on. I noticed tired lines around his hazel eyes as he scanned my monitors. Next, he looked at my chart and typed in his laptop on wheels.

I tried to talk, but it was useless.

The doctor put his hand on my shoulder and took a deep breath. "Mr. Sunday, my name is Dr. Collins. You've had a concussion and been in a coma for three days. Please be patient and don't move.

"The nurse will remove the tube we had to put in your throat. If you can drink on your own, we'll leave it out. We'll need to leave the oxygen in until we can do a blood test."

He tapped on his laptop several more times and said "Um." He said it several times before turning his attention back to me.

"I'm sure you noticed you're bruised and sore, but there are no broken bones. You've probably noticed a flush on your face. It's like a sunburn. The flash from the explosion caused that. As far as I can tell, there will be no permanent damage. You should be able to leave the hospital in a day or two. I'll leave you in Nurse Porter's capable hands."

He tapped on his laptop some more and turned to go. Although he'd touched me only once, he still took a sanitary wipe from the box by the door and wiped his hands.

Nurse Porter, my angel of mercy, reminded me of my maiden Aunt Maude. She was sturdily built with nondescript brown hair and pale blue eyes. She walked flat-footed and stomped over to my bed. I almost expected her to scold me for being untidy. She removed the tube out of my throat and smiled. She put a cup of shaved ice in my hand.

"Sir, you need to let the ice melt and run down your throat until you get used to drinking on your own again." She snapped the chart shut and stomped out of the room.

Once she left, Charlie pulled his chair closer to my bed with concern written across his face. He leaned in and I croaked out, "The doctor said—explosion?"

"Chance, do you have any idea what happened?"

I moved my head slowly from side to side, not daring to move too hastily.

"Someone blew an old hunting cabin to bits where you were parked. The blast was heard first, and the fire could be seen from the golf course clubhouse half a mile away. They called the fire department.

When the firemen got there, the cabin was completely destroyed except for the fireplace and foundation. The firefighters found you on the ground at the bottom of a giant oak tree.

"At first, they thought you were dead. They couldn't find a pulse. As they were walking away, one of the firefighters noticed your fingers twitch. They started CPR and continued it until the ambulance arrived a short time later. The ambulance brought you to the hospital and called the Pinedale sheriff. He called me when they found your PI license and address. I had called him earlier and told him Mrs. McIntyre had hired you.

"I have to tell you, you had me worried when you didn't wake up. The doctor kept telling me your brain was functioning, your vitals were good, and so was your prognosis. He said not to worry. Chance, that was a little too close. You may not think it, but you are one lucky dog."

"What happened? All I can remember is hearing a loud bang."

"The explosion and fire were caused by Thermate-TH3. The propane tanks at the house added to the explosion. We found some wiring and a piece of metal housing that didn't burn. This could have been the triggering device. The lab is checking on that as well. My guess is that it was triggered by a timer or cell phone.

"From the tracks on the soft ground and judging by where they found you, you must have been picked up by the force of the explosion and sent through the air into the trunk of the tree."

The melting water was loosening my vocal cords, but I was still hoarse. "I don't remember anything. I started walking toward the cabin, and that's the last I remember."

My throat felt scratchy, causing me to have a coughing fit. My insides were as sore as my outside. I took more ice and lay back on my pillow, exhausted.

"What were you doing out there?"

"I was searching for Laurel McIntyre. I received word that she might be hiding out in that hunting cabin."

It dawned on me what this meant. My heart beat faster. I grabbed Charlie's arm. "Was she in the cabin?"

"It's too early to tell. They found some pieces of bone. The lab's working on that now. Thermate-TH3 burns hotter than a crematorium furnace. We were lucky to find that much. The explosion blew out the windshield on your jeep. I had it replaced and towed to your house.

"Phil said he'll pick you up when they release you. He's worried about you. He's been here every afternoon and spends the night."

"Thanks, Charlie...for everything."

"I'll let you know if they think the bone they found is hers. Forensics got a DNA sample from her mother for comparison. The lab in Charleston is so backed up, it'll be a while before we know."

"Somehow, I doubt it was her. She's smart. My gut tells me this was a ruse. I feel like a couple of college kids played me. Is my face red or what?"

Charlie chuckled. "Nice to see you haven't lost your sense of humor. I'm going to leave now and let you get some rest. You take care of yourself and be careful. Don't go off on your own. Whoever these people are, it's plain they have no regard for life." He waved and left.

I couldn't stop the nagging feeling that someone timed that explosion for my arrival. Could it have been Laurel? There must have been someone watching or a trip wire or something that set off the explosion. The only one with the answers was the one who had steered me in that direction, Susie. She would be my first stop when they released me from this sterile prison.

The Pinedale sheriff arrived at the hospital as I was having my lunch of broth and cherry Jell-O.

"Well, well, Sunday, glad to see you're awake and back in the land of the living. Want to tell me what happened?"

"You probably know more than I do. There's not much I can tell you. I received word that Laurel McIntyre might be hiding in the hunting cabin. I went to check it out. From what I've been told, the cabin blew to smithereens right when I got there. That's all I know."

"Why didn't you pass your information along to us instead of going there by yourself?"

"I would have if I had known someone was going to blow the place up. I didn't know how accurate my information was, or if she was really there. I wanted to check it out myself."

He gave me the evil eye before he spoke. "You wanted to check it out for yourself, eh?" He screwed his face up and winked. "And maybe, just maybe, you wanted to spirit her away before we had a chance to question her. You know what I think, Mr. Sunday?"

He stood at the foot of my bed holding on to the bed railing and leaning toward me.

I pushed my tray aside and sat up straighter in bed. I didn't like the direction this conversation was headed. "No, what do you think, Sheriff?"

"I think the McIntyre family paid you to blow up the building. I'd say they wanted to confuse us long enough for the family to get her out of the country. You miscalculated and almost blew yourself up. That's what I think." The sheriff crossed his arms over his chest and gave me his bad-cop stare.

I hope he didn't think he was going to intimidate me with his routine. I've been on the other side of a hostile interrogation enough to recognize his attitude. You need a good cop in your routine to pull off a bluff like he was trying.

"Sheriff, personally, I don't care what you think. You do seem to have a vivid imagination though. Added to that, you must have a low opinion of me to think I'm so inept as to almost blow myself up. All I can tell you is, I had nothing to do with this.

"You can check my record. I used to be a cop, a good cop. I've never taken a bribe in my life. Evidence at the scene should show I had nothing to do with the explosion. And one more thing, just so you'll know, they couldn't pay me enough to pull a stunt like that. Now if you're through, my lunch is getting cold."

Nurse porter was standing in the doorway with her arms crossed. She gave the sheriff the benefit of her 'it's time for you to leave' stare.

"You haven't heard the end of this, Sunday. If I find out you had a hand in this, your friends in Parkersburg PD won't be able to save you. As an ex-police officer, I'm sure you know the penalties for aiding and abetting a fugitive. If you're hiding her, it'll go easier on you if you fess up now."

I tried my best to smile. "Good to know. I thought she was wanted for questioning. Have you issued a warrant for her arrest?"

He didn't answer me.

The sheriff picked up his hat from the foot of my bed and struck his leg with it. He shook his head and left. After he left, I wondered why he thought I would get myself blown up and almost killed to help someone I didn't know. The family was comfortable, but they were not well off enough to pay an enormous sum for a disappearing act.

Nurse Porter came in after the sheriff left and began straightening my room and bed. "I see the sheriff is one of your admirers," she said with a chuckle.

"Yeah, I figure when this is over, we'll be bosom buddies."

That sent her into a fit of giggles as she left the room.

Phil came to the hospital that evening. I signed myself out against the doctor's wishes. I had to find out what was going on as quickly as possible. Someone besides myself was in danger. If Laurel wasn't in the cabin, where was she? Why was she conveniently absent? There again, I felt Susie was the link. Both girls could be in danger, or maybe only one of them.

We made it home and this time I slept in the bed upstairs. I don't know how anyone gets better in a hospital. The beds are hard as granite. Someone wakes you up to take a sleeping pill, and nurses come in all through the night, waking you up to take your blood or your vitals.

From the time my head hit the pillow at home, I slept like a log. I woke up to the sun shining through my window. When I looked around the room, I saw Phil sitting in a lawn chair in the corner and

Boomer lying by the side of my bed. Phil opened his eyes, nodded, and left. I couldn't help but smile. Boomer stretched, gave me the once over, and followed him out.

I showered and dressed. The aroma of a caffeinated cloud wafting up the stairs drew me down to the coffeepot. On the counter sat a Styrofoam carton with eggs, bacon, and hash browns, along with my morning paper. I would have to remember to thank Phil. I can't think when I enjoyed a breakfast more. After breakfast, I took my coffee outside and sat down to enjoy the morning.

There's something about waking up in a hospital and making it out of there that causes you to be thankful for another day above ground. Phil came by and poured himself a cup of coffee. He sat down and drank it without speaking. When he finished reading the paper, he stood up to leave. I stood up as well.

He hesitated, turned around, and looked at me. "Who did this?"

"I don't know for sure, but I intend to find out. I'm going to wait until just before dark and pay another visit to Miss Susie Sharp. She lives on Alfred Street. If I don't make it home, you can call Charlie and let him know. I should be back late. Stop by later tonight; I may need your help."

He nodded and headed for his cabin.

Boomer followed me upstairs and lay down by my bed on guard duty. I slept the rest of the day. My alarm went off at six in the evening. I showered and dressed. By the time the clock struck seven, I was headed out on Highway 47 to Parkersburg with Boomer by my side. Phil had brought my truck back earlier from the bar and parked it in the garage.

My truck is black with tinted windows. I had removed the interior bulbs, so the lights wouldn't come on when the door opens. I kept watching my back, but I didn't spot anyone following me. If there was someone, he was very good.

I parked in the alley behind the apartment building, walked around to the street side, and down the sidewalk until I came to Susie's address. As I climbed the stairs, I imagined she wouldn't be too pleased to see me again so soon or at all.

I knocked on her door. She opened it a crack without putting on the chain. The crack was big enough to put my foot in. When she saw me, she gasped. "What ya want? I got nothing more to say."

"I need to talk to you. You've got some explaining to do."

"I don't have to talk to you. You're not the police. Go away."

She tried to slam the door, but my foot prevented it. I pushed harder, and the door flew open, sending Susie into the nearby chair. She slid down the front of the chair to the floor. I came through the door and closed it behind me. Sitting down, I waited for Susie to compose herself. It might take a while. She was on something, and it wasn't alcohol this time.

When she didn't have the strength to help herself up, I helped her up and brought her a glass of water in her cleanest dirty glass. While I was in the kitchen, I noticed a box of cinnamon apple tea. It was not there when I'd visited her earlier. By itself, this didn't mean anything, but I distinctly remember her saying she didn't drink tea. I noticed her glancing in the direction of the bedroom a couple of times. She chewed on her index fingernail and stared everywhere but at me.

I took a chance. "Susie, who's in the bedroom? If it's Laurel, I need to talk to her. That explosion didn't fool anyone. You're both in danger. I need to get Laurel to a safe house, and you need to stay with a friend or go to your parents. Your parents would be the best idea."

She gulped, licked her lips, and stared at the floor. "I don't know what you're talking about. Laurel was killed in that explosion. The paper said so."

"I'm having trouble believing you. You haven't been straight with me once. You aren't too broken up over your friend's death. Why is that? Susie, you and I know she wasn't killed in the explosion. However, I almost was. It's time for you girls to quit playing with people's lives and tell me what's going on."

I stood up and started toward the bedroom.

Susie jumped up, spilling her water, and grabbed my hand.

I took another step, pulling her with me.

"Stop, stop, you're confusing me. Sit down, please. I'll tell you what you want to know."

"Let go of my hand."

She shook her head and held on tighter.

"It's a little late for a confession. I'm going to find out who's in that bedroom. Any reason why you don't want me to look in there?"

Susie didn't say anything.

She continued to hold my hand, shaking her head, and glancing toward the bedroom door. I thought about dragging her across the room with me, but I decided to wait out whoever was in there. Truth be told, my energy was beginning to wane. I didn't think I had the strength to pull her across the room.

After several tense minutes, the bedroom door opened slowly, and a girl stepped out. It was Laurel.

"Well, well, it's a miracle. She's alive. Laurel McIntyre, I presume."

She nodded her head but didn't speak. She walked over to us, helped Susie up, and stood beside her. Both girls stared up at me without speaking.

Susie broke the silence first. "Laurel, I'm so sorry. I tried, but you know I can't keep a secret."

Laurel sighed. "It's all right Susie. It's not your fault. Don't worry about it. I'm the one in a mess."

"We'll talk about that later. Right now, I need to get you somewhere safe. Pack your bag and meet me in the back alley. Cut the light off in the hall. If someone's watching, they might not see you come through the door. My truck will be waiting by the gate in back. It's black with an extended cab. Climb in the back of the cab and lie on the floor. There's a blanket on the seat. Cover yourself with it. Now, Susie, you need to leave as well. Do you have somewhere to stay that's safe?"

Susie sobered up in a short amount of time. She nodded and began to gather up her clothes. She threw them in supermarket bags, not bothering to check if they were clean or dirty. When the girls were ready, I left to get my truck. Both girls came out the back in a rush. Laurel climbed in my truck's backseat. Boomer sat up and observed everything that was going on. Susie stuffed her clothes into the trunk of her Camry. She followed us out of the alley. We turned left, and she turned right. I felt a little better. Laurel was my first concern.

We rode for several miles until we were almost home without speaking. Once we arrived at my drive, I turned off the pavement and started up the gravel drive. I hit the remote, and the gate to my drive opened. Going up the drive, Laurel raised her head. I put my hand on her head and pushed her down.

"Don't show yourself. When we get to my house, I'll park in the garage. There's a breezeway between the garage and the house. It's screened in. Luckily, there's latticework halfway up. In case someone is watching, I want you to scrunch down and follow behind me. Boomer will walk on the outside. Once inside, you can't stand in front of a window or anywhere you can be seen.

"Someone's been trying to follow me, so we can't take any chances. Someone attempted to kill you in the explosion, but I think that same someone knows you weren't killed.

"There's a bedroom upstairs with a twin bed. It's ready for you. You can't turn the light on. You'll just have to fumble around. There's a bathroom next door to the bedroom. It doesn't have a window so you can turn the light on, but only if the door is closed. Do you understand?"

I heard a muffled yes and a whimper.

"I know this is scary, but we have to take every precaution. I'm almost to the garage now. Remember to keep out of sight. I'll tell you when to get out of the backseat."

The garage door opened, and the light came on. I pulled in and stepped out of my truck like I always do. I waited until the door came down and the light went out. Boomer jumped down after me. As I opened the back door of my truck, Laurel crawled out. We made our way to the breezeway door with Boomer walking beside Laurel on the outside. She bent down and began making her way crablike behind me, dragging her backpack. Once inside I sat her in a corner of the kitchen where she couldn't be seen. I made the round of the windows and closed the plantation shutters.

I came back and looked in my pantry. "Are you hungry or would you like something to drink? All I've got are colas and oatmeal pies. I usually order takeout. Sorry."

"That'll do fine, Mr....uh."

"It's Sunday, Chance Sunday. Call me Chance. If you didn't know who I was, why'd you come with me? That was kind of risky considering the trouble you're in."

"Susie said Mom hired a PI. I don't know why I trusted you. I could hear you speaking to her. Something in your voice made me think you could be trusted. Besides, I had to get out of there. Susie's been my friend since kindergarten, but you saw the apartment mess, and the mess Susie was in. I didn't realize she was that far gone."

Everything that had happened in the last few days seemed to come crashing in on her. She gave a sharp gasp and plopped down on the floor.

"What's happened to my life? I had everything planned for my future. I can't see any way out of this mess."

The tears started flowing in earnest.

I squatted in front of her and took her hand.

"Laurel, your mother hired me to find you. I'm going to try to get you out of this mess if I can, but you have to be honest with me. We'll take it one step at a time. You're safe for now, but you've got to tell me what's going on.

"Before we go any further, I want to make one thing clear to you. If I find you were in on these murders, then I'll turn you over to the police without a second thought. I told your mother as much."

She nodded.

"I understand. Please believe me, I don't know who those three people were. I still can't believe it happened. I knew the people in the lab. I would never do anything to hurt them. They were always so nice to me."

She began biting her fingernails. She looked like a little girl instead of the college senior she was.

"All right, I'll take you at your word for now. Finish your drink and oatmeal pie. You can go on up to your bedroom. We'll discuss this tomorrow when you're rested. Wait here while I check outside."

I stood in the shadows for at least fifteen minutes and checked the area. I didn't see any movement, not even Phil. I went back in the house and gave her the OK to climb the stairs. After I heard her leave the bathroom and close the door to her bedroom, I went outside to wait for Phil. I moved my chair to where I could see a wide area of the woods.

Shortly after midnight, he came through the trees as silently as a whisper. Boomer saw him first and began wagging his tail. I hadn't heard or seen a thing until Boomer looked in his direction. I watched him make his way to the patio. I would not have seen him then if I didn't know the path he always took when he was on patrol. He wore camo and blended into his surroundings as well as anyone. He walked up to the patio and sat down across from me. Boomer came over to me and put his head in my lap. I patted his head and looked across at Phil.

"I found the woman I was looking for. She's upstairs in the first bedroom. I don't think anyone followed me here, but we need to be vigilant. I have a feeling whoever is looking for her is not going to stop. There's too much at stake. I'll introduce you to her tomorrow. For now, I'll say goodnight and let you get back on patrol."

I walked through the door, turned, and watched the foliage swallow him.

Before Phil faded into the background, Boomer stood by my side staring up at me.

"It's OK, boy, go on patrol with Phil."

He wagged his tail and left me, heading up the trail Phil had just taken.

Phil goes to see a counselor once a week. It doesn't appear to have helped much. At least if he stays on his medication, he can keep his demons at bay for a while. There is a facility in Houston, Texas, that is making great strides in helping people with PTSD, but I can't convince him to leave the safety of what he knows. I've offered to pay for his treatments. All he will say is he'll think it over.

I closed the door, went back inside, and sat in my recliner. Too tired to read, the last thing I remember was closing my eyes. I awoke with the sun's rays filtering into where I lay.

I heard a rattle overhead and soon Laurel came down the stairs in her bare feet. She had on faded denim jeans and a T-shirt with the logo Plan B across the front. I hoped we had a Plan B. She slid along the wall until she saw me. I motioned for her to come on down.

In the kitchen were two Styrofoam cartons of eggs, bacon, and hash browns. Phil must have left them while I slept. Sometimes I think he might be a ghost or an alien. He never makes a sound. You think of him and there he is. The coffee finished dripping into the carafe.

"Phil left us breakfast. Dig in." I pushed a carton toward her. "What do you take in your coffee?"

"I don't drink coffee. I brought a tea bag."

She took a bag out of her jeans' pocket and held it up.

"Here's a cup. On the right side of the coffeemaker, you can put in water. Put your cup there and push the button. It'll be hot in no time. In the meantime, don't let your breakfast get cold."

We both ate without looking up.

She fixed her tea and sat back at the island. I hated to push her but there wasn't much time.

"Laurel, I need to hear your side of the story. I can't hide you forever. I have to think of my license. I'm obligated to tell the sheriff where you are. I can't delay much longer. He already thinks I helped you stay in hiding."

"Please, don't turn me in. If they put me in jail, I'll not live long enough to go to trial."

"If that's what you think, then you'd better explain in detail."

She cleared her throat and drank some of her tea. After sitting her cup down, she took a deep breath, and searched my face before beginning her story.

"I worked at the lab Mondays, Wednesdays, and Fridays, starting at seven in the evening. Janitorial work, mostly, but sometimes if I came in early, they let me help with their experiments. That's the main reason I started working there. I wanted the feel of a real lab. I was torn between research and teaching when I get my degree.

"It all happened on a Thursday. I wasn't supposed to be there. I'd asked Mr. Leslie earlier in the week if I could work a different night. I wanted to have a long weekend at home. You see, I'd had some personal problems. I needed to be away from Pinedale and my friends for a few days to get my head straight."

"Did anyone else know you were working that night?"

"I don't think so. I didn't tell anyone. I came in that Thursday night and began cleaning up as usual. I took my supper break, which is a half hour. I got a cola out of the refrigerator and sat down to study for my exam. It was scheduled for nine the next day. After that, I didn't have any more classes, and I could go home.

"It's usually very quiet. The scientists on the main floor of the lab go home at six, unless they have something critical. The lab in the basement is off-limits to me. They said they had to have a controlled environment, and they would clean it. I was always very careful not to disturb anything, but maybe they were afraid I'd steal their meth.

"Soon I heard a commotion in the outer hallway. If they were expecting a late delivery, they would have told me. One of the scientists would have been there to accept delivery. I stood up and peeked around the corner of the lunchroom doorway. Three masked men were coming down the hall. They didn't see me. I ducked back in the lunchroom and glued myself to the wall.

111

"At first, I didn't know what to do. I slid down the wall and crawled into the nearest corner. That's when I heard gunshots. Frantic, I looked for a place to hide. I happened to look over at the sink. The sink cabinet is large. I crawled into it and tried not to breathe.

"I heard footsteps, and someone came into the lunchroom. I could see through the slit where the cabinet doors came together. He looked at my open book, looked around the room, and left. Soon I heard running feet, and the outside door slammed."

"Were all three men armed?"

"I couldn't tell you. The first one had a gun. All I could see was the man in the lunchroom. I was so scared. After I heard running footsteps, the place became scary quiet. I stayed where I was for another five minutes at least. It felt like an eternity. Finally, I got up enough nerve to crawl out of the cabinet. I sat on the floor trying to breathe. My legs were too weak to hold me up. I took a deep breath and crawled over to the stairs going down to the basement."

I could tell from the expression on her face that she was living the whole experience again. Her eyes were large with fright, and her breathing was labored as she remembered. She shook her head to clear her thoughts and continued with her story.

"I-I saw Mr. Leslie draped across the steps at the bottom of the stairs. He was lying in a pool of blood. The door to the lab was open. I know I should have checked to see if anyone was alive, but I didn't. I couldn't. I was too scared."

She shook her head and looked down at her trembling hands.

"I just wanted to get away."

When she looked up, she had that haunted demeanor I had seen too many times.

"Could you see if any of the men had anything on that you could recognize? A logo on their shirt or, if they spoke, their voice, the color of their eyes and hair."

She shook her head.

"No...er...no. They were dressed all in black with ski masks, jeans, and dark hoodies."

"Why do you think your life is in danger if you go to the sheriff?"

"Because whatever they were doing in the lab was suspicious. One night several months ago about eight in the evening, a man dressed like a sheriff, or a deputy maybe, entered the lab. He came in without buzzing for someone to let him in. They had to be expecting him to leave the door unlocked, or they could have given him the combination for the door lock.

"He came to see the people in the basement. He didn't see me. I was in Mr. Carter's office tidying up. He went down the stairs as if he knew where he was going. I didn't see his face, only his back. When he left, he was carrying a briefcase. He didn't have it before he went down.

"Mr. Leslie took a trip to New York the next day. When he came back, he was happier, less worried. I didn't think anything about it. I just thought his experiments were going well. About a month after that, another man came after hours. He was carrying a small tote bag. It looked empty when he went down to the lab, but half-full when he left."

"Were they cooking meth in their private lab?"

"No, I don't think so. I know the smell and there was some of that, but it wasn't as strong as it should have been for a production lab. They had to make some to give to their test subjects. They were trying to come up with a drug to deal with meth addiction and a better treatment for a meth overdose. Their research was becoming more and more crucial. Dying from an overdose is a real possibility.

"So. no...they weren't cooking meth."

She shook her head, looked down at her hands, and took a deep breath before raising her head.

"What else could they have been doing?" I asked.

"They may have been doing something illegal, but I can't be sure. I hate to say it if it isn't true and ruin their reputation." She took a ragged breath and looked at me with the saddest eyes. "I believe they were smuggling something."

"They're dead. You can't do them any harm now. Their families deserve to know what happened. Why do you think they were smuggling?"

"They used Rhesus monkeys in their testing because they are the most closely related to humans. Their brains can serve as a model for the human brain. They kept four in cages. When I first came to work there, they took me on a tour of their facility.

"When they finished testing on a monkey, they euthanized it and ordered another. A new monkey came in about every four months from Africa. This was kind of unusual to get test subjects from Africa. They usually came from China. I didn't think anything of it at first. I thought they must be getting them cheaper from Africa. These animals came in wooden crates with metal bars."

Laurel stood up and walked around the room. She began to pace in front of the fireplace.

"I was taking the trash out one night when I accidentally bumped into one of the old cages. Two of the bars were loose, and something glassy fell to the ground. I picked it up. It felt hard and looked like rock candy. I put it in water, but it didn't melt or feel sticky. I have no way of knowing, but I think it was an uncut diamond.

"I checked the other cages, and each one had two hollow metal bars on each side, and they were loose on each cage."

She reached inside her pocket and took out a small plastic packet with her find in it.

I took it and held it up to the light.

"I can take this to a jeweler I know and get it checked out. That would certainly be a reason to kill. Uncut diamonds are the easiest to convert to currency. Did your employers give the impression of being more affluent than usual?"

"When I first came there, they paid me minimum wage and sometimes that was late. About seven months ago they gave everyone a raise and started paying me on time. They bought new and expensive, state-of-the-art lab equipment. I didn't think anything about it at first. I thought they must have had a breakthrough in their research and found more funding."

"Did you tell anyone about your suspicions?"

"I was afraid to say anything. I know my college bills are a burden to my parents. They were having money problems, and I didn't want to add to the mix. I wanted to help pay as much as I could. I couldn't afford to lose this job, but I didn't want to get into trouble either. I've been so worried. I didn't know what to do. I did tell Susie, but I don't think she remembered me telling her. She was too busy being Susie."

"She may have told someone. Did she tell you where she was going when she left last night?"

"No, but she has a friend over in Belpre. She would be the only person I can think of that Susie would go to. Her name is Gloria Rader, and she lives on Braun Road. It's the apartment building past the kennel. Hers is apartment B."

"I had better talk to her. If she told someone, they could be the ones who did this. We need something to prove you had nothing to do with the break-in or the murders.

"Here, write down Susie's cell number."

I handed her my notebook.

"First, I'm going to talk to the sheriff and tell him the circumstances. I may be forced to turn you over to him immediately. If I do, we'll get you a lawyer, and he'll insist on added security for you. In the meantime, try not to worry. Phil's here, and he knows about your trouble. If you need anything, call Phil's number. I left it beside the phone. We passed his cabin on the way up the drive, but don't go down there, don't leave the house, and don't call anyone else. And most importantly, stay away from the windows."

"Aye, aye, captain," she said and saluted me.

She managed to smile. I gave her a pat on the shoulder and left. As I came down the drive, I saw Phil sitting on his porch. I stopped by his place and told him my plans.

Chapter 7

The Do Drop Inn has the only working pay phone for miles around. I stopped there and phoned the sheriff. His secretary finally agreed to let me talk to him. I heard what sounded like angry mumbling in the background before he came to the phone.

"Sheriff Henry speaking. What do you want?"

"And a hello to you too, Sheriff. This is Chance Sunday."

"This day just gets better and better. I wondered when you'd be calling. Have something to confess?"

"I don't really have time for this. You can call Lt. Charles Parks if you still have doubts about me."

"Don't get on your high horse. As a matter of fact, I did call Lt. Parks. What do you want, or is this a social call? I'm a busy man."

The sheriff seemed to be enjoying himself at my expense.

"Sheriff, it's important that I talk to you and soon. I don't want to say this over the phone or in your office. Would it be possible to meet somewhere on neutral territory? When I explain, you'll understand why I'm being so secretive."

"I don't like this meeting in secret. I've talked to Lt. Parks, and he gives you a good name. That would be the only reason I'd agree to meet you. I'll let my secretary know where I'm going, but I won't say why or with whom. Does that satisfy you?"

"Yep, I'll take that. Where do you want to meet?"

"There's an Episcopal Church outside the city limits on the way out of Pinedale toward Parkersburg. It sits back from the road and has a big parking lot. I'll meet you there. Do you know the area?"

"Yeah, I know the place. The sooner the better."

"This had better be good. I'm taking a chance on you, Sunday. Can you be there in half an hour?"

"No problem. See you, sheriff."

I made it to the parking lot of the church before the sheriff. At least, I thought I did. I had the feeling someone was watching me. It was a large parking lot, a picturesque setting, but a long way from the nearest neighbor, which was a retirement complex. I came to a stop in front of the church office.

I only had to wait five minutes. The sheriff pulled up slowly and carefully. He drove around the parking lot in front and back of the church before he turned his attention to me. He drove around the parking lot one more time and came to rest beside my truck. I got out and stood by the passenger door of his SUV. He nodded and flipped the lock. I opened the door and slid inside.

"Well, I'm here. This better be worth my time. What's with all the cloak and dagger?"

He looked down and fiddled with the loose change in the console.

"Thanks for meeting me. I know this is unusual, but when I tell you why, you'll understand. I had to do it this way, so this conversation is between you and me until we decide what is best to do."

"What you mean is until I decide what is best to do."

"Sure, sheriff. I stand corrected. In the end it's up to you, but I have responsibilities as well. I don't want to argue over who does what. This is serious. As you know, I've been searching for Laurel McIntyre. And...as it happens, I found her."

The sheriff did not react. I would hate to play poker with him.

After several tense seconds, he raised his head to look at me.

"Good to know the combined forces of Pinedale and Parkersburg couldn't find her, but you did. So, she wasn't killed in that explosion. I thought that was a little too convenient. I suppose you want me to believe you just happened upon her," the sheriff said, and waved his hand impatiently for me to continue.

"I'm not asking you to believe anything. I'm telling you what happened. You can believe me or not. I had a little help in finding her. I'm trying to be straight with you. People sometimes talk to me when they won't talk to the police. She told me her story, and I'll tell it to you. I know you'll want to hear the story straight from her. I tried to get her to come with me today, but she's too afraid.

"She claims she was an innocent bystander. There were three men who entered and killed the people in the lab. They had on ski masks and hoodies and were dressed all in black. She hid under the sink, which is what saved her."

"Not new information. Same as the drug salesman told us. Tell her if she gives herself up, we can protect her. I'm not making any deals."

"We're not asking for a deal. She claims she's innocent."

"OK, for argument's sake, let's say she tells a convincing story. Just between you and me, what's your take on this, Sunday? Do you believe her story? It's a little out there. You would think after they saw her phone and textbook opened in the lunchroom, they would have searched the place."

"I'm not so sure. They'd just killed three people and stole something. I imagine they were in an all-fired hurry to get away. They had on masks so no one could recognize them.

"In answer to your question, it's my job to believe her. Her mother is my client. Nevertheless, I have to say, regardless of what you think, I believe her."

The sheriff grinned and shook his head.

"There's a sucker born every minute."

"Sheriff, I'm asking you to keep an open mind."

"All right, all right, go on with your tale," the sheriff said, with impatience spewing out.

"I'm coming to the why we're meeting like this and the part you will question without a doubt. She thinks the people in the lab who were killed were smuggling uncut diamonds. Did you find a meth lab when you investigated?"

"Not a full-blown lab. They had a small quantity and a log book detailing their use of the meth. It appeared to be just enough for their experiments. At first glance, everything is legal and aboveboard.

"I find it hard to believe respected scientists would be into anything illegal. I knew everyone at the lab personally. Leslie and I went through school together. Our families saw each other socially. I believe I would have known if he was into anything illegal."

I said nothing, but that was my thought as well.

"That seems to be the general opinion, but Laurel thinks they were smuggling diamonds in the hollowed-out metal bars of the research animal cages. She found an object on the ground. When she examined the cages, she found two of the bars on each side of the old cages were hollow."

I took the vial out of my jacket and let the sheriff look at it. He examined the vial, but his face did not register surprise.

"I was going to take it to a jeweler and let him evaluate it," I said.

"No need, I'll turn it over to the crime lab."

He took the vial and put it in a plastic evidence bag. We both signed it.

"Now, to my story and the part you're not going to believe. She said one night after business hours, she saw a man in a sheriff's uniform let himself in the back door. He walked down to the basement as if he had been there before. She says she only saw his back so she can't identify him, but he may think she can. If I have to turn her in and if this man is one of yours, her life will be in danger.

"When he left, he was carrying a briefcase. He didn't have one when he went in. You have to admit this sounds suspicious. Would one of your deputies have had anything official to do for the lab?"

The sheriff looked at me, swallowed hard, and then looked down at his feet. He removed his hat and ran his fingers through his hair. Clearing his throat before he spoke, he said, "Not that I know of, not out of my office. This might as well be the Syfy channel. She's sure he was in a sheriff's uniform?"

I nodded.

He stared at me and shook his head in denial.

"I find it hard to believe someone I work with is mixed up in this business. I will have to give this intel to the DA and let him decide what we need to do next. If what she says is true, she might be better off with you for the time being."

"I have a man with her now. He's watching her while I run down a few leads. Here's my card. I've written my home landline on the back, along with my address. My office and cell are on the front. As you know, cell reception is poor in my area. I think I can convince her to meet you if you want to hear her story in person."

"For now, I'll say no. When I want to speak to her, she must come in whether or not she wants to. Is that understood?"

I nodded.

"We'll meet here at the church. I think the padre will let me use a Sunday School room for a meeting place. I'll call you up and give you a time; I'll just say the same place, nothing else."

The sheriff chuckled.

"I take it back. It's not the Syfy channel. It's more like the Mystery channel. We sound like a couple of spies," he said with a grin.

He turned the key in the ignition and put his truck in gear. I felt the truck drifting backward. That must be my cue to get out. I stepped out of his SUV and watched him drive away.

Back in my truck, I found I had at least three bars of cell service. I tried Susie's number. She answered on the fifth ring.

"Hi, Susie, this is Chance Sunday. I was checking to make sure you're all right. Are you staying with a friend or your parents?"

"Yeah, I'm fine. I'm staying with my friend Gloria. No need to worry. I'll be careful. I may go stay at my parents this weekend."

"That sounds like a good plan, at least until Laurel's ordeal is over. I know Laurel talked over her problem with you and her friends at Thanksgiving. Did she tell you any more details about what she suspected was going on at the research lab?"

"She might have, but I don't remember. Why? What was going on?"

"It's best you don't know. Did she tell you about any other problems she was having, personal or otherwise?"

"If she did, I don't remember."

"If you think of anything, you've got my number. In the meantime, don't talk to anyone you don't know and stay away from town until I can get this sorted out."

"No problem."

She hung up.

Somehow, I wasn't satisfied. I guess I expected more questions from her and an offer to do anything to help her best friend. The hairs on the back of my neck were tingling. I thought Susie and Laurel were lying to me. I don't know why. Maybe it was a lie of omission. It was something in the change in the tone of their voices and the way Laurel didn't look me in the eye. I planned to pay Susie's apartment a visit later tonight. For now, I headed home to check on my charge.

I made my way up my drive, walked through the back door, and stopped in my tracks. I heard people talking, and I saw a scene I'd never imagined. Phil and Laurel were talking and laughing like old friends. I stood in the door with my mouth open. They turned and smiled at me. Boomer was lying at Laurel's feet, looking at me, and wagging his tail.

"You two are getting along nicely."

Phil saluted and left without saying another word.

"I like him," Laurel said and stared toward the closing door. "Anyone can tell he's damaged goods, but he's someone you can trust to have your back."

She looked away from me and hugged her chest.

"What did the sheriff say?"

"He said you can stay here for the time being."

Laurel sighed and looked relieved.

"When he's checked out your story as I told it about the smuggling, he'll eventually want to hear your story in your own words. For now, he's taking everything to the DA. He'll call me and let me know when they want to meet.

"I have to leave for my office. There are books in the library down the hall. No internet and no TV. You'll have to make do. I have a CD player and radio. The CDs are most likely not your kind of music. I like instrumental music, so you'll find most of my CDs are classical or old-time instrumentals."

"Not a problem. I like classical music too. Before I decided on chemistry and teaching, I took oboe lessons. I played in my high-school orchestra. My teacher said I had potential and for a time, I thought of going to the Juilliard School of Music. I applied and was accepted. Perhaps it would have been better if I had gone."

She looked so miserable and lost.

"Laurel, I'm sorry. I want to tell you everything will be all right, but I don't want to make promises I can't keep or have no control over the outcome. For what it's worth, I believe your story. I'm working to find out something that will help, but I don't have much to work with."

She managed a smile.

"Oh, well, water under the bridge. I feel better than I have since it happened. Don't worry about me. Go to the office. I'll manage. Phil's here."

"Good. I will see your mother tonight and tell her I found you. That should ease her mind, but it also puts you in more danger. She's liable to let it slip you're still alive. It would not take a genius to connect you to me and figure out how to find you."

"I'm willing to take that chance. I'm sorry for what I put her through. Thank you."

She reached into her jeans and handed me a note.

"I was going to ask you to give this to her. Please, will you take it to her?"

I nodded, put the note in my shirt pocket, and turned to go.

Before I went through the door, I turned back.

"Oh, Laurel, I forgot to tell you Phil will bring you supper if I'm late."

She waved goodbye.

While in the office, I took care of a security check for a small office downtown. Paid bills, sent out invoices, fiddled around, and drank too much coffee. I had accomplished what Mrs. McIntyre hired me to do, but I felt I had missed something. I'd found Laurel, but I was still uneasy. Something was nagging at me, something I'd overlooked. It was almost closing time. I processed some more paperwork until it was time to go see Mrs. McIntyre.

Driving over to 2114 Clark Avenue, I ran through what I would say to her in my head. I had no idea how she would take the news. Their house was in one of the better sections of town. It used to be the area everyone wanted to have a house in during the sixties. I had never seen the house in daylight, but it turned out to be a substantial two-story with gray brick halfway up and light green clapboards the rest of the way. The lot had a split-rail fence with an enormous oak tree at each corner of the front yard. A large picture window looked out on a covered porch with two white rockers. I saw someone moving around inside. I stepped up on the porch and rang the doorbell.

A heavyset man in his early fifties answered the door. His eyes were bloodshot. He was loose-limbed with a prominent beer belly. He held on to the door to steady himself with one hand and took out his handkerchief. He tried to blow his nose with the other hand, but all he managed to do was wipe his face. His open shirt was half in and half out of his sweatpants and there was a stain on his undershirt. His face was unshaven, and he had a sullen expression which didn't help his appearance any with the smell of cheap whiskey surrounding him like a cloud.

"W-what ya w-want?" He continued to hold on to the door in an attempt to remain upright.

"May I speak to Mrs. McIntyre?"

He slammed the door in my face, and I could hear him yelling for his wife. She peeped around the door and came through when she realized it was me. I couldn't believe it was possible for her to be tenser, but she drew herself up, visibly tighter.

Her husband made me uneasy. I looked over her shoulder to see where he was before I spoke. I glimpsed him pouring another drink at the dining room table.

"Mrs. McIntyre, I need to talk to you. Would you mind if we walk a ways up the street?"

She stepped out without saying a word and closed the door behind her. We walked without talking about a block and a half to the middle school. There were benches out front. We walked over to a bench under a street lamp, and she sat down.

She stared at me with eyes that had seen too much and had no hope. She hiccupped and took a deep breath. "I know what you're going to say. The police were here. They said Laurel was staying in that cabin that blew up. They found a piece of bone..." She looked away and stared off in the distance.

I took her hand in mine. Her hand was so cold, it didn't feel like flesh and bone.

"Mrs. McIntyre, I want you to remain calm and listen to what I have to say. The bone doesn't belong to Laurel. I found her...I found your daughter, Laurel."

"You found Laurel?"

"Yes, ma'am, she's alive. I have her in a guarded location. You can't tell anyone or let on that you think she's safe."

She hung her head and nodded as the tears flowed. I put my arm around her, and she turned into my chest. Her sobs racked her thin body. To anyone observing, you would think I had given her the worst news instead of the best.

"Ma'am, I talked with the sheriff. He left her in my care for the time being, until he talks to the DA."

I reached into my pocket and took out Laurel's note.

"I understand."

Grasping the note in her hand, she stared at it. At last, she swallowed hard and opened the note. She read it by the light from the streetlamp. After she finished, I set the note on fire and obliterated the ashes.

"Please tell her I love her too."

"I'll do that, Mrs. McIntyre.... Ma'am, it's none of my business, but I couldn't help notice your husband's condition. It looks as if he's been hitting the bottle a little hard. He might become abusive in his condition. Are you all right to be there alone with him?"

"Yes, I think so. I've begged him to get help, but he just cusses me and staggers off. He owns a construction company, and fortunately he has a good office manager and foreman. He goes in later and later each morning and some mornings he doesn't go in at all. I don't know what to do. I can't worry about him and everything else."

She wrung her hands and looked like a trapped animal.

"We'll work on one problem at a time. I can't tell you where I have Laurel stashed for safety reasons. I'll try to keep you informed, but I think it's safest if I drop by from time to time and update you in person."

She nodded her head and wiped her eyes.

"When the time comes, she will need a good lawyer. Not a public defender."

"You think she's involved in this terrible thing."

"I don't know, ma'am. She says she isn't. If the sheriff takes her into custody, we have to insist that she has extra protection. A lawyer is best equipped to do that. I'm thinking the finest criminal attorney in town is Walt Cramer."

"Yes, I went to school with him. He has a good reputation. When do you think I ought to talk to him?"

"As soon as possible. He needs to be prepared when they take her into custody, which should be soon. I'll be glad to talk to him if he needs my input. However, in case someone is watching, I don't think it's a good idea for us to be seen together going into his office. If the person who tried to blow Laurel up is watching, I want him to think he completed the job."

We stood up and walked back to her house. Along the way, she grabbed my arm and held on tightly until she could speak.

"I'll go see him tomorrow. I can't thank you enough for all you've done. I can't tell you how relieved I am," she said, and started to cry again.

"Mrs. McIntyre, you've got to pull yourself together. Laurel's safe for now. We're moving forward. I'm still checking leads that I hope will clear her of any involvement. Try not to worry."

She nodded and kept her head down.

We reached the house, and I walked her to her porch. As we stepped upon the porch, the door flew open, and Mr. McIntyre came barreling out. As he went by, he swung at me. I dodged his punch, but he hit my shoulder and almost knocked me down. As he flew past, he lost his balance and landed with a thud in the yard, skidding along the ground. He lay awfully still and quiet. When the surprise wore off, I stepped off the porch to check on him.

Mrs. McIntyre stood behind me wringing her hands and shifting from one foot to the other. I knelt down and felt his pulse.

"Oh, dear, oh, dear, is he dead?" she asked and hovered over my shoulder.

When I straightened up, I could see several neighbors standing in their front windows, watching the show.

"No, ma'am. His pulse is strong. I think he passed out. I'll help you get him back in the house. Where do you want to put him?"

"Oh, my, he's too heavy to get up the stairs. Perhaps the basement would be the best place to take him. There's a stair chair lift down to the family room. We could put him on the sofa."

"All right. If you'll help me get him into a standing position, I can get my arm around his shoulders."

The man weighed two fifty if he weighed an ounce. He was a dead weight. It was like shifting Shamu.

With Mrs. McIntyre's help, I half-dragged, half-lifted him through the door and managed to get him in the chair lift. He snored at full volume and blew out toxic fumes. It took both of us to keep him upright on the chair. We made it to the basement. I laid him on the sofa on his side with a pillow under his head. She covered him with an afghan, and we left him snoring deafeningly.

Back in the living room, Mrs. McIntyre collapsed on the sofa, shook her head, and wrung her hands. I wanted to help her, but I didn't want to be any more involved in their problems than I was already. Some families suck you into their mire of despair, and before long you're trapped with no way out. I have to keep reminding myself I'm here to do a job. A job I'm paid to do and nothing more.

I sat on the sofa beside her. "Mrs. McIntyre, are you all right?"

"I'm sorry you had to see that. He hasn't always been this way. The heavy drinking started about two years ago when his business wasn't going well, but not to this extent. He hasn't been sober since Laurel disappeared."

"Is there someone who could stay with you? I don't want to leave you here alone. He's in a dangerous mood. If he wakes up, he may be fighting mad."

"I'll call my brother. He lives in Marietta. I'm sure he'll come over."

"Good, I'll wait here until he comes." I went out on the porch and sat in one of the rockers.

About an hour later, Paul Weeks pulled into the drive. He came across the walk and up on the porch like a breath of fresh air with a smile on his face. He was a couple of years younger than Mrs. McIntyre. He stood over six feet, and from the way he carried himself, he looked like he could take care of an abusive drunk. We shook hands and walked into the house. Mrs. McIntyre was asleep on the sofa. He frowned at his sister and shook his head with concern. I explained why we'd called him.

"I'm glad you did. Of course, I'll stay until he wakes up, and I'm sure everything is all right with him. You did right to call me. Carol's got a hard row to hoe with that husband of hers." He looked back at his sister.

I inched my way to the door. He held out his hand, and we shook hands again as I prepared to leave. Paul walked me to my truck. Once out of the house, it was like walking from under a cloud to the sunlight of a new day. I didn't realize how oppressive the atmosphere was inside the house. No wonder Mrs. McIntyre was on her last nerve.

After I got into my truck, Paul kept standing there looking at me as if he had something on his mind. I rolled down the window.

"Mr. Sunday, how bad is he? I've tried asking my sister, but she just shakes her head and cries."

"He needs help. I'm not sure your sister has the strength to insist he gets it. He took a swing at me as I stepped up on the porch and then passed out in the yard. I don't think your sister can take much more with her daughter missing and no support from her husband. I'm worried about her."

"So am I. Thank you for your concern. I've tried to get her to come home with me, but she's determined to stick by her husband. She has too much pride and on top of that she's as stubborn as a mule." He snorted. "Don't worry, Mr. Sunday, I'll do my best to take care of her, and I'll talk to her husband for all the good it'll do.

"Is there any news on my niece one way or the other?"

"Sorry, but I have nothing to report so far."

I rolled up the window and waved goodbye. Through my rearview mirror, I watched him walk back in the house with his head bent. I didn't envy him his task. I have to tell myself I can't solve everyone's problems. One problem at a time, and right now that problem was finding out who knew about the diamonds and killed those people. My gut told me Susie or Laurel, or both, knew more than they were telling me.

Chapter 8

I made my way down Dudley Avenue and across town to Alfred Street. The parking area for Susie's apartment was about halfway down the back alley. I slowed and had almost turned my truck into a vacant parking space when I noticed a light on in her apartment. Not wanting to draw attention to myself, I cruised on by and turned at the end of the alley. I drove back onto Alfred Street and parked across from her apartment building on the street side.

Above her apartment building, farther up the hill, was a park on the next street. There was a set of steep steps rising from Alfred to the next street and the park. I climbed the steps. Hopping the fence into the Alfred Street alley, I made my way back to Susie's apartment house, where the light was still on. Someone had parked a familiar red Mustang with the top down in the parking area.

An old derelict garage butted up to the parking spaces. I tried the garage door, and it was locked. A child could have picked the lock. I took a piece of wire from the rubbish heap beside the front of the garage and worked my magic on the lock. The tumblers clicked, and I stepped inside. There was a dirty six-paned window in back. I pulled up a rusted barstool and listened to it creak as I sat down. I hoped it would bear up under my weight. Grabbing an old newspaper, I cleared a spot on one of the window panes with an unobstructed view into Susie's apartment.

Two shadows moved across the kitchen window. I watched as an arm went around one shadow, drawing it into what looked like an embrace. There did not appear to be a struggle. One shadow drew the person out of sight of the window, and the kitchen light went dark. A light came on in the bedroom and then went out. I sat where I was and waited.

I hated stakeouts. They reminded me too much of my previous occupation at the police department. It must have been two hours later when a light came on and roused me out of my boredom. There was another embrace, and one shadow moved from my view.

A short time later, Davis Howell came tripping down the walk and vaulted into his red Mustang convertible. He backed out, squealed the tires, and roared away. Throughout an investigation, you expect a few lies, but it appeared everyone in this little circle of friends had something to hide.

I turned back to my windowpane and saw the light was still on in the kitchen. Making my way in through the back door, I climbed the stairs to Susie's apartment. I knocked on the door and heard running footsteps. The door flew open.

"What did you forget?" Her smile faded when she saw me.

"I didn't forget anything, but you did. You forgot to tell me about your boyfriend. What else have you forgotten?"

She tried to slam the door in my face, but I again had my foot strategically placed. I pushed on the door and made my way into the room.

"Get out or I'll call the cops."

"You do that, Missy, and I'll tell them how you tried to get me killed with that explosion. You were the only one who knew I was going out there. On second thought, I think I'll call them myself." I took out my cell and started to dial.

"Wait, wait, no, no, don't call. I guess it's no use now. What do you want to know? I swear I knew nothing about the explosion. All I did was give Laurel a place to stay."

She sat down straight away and leaned back in the chair with her hand over her eyes.

"Laurel's my best friend in the whole world. I wouldn't hurt her, no way. I had no reason to hurt you either since you were trying to help her."

"Look, Susie, I don't care what your relationship is with Davis. I only care about Laurel and keeping her safe. I'm worried about you too. The last time I saw you, I told you to stay with a friend or your parents. What I find is you're keeping a rendezvous in your apartment. Don't you understand you're in danger?"

"I had to see Davis. I love him. We've kept our relationship a secret. No one knows except his parents, and they're not happy about it."

"Who knew you were hiding Laurel?"

"I don't know, no one. It was just the four of us. The four musketeers," she grinned sheepishly.

"That makes four people who might have told other people. Who are the four of you?"

"Davis, Laurel, Brian, and myself. We've been friends for years. No one would hurt Laurel.

"Someone must have followed me out there. I didn't speak to anyone except Davis and Brian, and they would not have told anyone. Laurel's mother didn't even know."

"Laurel couldn't call from the cabin, so I couldn't call her. She couldn't call out unless she walked for a mile to get a signal. There are no pay phones that I can think of where she could've called from."

"OK, if you think of anything, call me at once. Now, you need to get out of here right now. I'm serious. Get whatever you need and go to your friend in Belpre. I'll wait outside until you leave."

Susie nodded that she understood, but I don't think she grasped the seriousness of her situation. She walked me to the door. I made my way down the stairs. Her neighbor was waiting in his doorway. He waved to Susie.

"Is everything all right, Susie?"

"Yeah, thanks, Mr. Corn."

She stepped inside her apartment and slammed the door. Mr. Corn gave me the once-over and stood in the hall until I went out the back door before stepping into his apartment and closing his door. I hurried to the garage to watch the area.

I had an eerie feeling something was going to happen. The air felt electric. I sensed someone was watching the apartment house, but I didn't see anyone in the area. Looking up, I could see Susie moving around. I hoped she was packing. Next, I glanced around the back alley and the nearby houses. Nothing moved. No new cars since I'd come.

When I looked up at her apartment again, there was another shadow in Susie's kitchen window. It looked like the two were struggling. The second shadow was choking the first shadow. I ran for the garage door. What a time for the old door to stick. I braced my foot against the wall and jerked the door open, breaking the rotted door jamb. Racing up the walk and down the hall past Mr. Corn standing in his doorway, I made it to the stairs. I took the steps two at a time. By this time, people were standing in the hall.

I made it to Susie's apartment and tried the door knob. The door was closed and locked. I beat on the door with my fist and called Susie's name. Putting my ear to the door, I couldn't hear any noise in her apartment. I kicked the door in and fumbled for the light. The place was in even worse disarray than the first time I was there. Susie had put up quite a fight.

Standing in the doorway, I scanned the room. My eyes came to rest on her body. It was lying in a pool of blood halfway in the kitchen and halfway in the living room. It was not hard to tell even from across the room that someone had cut her throat. Seeing her vacant staring eyes, I knew nothing could be done for her. I backed out of the apartment, closed the door, and bumped into a group of her neighbors peering in the door opening.

"Ma'am, call the cops," I said to the woman nearest my left shoulder.

She stood immobile with her mouth gaping and eyes staring at me. The door to the next apartment stood open.

"Is it all right if I use your phone?"

She came alive enough to nod and point her finger to her door. As if of one mind, the group's eyes followed me into her apartment. I used her phone to call the police and report the murder. Next, I called Charlie on my cell while I waited.

Five minutes later, two policemen came up the stairs. The cops looked around at the growing crowd.

"Which one of you called 911?" the first officer on the scene asked.

Everyone turned in unison toward me.

I stepped forward. "I did, Officer." As I started to reach into my pocket for my ID, I saw the officer put his hand on his sidearm. I held up my hand. "I'm just getting my ID."

"See you do it slowly," he said, keeping his hand on his sidearm and his eyes on me.

He took my ID and wrote my registration number. After showing it to his partner, he handed it back to me. His partner patted me down. I was glad I didn't have a knife or bring my gun with me tonight.

The first officer looked around at the crowd. "You people go back to your apartments. We'll be by later to take your statement. No one is to leave the premises until we're through here."

I heard grumbling before the crowd dispersed.

He pointed at me. "You, private dick, wait here and don't move from this spot."

Since there wasn't a chair, I leaned against the wall. Too many long nights and no sleep had left me tired and sleepy. I slid down the wall to the floor to wait.

As they walked away, one of the officers asked the one in charge, "Why are you being so hard on the PI?"

"Two reasons. Number one, I don't like private cops who are nothing more than bottom-feeders at best and will do anything for a buck. Number two, the one to report the crime more often than not committed it."

Both of the cops looked back at me. My energy had drained from my body. I was too tired to care what they thought. A neighbor brought me a plastic lawn chair and a cola. I thanked her and sat down. By this time, it was past midnight, and I was getting more and more tired. I tried to ignore it, but I still felt weak from my concussion. My head ached, but I didn't have any of my pain pills. I dozed for a time, sitting up and leaning my head against the wall.

The long night was getting longer by the minute. The coroner arrived, and Charlie came behind him five minutes later. He nodded and went in the apartment to talk with the officers. However, I expected nothing less than endless questions and time at the police station before I would be allowed to leave.

Fortunately for me, the bloody footprints leaving the apartment did not match my shoes. Mr. Corn had heard the commotion and come out of his apartment. He and a neighbor had seen me run up the steps, break down the door, and back out hastily. One neighbor said she heard screams and what sounded like a scuffle before I came. She had come out in the hallway to see what the commotion was about. A hooded man had run past her on the stairs a short time before I ran up the stairs from a different direction.

However, no good deed goes unpunished. I spent the duration of the night in the police station being questioned, repeating my story a million times, and writing my statement. I felt a kinship with the people I had questioned when I was a police officer.

Charlie came in about nine that morning and took me into his office. He left me there and returned a few minutes later. When I looked up, he was standing in the doorway staring at me before shaking his head. He handed me a cup of strong, black coffee along with an 'I told you so.'

"What did I tell you? I said to let this one pass. You've been blown up, and now you've witnessed a murder." He gave me the disappointed stare of someone's father. "Not good, Chance. If I find you with a bullet hole in your head, I'll never forgive you."

"I would regret that too, Charlie. Thanks for the pep talk and the coffee. Am I free to go?"

"Yeah, yeah, get your sorry ass out of here. And Chance, be careful."

"I'm always careful."

"You can't prove it by me. I mean be extra careful. These people have a lot to lose, and apparently, they mean to clean up all loose ends. I don't see how this is related to the crime at the lab. Assuming there is a connection—the only connection we have found so far is that Laurel and Susie were friends."

"I don't see it either. Whoever did this must have thought Susie knew something."

I stood up, put my coffee cup in the trash, and left. No one offered to drive me back to my truck, so I exercised my right to use my own shoe leather. Walking in the morning, smelling the clean morning air, helped to lift my spirits and clear my head. By the time I made it to my truck, the morning was warming up.

Last night I'd told Charlie about finding Davis visiting Susie. The police must have paid him a visit by now. Boyfriends and spouses are the most likely suspects after the one reporting the crime. The next one on my to-do list was Davis Howell.

I had a few more questions for the boy, and I also needed to check on him. If there was a reason for killing Susie or Laurel, then Davis in all probability knew what it was. That knowledge put him in danger if he was not involved in the crime. I still did not have a solid clue to what was going on or who the perpetrators were. It had to be a trio, but who made up that trio? If I knew all the players, I would be halfway there.

When I arrived at his home, he had company. Someone had parked a 1947 Ford truck in the drive. It was completely restored and painted a dark, almost black, green with black fenders. I have always admired old cars, and classic trucks in particular, with beautiful grills and wooden slats in their beds. This one had bird's-eye maple slats finished to perfection. I couldn't help myself. I had to stop and admire the old truck.

If I had my choice, I would pick a 1932 Packard coupe with a rumble seat. When I was a kid, I remember a private detective on television named Miles Banyon. He drove a 1932 Packard. My grandfather had the television series on VHS tape. I think it was only on for one season. We used to watch it together every Friday night when I stayed with him during my school holidays.

As I was looking over the old truck, a man came out of the house. He was about the same age as Davis. A good-looking man in a James Dean sort of way. He had longish sandy hair combed away from his face and pouty, cruel lips. He stood a few inches less than six feet. Curious gray eyes glanced at me and then around at the area before returning to rest on me. He came over to where I stood.

"Hi, is this your truck?"

He nodded.

"She's a beauty. Did you restore her yourself?"

"Yeah, I've got a body shop over on 19ᵗʰ. My bread and butter is bodywork from accidents, but my real love is old cars. I restore classic cars in my spare time."

He stood beside me and raked his eyes over his project. It was plain to see he was proud of his work.

I held out my hand. "I'm Chance Sunday, by the way. Is Davis home?"

When he shook my hand, his grip was firm but his fingers were cold. His palm was damp.

"Yeah, he's pretty torn up. His girl just got herself killed."

"Yes, I know. I found her. What's your name?"

"Brian, Brian Moore. The name of my shop is BM Auto Restorations Old and New. Come by if you need any work done. I'll see you get the friends and family discount."

I nodded. "Thanks."

"Sunday, eh? Say, are you the private detective Mrs. McIntyre told us she hired?"

"Yeah, that's me. Do you have a few minutes to talk after I talk to Davis?" I asked.

"Sorry, I've got somewhere to be. Well, see ya around."

He hesitated and then gave me a half-wave before he slid behind the wheel of his truck. I watched him drive away. I couldn't help smiling. The old Ford purred like a kitten. I would take a classic truck over a new one any day.

Even now, companies are trying to put driverless cars on the highway. If you ask me, that takes the fun out of having a car. You might as well ride a bus. I wonder if there is an accident, will the police determine if it was hardware or software trouble, or will they have to call in a computer geek? Which one gets the ticket, hardware or software? If a drunk person gets in a driverless car, will the police still arrest him for a DUI? You read in the paper all the time that GPS has taken someone to the wrong address or gotten them lost. What if a blind person gets in the driverless car, and the driverless car takes him to the bad part of town? Maybe I'm an old dinosaur, but I'm not ready for driverless cars.

Taking a deep breath, I walked up to Davis's door and knocked. The front door was open with the storm door ajar. I heard someone groan, and I knocked again. From somewhere in the depths of the apartment, a slurred voice called, "C-come in."

I opened the door a little wider, stepped into the entry, and peered around the corner. Davis was perched halfway on the sofa, with the other half hanging off the edge. He blinked to focus his eyes and waved for me to enter. In waving, he overbalanced and rolled off the sofa. I helped him to a sitting position on the floor. He took a half-full bottle of beer off the coffee table and took a swig. After he'd wiped his mouth with the back of his hand and then wiped his nose, he looked up at me with tears in his eyes.

"Davis, do you remember me?"

"Y-yeah, you're that private detective. Monday or Tuesday or something..."

He stopped talking in mid-sentence and stared at the label on the bottle of beer. He began picking at the label, forgetting me. I cleared my throat, trying to get his attention.

"My name's Sunday, Chance Sunday. I'm sorry to hear about Susie. I'm the one that found her. I saw you leaving Susie's apartment before someone killed her. Was she your girl?"

"W-what's it to you? You accusing me of something?" Mumbling, he kept his head down, still picking at the label. He nodded and turned his eyes on me, but they were out of focus. He continued to pick at the label, seemingly without a will of his own.

"No, she was alive after you left. I talked to her. Do you know who she was meeting later that night after you left?"

He kept picking at the label with his head down.

"Davis, I need you to focus. I know you've had a shock, but I have to find out who did this to Susie. It would be a big coincidence if it didn't have something to do with the trouble Laurel's in.

"Previously when I talked to you, you said you barely knew Susie. I saw you at her apartment last night. What was she? A convenience?"

He threw his bottle at me. I ducked as it sailed over my head and crashed against the wall behind me. He stood up, swaying with his fist clenched. The effort was too much for him. He collapsed on the sofa at an angle. His head was resting against the back of the sofa, and his legs were sprawled out in front. Raising his hand, he watched his fingers move. I cleared my throat again to get his attention. He turned and looked at me as if for the first time.

He picked up the thread of the conversation at last.

"I know everyone thought she was easy, but she wasn't. She was my girl. I loved her. We were going to get married." He hiccupped, and a single tear rolled down his cheek.

"I'm sorry to pester you at a time like this, but Davis, you need to tell me the truth. Do you know why someone would want to kill Susie?"

He moved his head loosely from side to side. Sitting up on the sofa, he put his head in his hands. "It had to be some lunatic. No one would hurt my Susie."

"Did Susie tell you anything about Laurel's concerns with where she worked or what Laurel suspected?"

"We got together at Thanksgiving and discussed it. Laurel was upset about the people she worked for with the smuggling and all. She didn't know what to do. We told her to forget about it and keep her nose out of their business.

"I guess she should've gone to the police, but she was afraid. I told her the FBI would be better if she couldn't trust the locals. She said she would think about it. I guess she didn't think about it hard enough." He shrugged and fell back into the sofa with a sigh.

"Davis, do you know anyone who drives a black Tahoe with heavily tinted windows?"

He mumbled a no and slid farther down in the sofa.

"One more question. Was there anyone else there when you had this discussion besides you, Laurel, and Susie?"

"B-Brian, Brian was there. He's my best friend. You just missed him. He wouldn't have anything to do with this. He liked Susie. Susie used to be his girl."

"Did he know about you and Susie?"

"No, no one knew except me, Susie, and my parents. I told them we wanted to get married, but they didn't want me to get married until I finished law school. My father is the president and CEO of a small bank. They only have four branch offices."

He hiccupped and took another drink before setting the empty bottle on the floor.

"He's grooming me to take over when he retires. He said Susie wouldn't be a help in business. You have to be proper and above scandal," he mimicked his father.

"We had an awful yelling match. He never yells. He said if I married Susie, he would not give me another penny. I'd have to move out. He'd kick his only son out. I couldn't believe he would kick me out."

"I told Susie. She said we had to wait until we finished college, and we wouldn't need his money. We could just keep everything a secret until then. But I loved her, and I wanted everyone to know. I wanted to marry her. What do I do now? I don't see any point in going on without my Susie."

"Davis, you're young. You've got your whole life ahead of you. I know it's an old cliché, but it's true. Time heals the hurt. You'll have a scar, but as time goes on, you'll remember only the good times. Believe me, you will learn to live with the pain."

"How would you know?"

"Trust me, I know. Everyone copes differently. It's OK to feel angry, sad, confused. Do you have someone to talk to? A pastor, a parent?" Davis shook his head no. "Davis, I know you're feeling terrible now, but please help me if you can. If not for Laurel, then for Susie's sake."

I couldn't tell if he had been listening or not. He was somewhere far away in a world of his own.

"Why won't everybody just leave me alone? You don't know me. You don't know how I feel." He stood up, swaying and pointing at the door. "You better go, mister. I got nothin' more to say."

"Sure, I'll leave. I'm leaving my card here on the table. If you need someone to talk to, or you think of anything that will help, call me. Please listen to me. Davis, if the people who killed Susie think she talked to you, you're in danger too."

"So, what. I don't care. Don't you understand? I just don't care."

He unscrewed the cap on another bottle and took a drink. Leaning his head back, he managed to get some of it in his mouth. Mostly it ran across his chin and dropped on his shirt. He sat down and overbalanced again, almost falling off the couch.

As I was leaving, another empty beer bottle sailed over my head and crashed against a lamp. I looked over my shoulder and saw him pick up another bottle. Leaving quickly, I got into my truck and backed out of the drive.

Looking up the street, I saw the old Ford truck parked in a driveway about three houses on the right. I went on down the street and took a right on Fairview. Circling to the next block, I came up the street behind where Davis lived. I could see the old Ford truck parked in Davis' drive now. Brian must have been waiting for me to leave. I parked on the street behind another truck and made my way back to Davis's apartment. Keeping to the shrubbery, I found an open window and listened in.

"Davis, pull yourself together. What'd that man want?"

I heard the sound of slapping. Brian must have slapped Davis, trying to sober him. I don't know why people do that. It never works. Even coffee doesn't help much.

"He's a private detective. He wanted to know if I knew why someone killed...my Susie."

"What'd you tell him?"

I heard several more sounds of slapping.

"What'd you tell him?" Brian demanded through clenched teeth.

"Quit hitting me. I didn't tell him anything. I don't know anything to tell. I'm tired, and I want to sleep. There is no more light...it's gone."

I heard snoring sounds and someone muttering.

Ducking down behind a giant rhododendron on the corner of the house, I watched an obviously angry Brian stomp off to his truck. He got into the truck and just sat there as if he were thinking. He hit the steering wheel with both hands a time or two before he started the engine. Backing out, he turned left on Fairview and peeled off down the street.

I took a deep breath and made my way back up the street to my truck. That was an interesting development. I didn't know if it meant anything yet, but Mr. Moore bears looking into, and so does Davis.

Back on Seventh Street, I turned down Highway 47 and headed home. Stopping off at the Do Drop Inn, I picked up lunch. Today's special was Taco Salad. I turned up my drive and waved to Phil as I went through the gate. I found Laurel asleep in my chair with an open book on her lap. She woke up when I opened the refrigerator door. Yawning, she stretched, catlike, and stood up.

"You must have left early. I didn't hear you come in last night or leave this morning. Did you find out anything?"

"I found out more than I wanted to. Eat your lunch. We'll talk about it when you're through."

"You're making me nervous. Before I forget, your telephone rang, and the answering machine picked up. It was the sheriff. He said to meet him at the usual place at 11:00 tomorrow and bring the package. Do you know where or what he means?"

"Yeah, come on over and eat your food. You're the package. He wants me to bring you. My guess is they'll want to take you into custody. I talked to your mother, and she's looking into a lawyer for you. She said to tell you she loves you. I'll phone her tonight and let her know about tomorrow."

We ate in silence. I found it hard to eat, knowing what I had to tell her. There's no easy way to tell a person someone has murdered their friend. I waited until she had eaten before I told her about Susie.

"Laurel, I'm afraid I have some bad news. There's no easy way to say this, but your friend Susie is dead. Someone murdered her last night."

She jumped up and ran into the middle of the room. "No, no! Why? How?" she asked, and bent over, holding her midsection.

"I found her last night. Unfortunately, I was a couple of minutes too late to save her. I don't know the why or who, but I think it's time you told me everything. I know some of it, but you haven't told me everything."

"Yes, I have." Sitting down on the hearth, she put her head in her hands and sobbed until she had no more tears left.

I sat in my chair and waited for her to calm down. "Laurel, I thought Susie was your friend. Surely you want whoever did this caught?"

"Of course, I do. Quit badgering me." She stood up with her fists clenched at her side and ran up the stairs to her room.

I heard the bedroom door slam. Maybe she needed time. I'll try to be patient, but she has to talk to me before they take her into custody.

Then access will be restricted, especially if they think her life is in danger.

I had to make several phone calls, and I didn't want to use my landline. I listened and didn't hear any noise coming from Laurel's room. As I stepped onto the patio, Phil was coming up the drive with Boomer at his side.

"Phil, I have to go down to the Do Drop. I'll be back as soon as I make a few calls. Did she leave the place at any time while I was gone?"

Phil shook his head no.

"Good. I've had a little trouble. If you don't mind, hang around until I get back."

He nodded and sat down on the patio. Boomer stood and looked from one to the other of us as if he were trying to follow the conversation.

"Keep an eye on Laurel for me. Anything you want me to get while I'm there?"

He shook his head and stared up the mountain trail he always took. He didn't like an interruption in his self-imposed schedule.

I jumped on my ATV and went through the woods. Down at the Do Drop Inn, I called Mrs. McIntyre on the pay telephone.

"Hello, ma'am, this is Chance Sunday. Have you found a lawyer yet?"

"Yes, I talked to Mr. Cramer today. He's willing and wants to talk to you."

"Good, I'll call him. Keep a good thought. I'll come by to see you tomorrow."

She hung up without saying anything else.

I called Cramer next.

"Hi, Walt. This is Chance Sunday."

"Chance, you old soldier. I'm glad you called. I have a few questions."

"I figured you would. I'm calling from a pay telephone. Someone has been trying to follow me. I don't want to take a chance someone tapped my landline. If you need me, be careful when you call me at home."

"Sure, I understand. Do you have any idea who could be doing this?"

"Yeah, Walt, I'm afraid I do. If I'm right, Laurel will need protection. I think it involves someone in the sheriff's department. I don't know to what extent. The sheriff wants me to bring her to the Mountain View Episcopal Church about two miles out of Pinedale coming toward Parkersburg. I'll have her there by eleven. Will you be able to make it?"

"Of course, I'll be there. Not that it matters one way or the other. I'll give her the best defense I can, but do you think she's involved?"

"Walt, I hope not. If she is, it will kill her mother. Laurel tells a convincing story."

"Her mother said she saw the men, but they wore masks."

"Yes, that's what she told me. She says she ran because she feared for her life. She didn't say it in so many words, but Walt, she thinks one of them could have been a friend. I think she knows more than she is telling. If I find out anything, I'll let you know."

"That's what worried me when I talked to her mother. I'll represent her regardless, but I hate going into court blind with my hands tied. Clients always lie to their lawyer and their doctor. The two people to whom they should invariably tell the truth. Chance, be careful, and I'll see you tomorrow."

After I'd called Cramer, I talked to Elsie for a while, wasting time until supper was ready. Tonight's special was chicken-fried steak with a baked potato and salad. I wanted to give Laurel time enough to decide to tell me what she knew on her own. I returned home, waved to Phil and Boomer as they headed through the woods, and settled in to read my book.

Chapter 9

After a while, I ate my supper and waited for Laurel, but she didn't come down. I put her dinner in the refrigerator and sat down with my book.

I was getting drowsy and about ready to fall asleep myself when she came down the stairs, hesitating on each step. She made her way over to the hearth and sat.

"I'm sorry, but I guess it was the shock. I can't believe I'll never see Susie again. What do you want to know?"

"Did you know Davis and Susie were planning on getting married?"

"Susie and Davis? I always thought it was Susie and Brian. I know they dated until last November. You're sure it was Davis?"

"Yeah, I got it from the horse's mouth. He's pretty torn up. He's been drinking ever since the police told him about Susie. I tried talking to him, but I couldn't get anything sensible out of him. He's in shock and pain now. Later, he may remember something that will help."

Laurel let out her breath and looked up at me. "Then it couldn't have been..."

"Couldn't have been Davis, who killed her?"

She stared wide-eyed at me with her hand across her mouth.

"No, Laurel, it wasn't Davis. Why did you think it was him? This is important. Who did you tell about the diamonds?"

"I didn't tell you the exact truth. I did tell Susie, but I also told Brian and Davis. We discussed it when we were all home for the Thanksgiving holidays. They told me not to go to the police. To just keep my head down and do my job.

"I knew what they were doing at the lab was wrong, but they weren't doing it for themselves. They increased everyone's salary and bought new equipment for the lab. Equipment they needed badly."

"You realize you're rationalizing. As the old saying goes, 'You can't make a silk purse out of a sow's ear.' Did you tell anyone else? Someone at the college or your dorm roommate?"

"No, those are the only ones."

She looked up at me with pleading eyes. "You can't think it was one of them. I can't accept that or that one of my friends would try to kill me and kill Susie. Susie never hurt anyone."

"It has to be one of them or someone they told. It can't play out any other way. I want you to think about the people who came in the lab. There must be something you saw that would tell us who they were."

"No, no, no!" She ran up the stairs and then halted about halfway. She turned and came down the stairs little by little. When she reached the bottom step, she sat down and held on to the newel post. "Why do you think it was one of them?"

"I'm asking you to consider what I just told you. It has to be one of your friends. They're the only people who knew about the diamonds outside of the three people in the lab and maybe a deputy sheriff. However, we don't know for sure what he was doing there. No one would have connected Susie to you and the robbery if it were someone at the lab. Who else would have known where you were staying? You do realize someone tried to kill both of us?"

"No, no! There has to be some other explanation."

She stood up and looked ready to run. I didn't say anything. I waited for everything I said to sink in.

"What are you saying? It's my fault Susie is dead?"

She backed up against the wall, shaking her head. She looked at me crestfallen. Putting her hand over her mouth, she turned her face to the wall.

I walked over to her, put my hands on her shoulders, and turned her around.

"Look at me, Laurel. I'm not saying that, but at the very least, she had to tell someone. Can't you see that the incidents are connected?

I'm not sure how yet, but I have a pretty good idea. Tell me everything, even if you think it's unimportant. Let me have the rest of it."

She took a deep breath, and the words came in a rush.

"The man who picked me up let me out at the Kroger store. I walked on up Fairview and then Hemlock to Davis's apartment. He wasn't home. I waited and hid in the shrubbery until he came home. It must have been at least an hour later. I stepped out of the shadows and scared him as he was getting out of his car.

"He asked me in. I told him I needed a place to crash for the night. I didn't say why and he didn't ask. I don't know why I didn't tell him, but I was still confused and scared, I guess. Usually, I can talk to him about anything, but he gave the impression he had something on his mind. He barely spoke when I tried to talk to him. Anyway, I told him I'd take the sofa, but he insisted I take his bed."

"That's interesting. Davis told me he was watching TV when you knocked on his door."

"That is strange. I don't know why he would say that. I had to wait for him to come home. After he said it was OK to stay, he loaned me a T-shirt to sleep in. I was getting ready for bed, and I went into the bathroom.

"I gave Davis a small peace symbol for his birthday one year. It's the kind you put on your zipper tab. I found it at one of those retro stores. The man who came into the lunchroom at the lab where I was hiding had the same symbol on his hoodie. I could see him through the crack where the doors met. That's why I was afraid to come forward. I couldn't believe it was one of my friends. I didn't know what to do.

"Davis gave me a spare toothbrush. I started to brush my teeth when I looked in the mirror and saw the clothes hamper behind me. Hanging out of it was a black hoodie with the peace symbol on the zipper. Too stunned to move, I almost choked on my toothpaste. Somehow, I finished brushing my teeth and went back in the bedroom. By this time, I was wide awake.

"When I heard Davis snoring, I dressed as hastily and quietly as I could. Carrying my shoes, I slipped out of the bedroom and tiptoed past Davis asleep on the sofa. There's a door across from the sofa in the living room that leads to the basement garage. I took it and slid out the side door. Once I was outside, I put my shoes on and ran all the way to Susie's."

"Did you tell Susie about the hoodie with the peace symbol?"

"No, I told her I was in trouble and about what had happened at the lab. I didn't say anything about Davis or what the men were wearing. I didn't want to believe what I saw. It didn't have to be him. I couldn't see anyone's face. I told myself anyone could have that symbol.

"When I ran out the door, it was dark. The three men were too far away to see who they were. Even if I could have seen their faces, I was too scared to recognize anyone. My only thoughts were to get away from there. I couldn't think Davis would do anything like that. I've known him forever. What reason would my friends have to do something so appalling?"

"Laurel, I had my friend Josh run a program that estimated how many diamonds and what carat size could be hidden in the animal cage's hollowed-out bars. He also made an estimate of the number of cages, assuming the previous cages' cargo had already been sold. According to the program, and this is only an estimate, there could have been ten million dollars in uncut diamonds concealed in just four of those cages.

"So, I'd say someone had about ten million reasons to get rid of any witnesses. Did Susie ask you if you recognized anyone?"

"Now that you mention it, she didn't ask much about anything. I sat down trying to catch my breath. She walked away and got a beer out of the refrigerator and handed me one. She sat back down and turned on the TV as if it were common for me to come to her apartment in the early hours of the morning. I figured she was just being Susie."

"Do you know if she told anyone other than your friends that you were at the cabin?"

"She didn't say if she did. She could have told Davis, I guess. I don't want to think it was Davis or Brian. I can't believe they could do anything so terrible."

"I'm not saying it was either one of them, but they could have talked to someone else. We have to find out. I know you don't want to believe it, and I understand. The evidence says it has to be someone in your clique of friends who told someone else or is in on it. Not one of your friends admits to knowing anything about it. Even Susie denied knowing about the diamonds."

"I told everyone at Thanksgiving. They all knew about the diamonds. I don't understand any of this."

"Regardless, we have to make plans. When I take you to Pinedale tomorrow, the sheriff will take you into custody. When that happens, they'll take your cell phone. I have a burner phone that is fully charged. It's turned off. Don't turn it on unless you need me." I took it out of my shirt pocket and handed it to her. "Go up to your backpack and slip it between the shell and lining at the bottom. Secure it in place with this double-stick tape."

I handed her the tape, and she started up the stairs.

"When you know where they're taking you, send me a text. I put my office, cell, and home number in for you. Once you send the text, turn the phone off straight away. This is very important. Call no one except me, not your mother, not any of your friends. You can't trust anyone or that your conversation won't be overheard. The fewer people who know where you are, the better. I'll update your mother in person. Do you understand what I'm saying?"

She nodded and started biting her nails again.

"If you're scared or uneasy about the people guarding you, call me right away. If I don't answer, leave a message."

She sighed, and I watched her shoulders relax.

"Thanks, I feel better. I'm really nervous about turning myself in. I've never been in trouble before."

"That's understandable, but I'm going with you. Your lawyer, Walt Cramer, will be there too. Your mother hired him. He's one of the best. You'll be in good hands."

She walked over to the kitchen and took a cola out of the refrigerator and an oatmeal pie out of the pantry. "Well, I guess I'll go to bed now." She started up the stairs and turned back toward me. "It can't be one of my friends. There has to be another explanation."

I nodded. "Goodnight," I said, and waved to her.

I watched her go up the stairs, but I still had an uneasy feeling. I had missed something. The next morning it was a somber Laurel who walked down the steps. When it was time to leave, we took the same precautions getting back into my truck as we had coming in. I put her in the back seat and covered her with a blanket. Boomer was up front on guard duty.

Laurel stayed covered up in the back seat all the way to the rendezvous. When we arrived, the sheriff's truck was the only auto in the parking lot. I felt my stomach tighten. I'd expected to find several cars. He was parked by the office door of the church.

"Laurel, I see the sheriff's truck, but no one else is around. You stay where you are and don't move until I investigate."

I got out of my truck and locked the door. Strolling up to the office door, I kept my hand on my gun in the shoulder holster and scanned the area as I went. I saw Sheriff Henry open the office door of the church. He stepped out on the stoop, stretched, and looked around the area.

I kept my hand on my gun.

"Come on in. You can take your hand off that gun." The sheriff grinned, looked me up and down, and then looked at my truck. "Where's our witness? I took a chance on you, Sunday. This better not be a dry run. I'm not in the best of moods."

I studied his face before I answered. "Don't worry, I brought her. I wanted to check out the area first. Where is everyone?"

"You're a suspicious son of a gun, aren't you? We're all in the conference room waiting on you and Miss McIntyre. Everyone parked in back to avoid drawing attention to what's going on. Considering what you told me, we're trying to be as discreet at possible."

I relaxed a little and took my hand off my gun.

"I appreciate the thought. Wait here and I'll get her."

I went back to my truck and unlocked it. I took Laurel's hand as she climbed out of the back seat of the truck and felt her tremble.

"Try and stay calm. They're all in the conference room," I whispered.

She stepped down, but she grabbed hold of my arm and wouldn't let go.

I took her through the office door. We followed the sheriff down the hall to a Sunday School room. Everyone was gathered around a table in the middle of the room. All eyes were on Laurel when we entered the room. I recognized DA Webster. He had someone in a city police uniform standing behind him that I didn't recognize.

Webster stood and pulled out a chair. "Please have a seat, Miss McIntyre." He motioned with his hand.

She let go of my arm.

Laurel sat down and looked around the room. She wet her lips and looked up at me. I put my hand on her shoulder to reassure her. She grabbed and held my hand as you would a lifeline.

"Please wait outside, Mr. Sunday. We'd like to talk to Miss McIntyre alone for now. I'll be getting your story later."

Reluctantly, she turned her gaze from me to all the officials sitting there looking back at her. I pried her hand from mine.

I tried to give her a hint. "I don't think she should say anything until her attorney arrives. His name is Walt Cramer, and he'll be here shortly." I hoped Laurel understood she didn't have to say anything if it would incriminate her.

Against my better judgment, I left and went outside. I walked around the church and saw two Weston police cars parked in the back. One had two officers in the cruiser, and the other had one. I heard one of the doors open. When I turned and started back around to the front, I heard his door close. Another car turned off the road and came to a stop beside my truck. I felt a sense of relief when I recognized the driver. Attorney Cramer stepped out of his car and walked toward me.

"Boy, Walt, am I glad to see you. She's inside in the conference room. They insisted I leave while they talked to her. I tried to clue her in that she shouldn't talk without you present. She is so scared she may not have caught my hint. When you're scared, you blurt out things that are best left unsaid."

"Don't I know it. Thanks, Chance. Show me the way and we'll see what's going on."

I took Cramer to the conference room. He knocked, and the sheriff admitted him. The sheriff motioned for me to turn around and leave. I went outside, where I sat on the steps of the porch. A short time later, Sheriff Henry called me to come back in. I passed Cramer in the hall on his way out. I told my story three or four times and answered all their questions.

"For now, and until we can finish checking out Miss McIntyre's story, we will take her into protective custody," Webster said.

"That's all well and good, but she needs around-the-clock protection."

"We're aware that she needs protection, Mr. Sunday. Her attorney, Mr. Cramer, has made that abundantly clear. Since she has made an accusation against the sheriff's department, we are turning her over to the Weston Police. They will be responsible for her safety and protection. It satisfies Mr. Cramer, and you should be satisfied too. There will be two officers with her at all times in an undisclosed location.

"Chief Roberts will collect her things from your truck."

The chief moved to my back as we were talking. I stood up, and he followed me out the door. The chief walked ahead of me to my truck.

Boomer stood up and bared his teeth with a low-down growl. The chief backed up a step.

"What are you doing with a vicious dog?" the chief asked and put his hand on his gun.

"He won't let anyone around my truck or my home if I don't give permission first. If you'll permit me, I'll get her backpack for you. Otherwise I can't be responsible for what he might do."

The chief backed up several steps without taking his eyes off Boomer.

I had to grin as I unlocked my truck. I gave Boomer a pat on the head and handed Chief Roberts Laurel's backpack. He searched her backpack without delay, looking for a phone or a gun. When he found her regular cell phone and no gun, he confiscated the phone. He didn't find the hidden cell phone, and he didn't look any further, as I had guessed he wouldn't.

I stayed in the parking lot with Cramer and watched them drive her away. She didn't look at us but stared straight ahead. Somehow, I felt I had failed. I drove home. There was one more person I needed to talk to before I called in my friend Josh. Cramer had agreed to subpoena the financial records for the four young people and the sheriff.

My friend Josh is a whiz on the computer, with degrees in accounting and computer science. He looks like the kid next door, average height, with brown, longish hair and brown eyes. He's good-looking in a nondescript way. Looking at him in jeans and a T-shirt, you wouldn't guess what a genius he is. He'll look their financials over for any anomalies.

I was getting tired of keeping the roads hot, but I had to talk to Brian. I headed back down Highway 47 on my way to 19th Street. It was the middle of the afternoon, and the shop appeared to be closed. I heard hammering in the back and made my way around to the garage. On the way, I passed a black Tahoe with mud-smudged license plates.

I tried the gate to the yard, but it was locked.

"Brian, you there?" I yelled and waited.

The hammering stopped, and I yelled again.

Brian came through the door of the garage. From his expression, he was not pleased to see me. He put his hammer down and came over to the fence. "What can I do for you?"

"I'd like to talk to you about your friends."

"I got nothing to say. Get off my property." He turned to go.

"Look, Brian, I'm just trying to help them. What have you got to lose by talking to me? You never know, you might help. I've got a couple of questions is all. Laurel's been taken into custody."

He turned back, unlocked the gate, and stepped outside the fence. "So, she wasn't killed in the explosion. Why are you bothering me? I don't know anything." He waited with his arms crossed and his mouth a tight slash across his face.

"No, she wasn't killed as everyone thought. I've been keeping her under wraps until she could tell her story to the sheriff and the DA. They have taken her into protective custody.

"I know that you and your friends talked over Laurel's problem with her job. Everyone's advice was for her to keep her head down and mouth shut. Did you tell anyone what she discussed with you and your friends about the diamonds and smuggling?"

"No, man, why would I do that? I keep my nose clean and mind my own business. I wish everyone else would do the same." He turned to go back through the gate.

I held onto the wire fence and called to him. "You can't think of any reason why someone would want to kill Susie or try to kill Laurel?"

He turned back around, and his hard eyes bored into me. "How would I know that? Since they all went away to college, I scarcely ever see any of them."

I noticed something akin to resentment in the tone of his voice. He came outside the gated area again.

"You're friends with Davis. I saw you at his house. I thought the four of you were friends from way back. From what I hear, you were sweet on Susie at one time. Davis stepped in and took your girl. That must have ticked you off."

"I split with that pothead in November of last year. Davis was welcome to her."

I thought I might take a stab in the dark since I had him riled up. "From what I hear, you still called her. That doesn't sound like it was over for you. Maybe it was for her. Are you the one that tried to blow Laurel up when I started asking questions? Do you know anything about the robbery and murders?"

His face was getting redder by the minute, and the vein in his forehead was pulsing. He clenched and unclenched his fist at his side. He strode up and came at me until he was less than a foot away. It didn't take him long to decide to take a swing at me. I saw it coming and blocked his fist.

He lost his balance and landed in the debris pile from his body shop. Jumping up, his fist was wrapped around an iron pipe. He lunged at me again. I dodged him and landed my own punch to his midsection as he flew by. He doubled over in pain. I took the pipe away from him and helped him to sit up. I squatted in front of him so I could see his face.

"I wasn't sure before if you knew anything about this mess, but I am now. My advice to you is to come clean. If you told someone about the diamonds, then they're the ones I need to talk to. If you're mixed up in this, you need to come clean before you end up like your friends." I stood up and waited.

He would not look at me.

"By the way, Brian, whose Tahoe is that?" I pointed at the black Tahoe.

Brian spit out some blood and looked up at me with hate in his eyes. "It's a customer's truck. I'm working on it. I told you I don't know anything. Get off my property before I call the cops."

"Sure, you call the cops. I think they might be interested in that black Tahoe in your yard and your relationship with Susie. Tell whoever is following me to get off my back."

"Why, you son of a—" He doubled over and coughed.

"By the way, where were you on the night in question from ten to midnight?"

"I was at home asleep like I am every night. That's all I'm saying without a lawyer present. You're not hanging this on me. You need to check into Davis and Laurel. Leave me alone."

I thought I'd made my point and it was best to leave. Since I was in town anyway, I crossed the Ohio River and made my way to Susie's friend Gloria in Belpre. As I stepped up to her apartment door, I heard music blaring out of her open window. Knocking loudly, I was surprised by the bouncy girl in a leotard who answered the door. She smiled at me and let her sultry eyes roam over my frame before she spoke.

"What can I do for you, mister? Anything at all."

She leaned against the corner of her door with a smile and a gleam in her eyes. I felt like I might be on the menu for supper.

"Er...my name's Chance Sunday. I believe Mrs. McIntyre told you about me. I'd like to ask you a few questions."

After I flashed my ID, she stepped back from the door and motioned me in. Asking questions is a risky business.

"Susie was my friend. She told me about you." She looked me up and down. "Umm...you look the way she described you. She said you were good looking. I like older men." She licked her lips, turned with a flounce, and sat at the kitchen counter, displaying her body to advantage. "I don't know what I can tell you. Susie and I were friends at school, and we went clubbing a few times, but her real friend was Laurel McIntyre."

"Yes, I understand. She told me she came here the night before someone killed her. Did she come?"

"Yeah, she did, but she got a phone call a little after ten and said she had to leave. She didn't come home until late. I heard her coming in about two or three the next morning.

"The next night she got another phone call, and she was half way to the door before her phone rang again. I don't know who was calling her. From what I heard, the second call didn't sound like she wanted to talk with this person, but I heard her agree to meet them later that night. When she left, she had a frown on her face."

That was a point I'd overlooked. Her cell phone was nowhere in the apartment. I would have to check with Charlie to see if he could find out her provider and get any information from them. He might even be able to backtrack where it had been.

"Did you know she was seeing Davis Howell?"

"No, really...Davis, you're sure? I thought she was going around with that Brian character. They broke up before Thanksgiving of last year, but I got the idea from her he still called her. I would have thought Davis was too straight an arrow for Susie."

"Did Susie tell you anything about her friend Laurel? Laurel was having trouble at work. Did she mention anything about that?"

"If she did, I don't remember. When we met, we typically talked about school or guys. I'm sorry; I wish I could help. I liked Susie. When she asked to stay, she said she was in a little trouble. I thought it was man trouble.

"She was a little flaky, but she was a friend. Susie was just a carefree soul. If it didn't concern her, she didn't get involved."

"Thanks, Gloria. I appreciate your time." I made my way to the door.

She moved up close and looked up at me. "Come back any time. I like older men." She put her index finger in her mouth and winked.

"Yes, you said that. I appreciate the offer, but I'm old enough to be your father. I'll have to decline."

Waving goodbye, I left. I couldn't wipe the smile off my face.

Chapter 10

My thoughts turned back to Laurel's three friends. I needed to tackle Davis again, but he could wait until tomorrow. Rest and a little time to think were what I needed. I headed out Highway 47 toward home. Driving unhurriedly, I couldn't get the friends out of my head. I started thinking and running everything over in my mind. I had seen and heard from all the people Laurel could have told about the diamonds. Several of their answers were suspicious, but nobody stood out.

Trying to solve a problem while you're driving is perhaps not a good thing to do. I crossed the county line and looked in my rearview mirror at a flashing blue light. I checked my speedometer, and I was five miles under the speed limit. I couldn't think what I had done. The deputy hit the siren, and I pulled over.

I watched him strut up to the driver's side, with his chest puffed out like a stuffed turkey. He had his aviator sunglasses on although the sun had almost disappeared. I had my license and registration ready. I rolled down the window and handed them to him.

"What's the trouble, Officer?"

"Do you know how fast you were going?"

"Yes, I was doing fifty in a fifty-five. Why did you stop me?"

Without answering me, he walked back to his car and gave the impression he was talking over the radio. I listened, and I didn't hear the normal chatter. He came back and handed my license and registration to me. He still said nothing. I watched him in my rearview mirror as he walked around my truck. He bent down, out of sight behind the bed of my truck. I heard breaking glass on the far side of the truck.

He came back around to my side looking pleased with himself. "I'll give you the benefit of the doubt for speeding. Just watch it when you're on my stretch of highway. There's a Parkersburg address on your registration and license. I've seen you out here quite a bit. Where do you live when you're not in Parkersburg?"

I handed him my business card. "Look, Officer, I'm a business man. I have a residence in Parkersburg and an office address there also. That's all the information you need. If you need more, contact Lt. Charles Parks of the Parkersburg police. Are we done here?"

He wrote in his ticket book, ripped off a ticket, and handed it to me. "Better get that taillight fixed. You have ten days to comply." He snapped his book shut and turned to go.

Some days it doesn't pay for me to leave the house. This was one of those days. I should learn to keep my mouth shut, but sometimes your mouth is in gear before your brain.

I leaned out of the window and stared back, but the deputy kept walking to his car.

"I heard you break the taillight. This is a bogus stop, and you know it. I'm going to lodge a complaint with the sheriff. I think the only reason you stopped me was to harass me and find out where I'm staying when I'm on your turf."

He turned and came striding back to my truck. He reached in and grabbed me by the front of my shirt, pulling me close to his face.

"Listen, jerk, I don't care what you think or what you lodge. It's your word against mine. So, what if I broke your taillight? This is my neck of the woods, see. I do what I want. Who do you think they'll believe? Me or some sleazy private dick? Mess with me, and I'll lodge this stick where the sun don't shine."

He let me go with a shove backward and stomped back to his cruiser. Squealing the tires and stirring up a dust cloud, he pulled away and headed down the road. He shouldn't have called me sleazy.

Oft times I get disgusted with this technological age and all the silliness or self-centered shenanigans that go on. Today wasn't one of them. I have a camera in my rearview mirror that picks up what's in front and a dashboard camera that picks up what goes on inside. I won't know until I get home and check, but I believe I just made the deputy a star in my video.

When I entered the Do Drop Inn, I still had a smile on my face. I made my way to the bar. Before I could get settled on the barstool, John had a cool one in front of me.

"Chance, you're looking mighty pleased with your bad self."

"Yes, I am, as a matter of fact. Tell me, John, you ever have any dealings with Deputy Sheriff Hollis Evans?"

"That jerk, yeah, I know him. Many times, I've thought of making a complaint. The way he struts in here. He orders something to drink or eat, and do you know what he does?" I had a good guess, but shook my head and took a drink of my beer.

John leaned in. "I'll tell you exactly what he does. He never pays. What he does is walk out like he owns the place. He thinks he has privileges since he's a deputy." John's eyes became hard thinking about Evans. He had his bar towel twisted into a tight knot.

"Why don't you lodge a complaint with the sheriff? I'm going to."

"That may be all right for you. We have to do business here. We have to stay on the right side of the law, but someone like that makes it hard. If I read him properly, he's a vindictive prick riding on the sheriff's coattails."

"What do you mean, riding on the sheriff's coattails?"

"Don't you know who he is?"

I shook my head.

"He's Sheriff Henry's son-in-law. I think he's originally from Parkersburg. He met the sheriff's daughter when he attended WVU. He planned to study law but washed out of the university after two years. The sheriff gave him a job when he married the daughter."

"Very interesting. John, my friend, give me a fish sandwich, slaw, and fries to go. If he comes in here asking about me, don't tell him where I live. Pretend you don't know. Tell him you think I live about a mile down the road in the other direction."

John winked at me and grinned. I took my dinner and went out to the parking lot. When I got to my truck, I fumbled around and dropped my keys and supper. I knelt to pick them up. It wasn't more than a split second after I bent down that a shot rang out and shattered the glass in the door of my truck where my head would have been. I hit the ground flat and slid under my truck.

I heard tires squeal, but I couldn't see anything. By this time, everyone was out of the bar and in the parking lot. John helped me up and handed me my dinner. He called for Elsie to bring a dustpan and broom. She came out and started cleaning up the glass in my truck seat.

"Did anyone see who did this?" I looked around at their faces.

Most of them shook their head no. The rest stared around the parking lot.

One man came forward. "I was coming through the door when I heard the shot. I'm pretty sure it came from the other side of the road a little farther up the hill." He pointed at the spot where he figured someone took the shot.

"It was a dark truck, maybe black or dark blue. It's hard to tell in this light, particularly since its headlights were off. I'm sure that's where the flash from the gun came from. Anyway, I saw the truck burn out of here damn fast without its lights. It was too dark to see anything. Sorry, Chance," Holden said, and patted me on the back.

The crowd dispersed. Elsie had my seat cleaned by this time. After the bullet had hit my window, it had deflected downward. I went around to the passenger side and dug the bullet out of the door. I put it in a plastic bag. Elsie and John signed the bag as witnesses. I slid behind the wheel of my truck and turned the key.

John frowned at me. "Aren't you going to call the cops? Chance, this is serious. Someone took a shot at you. You could have been killed."

"Don't you think I know? Who do you think would come to investigate? I've already had one run-in with Evans earlier. I'm too tired to fool with him again tonight. Besides, I've got a better plan. I'll see you."

Backing out of my parking place, I drove home.

I activated the remote control on the gate and drove through. Once I was past the bend in the drive, I saw Phil standing there waiting for me. He came around to my side as I started to roll down the window. Oh, yeah, I'd forgotten. I didn't have one. Phil looked over the damage and shook his head.

"I thought you might want to know a deputy drove up to the gate as I was passing earlier this evening and flagged me. He stopped at the gate when he couldn't get it open. He asked me who lived here. I gave him my name and told him I was the renter. I figured I'd better say that since he could always check and see it wasn't my property. He wanted to know who owned the property. I just walked off with him standing there. You in trouble, Chance?"

"I am, but I don't know why. That jerk deputy, Evans, stopped me and tried to give me a speeding ticket. He settled for breaking my taillight. Most likely, it was a ruse to find out where I live or maybe a spot of intimidation. Someone took a potshot at me a few minutes ago.

"I'm getting more and more nervous about letting Laurel go with that bunch. Something is definitely not right. Stay as far away from that deputy as you can. If you see him trespass, call 9-1-1 and report the intrusion just like any concerned citizen. If you don't invite him in, he must have a search warrant. His name is Hollis Evans. He looks like another one for Josh to check. I think I'll call the DA and then Laurel's lawyer."

I went on up to the house and started to call Webster when I decided to do it from the Do Drop Inn. Maybe I'm getting paranoid. If he thinks this is where I live, I wouldn't put it past him to put a tap on my line. Like the saying goes, "Just because you're paranoid doesn't mean someone isn't trying to get you."

My ATV was out back. I felt every one of my forty-two years as I climbed on and went through the woods to the bar. The district attorney had left for the day, and no one would give me his home number. I left a message. I would call him in the morning. I had better luck with Cramer.

The phone rang six times before someone picked it up.

"May I speak to Mr. Cramer?"

"This is he. Is that you, Chance? Is something wrong?"

"Yeah, it's me. Glad I caught you."

"What's wrong?"

"I don't know if anything is wrong or not, but the sheriff's son-in-law, Hollis Evans, is trying his best to find out where I live. He stopped me and tried to intimidate me. He broke my taillight and drove up my drive to the gate and tried to get in. Good thing it's always locked, and I have Phil keeping watch.

"Phil asked him if he could help him. The deputy wanted to know who lived there. From his description, it had to be Hollis Evans. All Phil told him was he lived there, and he was the renter. The deputy then asked for Phil's name. At that point, he wanted to know who owned the property.

"Phil just told him he was the renter and walked off with Boomer. He left Evans yelling after him. The gate was locked, and he didn't have a search warrant.

"Phil stopped him before he came in this time, but I don't think it will be long before he pays me another visit. Someone took a shot at me this evening and missed. However, the shot broke the window in my truck."

"Sounds like you've had a busy day. What can I do?"

"Can you get Laurel moved to Parkersburg? Her safety is my biggest concern now. I'm going to see the sheriff tomorrow about his son-in-law. I got most of his little tirade on video. Tomorrow I'll get my window and light fixed. I plan on taking the taillight bill to the sheriff for reimbursement."

"Chance, believe me, I understand why you want to do this, but do you think it's wise, considering he's the son-in-law? Do you want me to come with you? I'd be glad to come."

"No, I'll do this on my own. In case something happens to me, I wanted to make sure Laurel is taken care of, and you know what and who's getting on my last nerve. Just in case I turn up missing and or dead, you'll know where to look."

"Chance, I don't like this. You're making me nervous now. I'll see what I can do about moving Laurel. Call me when you get back from the sheriff's if they don't throw you in jail."

He chuckled and hung up.

I stayed in the bar for a couple of pints and headed home on the ATV. When I arrived, the hairs stood up on the back of my neck. My place is always quiet, but it seemed too quiet. There was not even an insect making a noise. I took my gun from the lockbox in the garage and made my way to the house. I slid inside the door without turning on the light. When my eyes adjusted to the lack of light, I saw my place had been tossed. I don't know what they hoped to find. I don't have anything. Whoever it was broke my coffeepot and stomped on my only two cups.

Then I remembered Phil. He would have stopped this if he were able. I ran back outside and called his name. It was still dead quiet. I picked up my flashlight from my truck and started in a run toward his cabin. Halfway there, I heard a groan. Following the sound, I found him in a drainage ditch unconscious. Close to Phil, Boomer was lying, not moving.

Jumping down in the ditch, I raised Phil into a sitting position. He was still unconscious but moaning. I felt the side of his head. There was a large bump forming above his ear. When I brought my hand away, I had something warm and sticky on it. I wiped the blood off my hand on some plants. I looked around for his rifle and found it in the ditch about six feet away.

Next, I knelt beside Boomer with my heart pounding in my ears. When I touched him, he felt warm and one of his eyelids flickered. I felt his heart, and it was beating. I stopped holding my breath. He was alive. I ran back to my house and backed the Jeep out of the garage.

Phil was a slim man, but it was a Herculean task to get him in the back seat. At last, I got him situated. I laid Boomer in the cargo area of the Jeep along with Phil's rifle, and we were on the road to the Parkersburg hospital. The emergency-room crew whisked Phil away. I told them I would be back before long. Next, I flew to the emergency veterinary hospital at the end of Seventh Street.

I carried Boomer inside. A receptionist called to the back for help. She looked at me as if I had done something.

"What happened?"

"I don't know. When I came home, I found him on the ground passed out. I can feel his heartbeat, but it feels slow. What could be wrong with him?"

"You wait here. I'll take him in the backroom and have the doctor check him out."

Two hours later, the doctor came through the door. "Your dog is awake now. Apparently, someone drugged him. I couldn't find anything else wrong. I gave him an antidote. He should be up in a couple of hours. We'd like to keep him until tomorrow, and then you should take him to your own veterinarian."

"Thanks, Doc. May I see him before I leave?"

The doctor took me to a room in the back. Boomer lay on the floor with an IV in his leg and an oxygen tube down his nose. I patted his paw. He opened his sleepy eyes and then closed them. He tried to wag his tail, but all he could manage was a small flutter.

"I'll be back to get you tomorrow, old boy. Phil's in the hospital. I have to go check on him now."

Standing up, I turned and went through the door without looking back. I hated to leave him, but my next concern was Phil. I gave the vet my credit card and phone numbers and left for the hospital and Phil.

When I reached the hospital, the doctor was still working on Phil. After several more hours, he came out and looked around the room for me. I stood up and went to the desk.

"I'm Dr. Digman. I have a few questions. First off, how did this happen?"

"I have no idea, Doctor. Phil is my handyman. I came home and couldn't find him. I searched and found him in a ditch. Is he going to be all right?"

"Yes, we've x-rayed his head and nothing appears to be broken. He has a slight concussion. He sustained a wicked blow that jarred his brain. So far, we cannot detect any bleeding. He regained consciousness a few minutes ago. We'd like to keep him under observation for twenty-four hours. We'll need to wake him up every couple of hours. It's best if he stays here."

"Sure, whatever you need. May I see him before I go?"

"They'll be taking him up to a room in a few minutes. A nurse will come and get you when you can go up. Sir, please don't stay more than a few minutes. There is nothing more you can do. We'll call you if anything unforeseen happens. What is your number?"

I handed him my business card and wrote my home number on the back. He disappeared behind a swinging door. I waited another hour. As I stood up to complain, a nurse motioned for me to follow her. She took me to room 342 and Phil. It was a two-patient room, but no one was in the other bed. I hoped it stayed that way. Phil doesn't do well with people he doesn't know.

I eased through the door and made my way over to his bed. He opened his eyes and tried to focus. "How are you feeling?"

He touched the bandage on his head. "Like my head's the size of a basketball and I've got the grandfather of all headaches. I can't get my eyes to focus."

"I'm sorry, Phil. You've got a concussion. Your eyes should clear up by tomorrow. The doctor says there's no damage done to that hard skull of yours. Do you know who did this?"

"I don't remember much. I was walking along the drive when I saw something shiny in the road like a mirror. I bent down to pick it up, and that's the last I remember. Doc said I may remember something a little later. I keep seeing bits and pieces like a puzzle. The doc says it'll come together in a day or two. I think I might have seen a face in that mirror before he coldcocked me.

"Don't look so worried, Chance, I'll be fine. What about Boomer? I wondered where he was. I hadn't seen him in two or three hours. That wasn't like him. I called him and when he didn't come, I went looking for him. I'm almost sure I remember seeing him by the side of the road before this happened."

"You probably did. Don't worry about him. The doc thinks someone drugged him. I'm sure all the pieces will fit together later on. I promised the doc I wouldn't stay more than a couple of minutes. He wants to keep you here for twenty-four. I'll be back to get you tomorrow. Boomer'll be OK too. I'll pick him up tomorrow along with you.

"Even if your memory comes back, keep this under your hat for now. I don't want this going through the Pinedale sheriff's department. I will report everything that happened to Charlie just to get it on record. If anything should happen to me, go see Charlie and tell him everything you know. Charlie is the only one I can trust right now."

I gave him a pat on the shoulder and left. Before I closed the door, I looked back and saw him shut his eyes. This will almost certainly be the only time he's slept at night since he returned from Iraq.

I told myself I could not have predicted this, but I felt responsible. Making my way to the nearest motel on Seventh Street, I rented a room. I needed rest and safety for at least one night.

The next morning, I went home to pick up my truck. I took it back into town to the General Glass Company and got two separate bills, one for the door glass and one for the taillight.

I had lunch at the Third Street Deli and headed for the Pinedale sheriff's office. His office is on the second floor of the courthouse. I found the sheriff in. Next time I looked up; he was standing in the doorway watching me. After letting me cool my heels for thirty minutes, he agreed to see me.

"Well, well, Sunday, come in. Have a seat." He waved broadly and pointed at a chair. "What do you want? If you want to talk to that little girl, no can do." He crossed his arms over his belly and smiled smugly.

"I didn't come about that, but I have a little video I want you to watch." I took out my flash drive and inserted it in the sheriff's computer.

"What do you think you're doing?"

"Be patient, Sheriff, and all will become clear. Isn't today's technology a hoot?"

The video loaded up and began to play. The sheriff's eyes became big as saucers and his mouth flew open. He sputtered and sat down in one of the visitors' chairs. When the video finished, I took the bill for the taillight out of my pocket and laid it on his desk.

"Do you know who that deputy is?" I asked with all the innocence I could muster.

"Yes, unfortunately I do. I do believe he's family," the sheriff said, and shook his head.

"Someone broke into the house of a friend of mine last night. That same someone knocked him unconscious and put him in the hospital. He looks after my dog when I'm involved in a case. I found my dog drugged and my friend in a ditch. Someone took a shot at me last night as well.

"I've informed the Parkersburg police, and now I'm reporting it to you. My friend is not pressing charges because he has no proof, and he's not accusing anyone. I don't think I'd have to look too far to find the one responsible, do you?" The sheriff sputtered again.

I ignored him. "The fact remains that your son-in-law stopped me for no reason, vandalized my truck, and tried his best to find out where I live, although I gave him my Parkersburg home and office address. He stopped at my friend's house earlier in the day and asked questions about me. I don't know what his problem is, but I expect to be reimbursed for the $328.45 the taillight cost me."

I stood and watched him process what I told him as clearly as if he had been doing it on paper. He reached for his checkbook, but I stopped him.

"I don't want the money from you. I want you to call Evans in here, and I want him to give me the money for my taillight. And if he makes good on his threat to put his stick where the sun don't shine, I want you to stop him with a bullet." It was my turn to smile smugly.

Henry hit the top of his desk with his fist, jumped up, and went through the door. He yelled down the hall, "Someone get me Evans. I want him in my office in fifteen minutes." He returned to his desk still shaking his head.

"Sunday, I'm sorry this happened. Believe me, I had no idea."

"I know, Sheriff, but he's the one who needs to apologize and pay up."

I kept my eye on my watch. It was seventeen minutes later when Evans strolled into Henry's office. He took a step back when he saw me sitting by the sheriff's desk. I grinned at him and kept my seat. The sheriff stood up and walked until he was almost nose to nose with Evans.

"I've just been watching an interesting video. Sit down and I'll let you view it."

He went behind his desk and started the video again, turning the monitor to where Evans could see it. Evans opened his mouth to speak, but the look on the sheriff's face said he would be wise to sit there and watch. The video ended, and the sheriff walked around his desk. He sat on the edge of his desk in front of Evans.

"You will give Sunday here $328.45 in cash this instant. If you don't have it, cash a check at the cashier."

Evans stood up and felt in his pocket and came out with three one-hundred-dollar bills and two twenty-dollar bills. I'd expected him to do just that. I had the change ready. I took his money and put it in my pocket. "Thank you, Sheriff. Nice doing business with you, Evans." I saluted and left. Although I didn't get an apology, I got my money and made my point.

While in the sheriff's office, I'd noticed a side door opening out to the hall. I made my way there and leaned against the wall in such a way so I could eavesdrop.

"Hollis, you're an idiot every day of the week. Why couldn't you take a day off just this once? You blasted moron, don't you know Sunday used to be a cop? A traffic stop, really...what were you thinking?

"I don't doubt you're the one who assaulted his friend. You stay away from him and his friend. I don't know what you've got against him, but it ends here today. This could be trouble with a capital "T". Get out of my sight for the rest of the day pronto. Why are you standing there taking up space? I said, get out of my office."

"But sir...you know me..."

"Yeah, I know you all too well. I don't want to hear whatever you've got to say. If my daughter didn't think the sun rose and set on you, I'd fire your sorry ass on the spot."

I heard a door slam and loud footsteps. I made it to the back stairs in two steps and hurried out to my truck. Despite his father-in-law's warning, if he saw me, there would be trouble. He was wearing a uniform and a gun. I wasn't. I left Pinedale as speedily as possible.

Hollis had to be tied into this somehow. I had to find the link. There was no other explanation for what he did or the words the sheriff had with him. It had not occurred to me until now that the sheriff could also be linked to the murders. I thought, Charlie's right. I've stepped in it this time.

On my way in to pick up Phil, I planned to stop at my office and talk to Josh, my friendly neighborhood hacker. I'd called him earlier and told him about Evans. He would have to hack the bank to get his financial records since Cramer had no reason to subpoena them.

Josh said he would be in the secure room where I kept my server, paper files, and data backups. The room is sound- and fireproof. I have security wire in the ceiling to prevent a break-in from above. The best you can do is the best you can do. There is always someone who can do better than anything you can do. At least, whoever tried to break-in wouldn't have an easy job.

I parked behind my office building and took the steps two at a time, hoping that Josh would have found something to help me. When I reached the office, I noticed the door to the reception area was ajar. Little by little, I pushed the door open wider. Upon entering, I couldn't believe what I saw. Someone had tossed everything. I have dummy, old-fashioned green file cabinets in reception and my private office. I don't keep anything of importance in them. It's mostly blank forms and paper for the printer. My office looked like a case of malicious vandalism, but I doubted it.

My laptop was on the floor; it looked as though the heel of someone's boot had been in the middle of the monitor. Someone had smashed the battery against the wall. My hard drive was lying by an overturned cabinet, also smashed. I stood in the doorway between the two offices too stunned to move. When I came to my senses, I went through the door that looked like a closet. I could see where the closet door had scars from being kicked. A panel in the wall of the closet opened backward, giving entry into my secure room. It did not appear to have been breached.

I pushed a button that activates a signal light inside the room to let Josh know I was at the door. I waited for him to open the door. When he didn't, I slid the coat hook to the left, and the door slid back gradually. I peered in, but I didn't see anyone.

"Josh, you in here? It's me, Chance."

I saw one hand come around the storage rack and then the rest of the body.

Josh sighed and grinned sheepishly. "Chance, am I glad to see you. You had a visitor not more than fifteen minutes ago. I slipped into the server room when I heard what sounded like glass breaking in the outer office. I was afraid if your visitor knew I was here, I'd be in trouble.

When you had the dead bolts installed, I thought that was overkill, but I'm glad you did. I threw the two dead bolts and slid the iron pole in place to hold the panel even if they found the release for the panel door.

"Seems it's dangerous to know you. Speaking of which, I went to see Phil today. He's itching to go home. Do you know who did this?" He peeked around me at the mess in the office.

"Not for sure, but I've got a pretty good idea. Say nothing to anyone about it. I'll replace the laptops and fix the damage on my own dime. I don't want the police crawling all over my office and finding my safe room. Before I go get Phil, did you find anything?"

"At first glance, everyone's financials are about what you would expect. The college kids' parents put money in their accounts the first of each month, and they buy the usual. No unusual deposits.

"Sheriff Henry gets his paycheck direct deposited every month, and he lives within his means. I couldn't find any evidence that he bought a house out of his pay scale, a fancy boat, or a luxury car. He looks good.

"Hollis Evans is a different story. He and his wife have their checks direct-deposited. They have their mortgage, which is within their means, taken out each month, along with utilities and cable. The majority of the leftover balance is deposited into a 401K at the end of each month."

"Blast, Josh, all that looks open and aboveboard."

"Pay attention. That's all that's taken out of the Evans account. He doesn't write a check or debit his account for groceries, gas, clothes, or whatnot. I can't find any other means of income. Both his and his wife's parents are living. No bequests from a relative. He has to be getting kickbacks somewhere. He has credit cards but only uses them enough to keep them active." Josh rattled through papers until he found the printout he wanted.

"Now we come to Brian Moore. His business is failing, but he pays his bills on time, makes his posh apartment rent, and continues to restore old cars, which, as you know, is an expensive hobby." Josh turned back to his computer and motioned for me to look at the monitor. "I noticed that Evans had purchased an airline ticket one week before the robbery on his credit card. I checked that same time for Brian and nothing. However, Davis purchased a ticket on his credit card at the same time, identical departure date. I cruised the airline bookings and found they went to Panama.

"I'm thinking offshore banking. It's a closed system, and I can't hack into any of the banks they would do business with to check. They only stayed for three days and returned. What's more, one day after the robbery and murders, both booked tickets to New York City, stayed two days, and returned."

"That makes no sense. I didn't check before the robbery, but Davis was still going to classes the week before the murders. He couldn't have used that ticket. He was also in class at the time of the New York trip. What's going on?"

"That's what I thought. Great minds think alike." He poked his head with his index finger.

"I checked the airlines to verify who used the ticket. I called and said my luggage was damaged. We did a song and dance, until at last she said, Mr. Moore, I'm sorry, but you did not report the damage when you returned. You'll have to bring in the luggage and fill out a report.

"Now I come to the most interesting part. One week after the robbery/murder, Brian drove his car to Brownsville, Texas. That's the last time he used his credit card in the United States. Three days after that he buys a ticket in Panama City and flies to Brownsville. From there he drives his car home. I believe he took a boat to Panama so as not to have to go through US or Panamanian customs at the airport. If I were a betting man, I would bet they took the diamonds to New York and sold them. After that, Brian took all the money and put it in a Panamanian bank.

"Davis bought the tickets for both the New York and Panama trips, but Brian Moore used them. Very curious. If you're looking for three, I'd say you have the connection. I checked Moore's credit card and the last ticket from Panama and the trip to Brownsville are the only charges on it. He has a credit limit of $12,000, which means he has an excellent credit rating despite his failing business. Where's he getting his money?"

"So, Davis bought the tickets for Brian Moore. Moore does the bank work because they already set the account up from his and Evans's previous visit to Panama. Moore, Howell, and Evans make three. In all probability, the reason Evans didn't take more time off is his father-in-law would ask questions. Howell had classes. Now we're getting somewhere."

I couldn't wrap my head around Davis Howell as one of the gang. "However, it doesn't make sense that Davis would kill Susie. You should have seen how torn up he was at her death. And don't forget, I saw him leave that night. He looked happy. No, it couldn't be Davis."

"Chance, don't let your personal feelings override your common sense. You like Davis Howell, and he's going through some of what you did. You're forgetting we're talking about perhaps ten million. Murder has been done for a lot less. Maybe Susie was just a loose end. A goodbye shag."

"Or Susie was getting wise to what they tried to do to Laurel, her best friend. Someone tried to kill Laurel and me. I don't understand why Brian asked Davis to buy the tickets for him. That's something I'll have to find out.

"Thanks for your help, Josh. Are you sure you won't get into any trouble over hacking the airlines and Evans's bank?"

"No, man, I'm no amateur. I masked my IP, bounced through several servers around the world, and went on a VPN site that guarantees anonymity. If I told you how I did it, I'd have to shoot you."

He made a gun out of his hand and pretended to shoot me. I heard him laughing as I headed down the steps.

I called up the stairs, "OK, send me your bill. I'm late picking up Phil. Lock up for me."

Chapter 11

After I'd picked up Phil at the hospital, we drove home in silence. I wanted to find out if he remembered anything else, but he was too groggy to be questioned. If I waited for a day or two, he would feel better, and with a bit of luck, remember more. As we drove up my drive, I came to a stop by his cabin and glanced over at him. His eyes were closed, and his facial muscles relaxed. I hated to wake him up. He looked so peaceful.

I touched his shoulder. "Phil, I think I should take you up to my house, so I can keep an eye on you."

He sat up and stifled a yawn. "That won't be necessary. Leave me at my place. I've had worse than this in the Marines and lived through it. Semper Fi."

"Oorah!"

He looked at me through half-closed eyelids and smiled. "You worry too much." He looked around the truck for the first time and back at me. "Where's Boomer?"

"I dropped him off at the West Hills Kennel before I picked you up. He had an overdose of a tranquilizer someone slipped him and almost died. The vet said I got him to her in the nick of time. It was touch-and-go there for a while. I'm leaving him at the kennel until this is over. I can't take a chance on someone doing that to him again or worse."

Phil nodded and stared out his window. "He's a good soldier."

I nodded. He sat in my truck without moving. I went around to his side and opened the door. Phil stepped out and stumbled, but I caught him before he fell. I didn't want to leave him in his cabin alone, but he didn't give me a choice.

I helped him into his house. You can't force a grown man to do something if he doesn't want to do it. I stayed long enough to see he made it to bed. I put water, his medicine, and his phone on his nightstand alongside his gun.

"Just rest. I'll get supper. Tonight is spaghetti. OK with you?"

Phil nodded, and I left. I had to clean up my house. I hadn't been inside since someone had trashed the place. The longer I thought about it the more I decided Davis was the key to this. First, I wanted to visit Susie's apartment and then talk to Davis, but he could wait until tomorrow.

After I cleaned up most of the mess, I sat down in my recliner and fell asleep. When the sun set, it left a chill in the house. I woke up and made the supper run to the Do Drop Inn.

After my patient and I were well fed, I locked Phil's cabin and made my way home. I rarely bother locking my door. However, on my return home, I locked up, checked the windows were locked, and closed the plantation shutters. Making my way upstairs to the guest room, I put my gun under my pillow and fell asleep almost immediately.

The next morning was a clear, sunny day. I sat on the patio and drank my instant coffee in my travel mug. Listening to the birds sing, I glimpsed a cardinal settled on a rhododendron at the edge of the patio. Its mate perched two branches down. He joined her, and both flew away. A doe with twin fawns grazed in the meadow alongside four young bucks. A gentle breeze came off the mountain and gently whirled around my head.

The wind felt almost seductive. If I closed my eyes, I could see my wife and feel the way she used to massage my temples when I came home tired and sore. Her fingertips had rubbed my temples in slow, soothing circles. I never thought of her without joy and sadness at the same time. My son would have been eleven this coming Friday. Sometimes I can go days without thinking of them and then the memories come at me in a rush. Keeping the pain at bay is a full-time job.

I looked around and wondered why I had to go into town again when I had such peace here in this place. Phil came up the trail in behind the house with his coffee already in an insulated cup. He looked tired, but being tired never stopped him making his rounds of the property. He sat down as usual, drank his coffee, read the newspaper, and left without saying a word.

I locked up and climbed into my truck. With a sense of dread, I made my way to Alfred Street and Susie's former apartment. I knocked on the manager's door and heard chains rattling. The manager opened the door a crack. When he saw me, he opened the door a little wider.

"What can I do for you, mister?"

"Mr. Corn, you may not remember me. I was here the other night when Susie's body was found. My name's Chance Sunday, and I'm a private investigator. The police finished with her apartment. I would like to have a look around."

He scratched his head, closed one eye, and looked at me. "I don't know about that. Her parents paid for another month's rent until they can pick her stuff up."

"I won't take anything. You can watch while I look. I'll not disturb anything, I promise. I want to make sure the police and I haven't missed something important."

He looked down and scuffed his foot in the worn carpet. "You know, I don't get much for looking after these apartments. I get a reduction in my rent, but that's all. A man has to pay bills."

It didn't take a genius to see what he was after. He let me in for twenty dollars. It looked the same as the last time I saw it. No one had cleaned up the mess or packed her clothes. He stood in the doorway and watched me search. I went into her bedroom. I found, stuffed in a corner of her closet, two black pairs of sweatpants and two black hoodies with matching ski masks. Both had peace symbols on the zipper tab.

Susie was below average in height. I would say five foot two or three. No way would Laurel have mistaken her for Davis, even scared to

177

death. I felt sure she would not have run to her for safety if she suspected her. I held the items up. One outfit came closer to fitting me than her, but the other would have fitted her. When I finished searching, I still could not find her cell phone.

I took out my cell and called Charlie.

"Hi, Chance, what can I do for you?"

"Did you find Susie's cell phone yet?"

"We haven't found it. Do you know her number? I tried to get her number from her parents, but they were in such a state I didn't press it. I will check with them again after the funeral."

"You're in luck, I have it. Her number is 304-555-8931. Do you think you can find out who the carrier is?"

"Finding her provider won't be too hard, but getting her information will be difficult, as you know. I'll have to have a subpoena, and that will take time."

"Yeah, I know. Time is something we have little of. Do the best you can. They may be able to track where it's been. If you can ping it, you can get a location of where it is now."

"I'll do what I can, but Chance, I can't give you any information."

"Yeah, I know you'll do your best. All I'm asking is that you keep me in the loop. Let me know if you get anything that will help. And thanks, Charlie."

I stood in the middle of the room and looked around, making sure I hadn't missed anything. I knew the police had gone through here, but they weren't really looking too hard at clothing. If they'd found the sweat outfits, they didn't realize the significance. Their thoughts were centered on finding who murdered Susie not a robbery in another county.

My eyes came to rest on Mr. Corn standing in the doorway with his little eyes taking in every detail.

"Mr. Corn, did she have a lot of visitors?"

"Not many. Mostly that girl they're looking for and them two boys."

"What two boys?"

"Don't know their names but I can tell you what they drive. One of them had a red Mustang convertible. He always made a racket when he pulled out. Never made a bit of difference to him what time of the night it was. Young people got no consideration these days.

"Then there was that one what drove an old Ford truck. I remember my daddy having one just like it only not in as good a condition. They never come at the same time. Don't know how she kept both of them separated. The Ford truck regularly came after the red Mustang left and always much later at night.

"Did you find anything to help?" Mr. Corn asked. "I sure hope they catch whoever did it. She never gave me any trouble. She always paid her rent on time, which is more than I can say for some."

"The police did a thorough search of her apartment, but her phone hasn't turned up. If you find her phone, let the police know." I handed him my card. "If you think of anything that might help, call me or the police. Thank you for your time, Mr. Corn."

He looked at my card and put it in his wallet. He shook his head. "I'm gonna miss that little girl. She always stopped to say hello or wave at me when she was leaving."

I watched him lock her door. We walked down the stairs together. At the bottom of the stairs, I held out my hand and shook his.

"Thanks again. I'll be going now."

I gave him another twenty and watched him go back in his apartment before I left.

Contrary to common belief, she had not finished with Brian. The only one who knew the true story would be Brian.

After leaving Susie's apartment, I headed for the church. Susie's funeral was today. I slipped through the door of the chapel as the pastor stepped behind the pulpit. I slid into the last pew in the back on the right. The church was filled with flowers and friends. Brian and Davis were conspicuously absent. Her bereaved parents were up front holding on to each other.

After the service, we all filed outside and stood around like people do. Most people like me want to get away as soon as possible but are not sure when they can or how to do it. The mourners moved to their cars, and the funeral procession started for the cemetery. I let everyone get ahead of me. This was the hardest part of my job. I never went by a cemetery without remembering my personal losses.

The day was sunny. Not a cloud in sight. I still feel if you're having a burying, it should be raining. The pastor said a few words over the grave, and everyone began to leave. The men filled in the grave. Susie's parents got into their limousine and left. There's nothing quieter than a cemetery when everyone is gone.

I stayed in my truck until everyone left before I walked up to the grave and paid my last respects. I hadn't known her, but this should not have happened to one so young. As I drove away, I passed Brian going in the direction of the cemetery.

I left and headed for Davis's apartment. He hadn't been at the funeral or the graveside. I found his Mustang parked out front, but he was not in the apartment. When I found him, he was sitting by his parents' pool dangling the pool skimmer in the water. He had several days' growth of whiskers; his hair looked like it hadn't been combed in two or three days. He had on the same clothes from my previous visit. I walked up, but he didn't notice me until I sat down beside him.

"Hello, Davis. Remember me?"

"Yeah, man, why don't you leave me alone? Today's not the day to talk to me. I keep telling you I don't know anything."

"I'm still trying to help Laurel. When I find who the people were that stormed the lab and killed everyone in sight, it'll help Laurel, and also, I believe it'll find Susie's killer. You want Susie's killer found, don't you?"

"What good would it do now? Nothing you do is gonna bring her back. I guess you think I should have gone to the funeral. I didn't, and I'm not going to the cemetery either. Just go away and leave me alone."

"If you want to wallow in your grief, that's up to you. Speaking of the funeral, why didn't you go?"

"What would be the point? It's just a meaningless ritual." He stared off in the distance while tears rolled down his cheeks. He took a deep breath, turned his head, and stared at me. "Truth is, I'm a coward. I couldn't get up the nerve to go. If I don't see her grave, then she can't be gone. I'll go by her apartment and she'll still be there."

"It might help you move past this point in your life by accepting the truth. She is gone, and no one can bring her back. A funeral is more for the living than the dead. It usually gives you some closure. Going by the cemetery and leaving flowers might help you say goodbye. Knowing she received justice even though nothing brings her back might ease your mind. I think you know something you can tell me. Maybe you don't even know you have the key to this."

Davis shook his head and stared off in the distance. He continued to dangle the skimmer in the water and stare down into the depths of the deep end of the pool. His mind was somewhere far, far away. I cleared my throat and spoke a little louder, hoping to get his attention.

"Davis, listen to me. Let me lay it on the line for you. Everywhere I turn, left, right, and center, your name crops up. Either you're mixed up in this, or you know who is. Is that what's eating at you? Are you going to wallow in your pain or are you going to help me?"

"I told you before, I don't know anything," he shouted and stood up.

He threw the skimmer in the pool and turned toward me with his fist clenched. I stood up too and backed up two paces.

"You told me the night of the robbery you were in your apartment watching television when Laurel showed up. Laurel says she waited over an hour for you to show. Who's telling the truth?"

"What difference does it make now?" He looked at me with a scowl. "All right, if it'll make you go away, I'll tell you. Laurel told the truth. I had a standing date with Susie. She called it off at the last minute. I'm ashamed to say I went to her apartment anyhow. I was afraid she was cheating on me with Brian. She wasn't there. She hadn't come back, and it was after midnight. I gave up and left.

"I cruised by Brian's place, but he wasn't there either. I didn't know what to think. When I came home, I found Laurel waiting for me here at my apartment.

"Look, man, Susie's and my relationship had to be kept secret. My parents forbid me to see her. I didn't want what I did getting around, or my parents finding out. If Susie found out I was checking up on her, then it'd look like I didn't trust her. I didn't tell the truth when you asked me because I didn't want our relationship getting back to my parents. I guess it doesn't matter now."

"No, I guess it doesn't. Do you have any other secrets I should know about?"

He shook his head and walked to the edge of the patio. He bent down and picked absentmindedly at some weeds pushing their way through the tiles.

"Look, Davis, I think your friend Brian and his friend Hollis Evans are involved in this."

"You're crazy. Not Brian, of all people. No, you're way off base. He loved Susie. He wouldn't do anything to hurt her or Laurel."

"After the robbery/murder, you bought a ticket for Brian to go to New York. Why'd you do that?"

"Man, you don't give up, do you?" He shook his head and took a deep breath. "It's none of your business. I don't know why I should tell you. It's no secret Brian's business is failing. He didn't have the money for a ticket, and his credit cards were maxed out. Brian needed to talk to a man in New York about buying one of his restorations. I'm not worried. He'll pay me back when he gets the money."

"Is that what he told you? You're sure about this. And you believed him?"

"Of course, I believed him. Why shouldn't I? Brian's my friend."

"Do you know Hollis Evans?"

"Sure, he's Brian's cousin. He's a deputy sheriff in Pinedale. He wouldn't do anything like this either. You're barking up the wrong tree."

"I don't think so. Let me give you a few facts. New York City has a big diamond district. A deputy sheriff would know where to go to unload some hot ice. Uncut diamonds have no way to be traced as to ownership. If someone were interested in a restoration of Brian's, he'd come to see him and the car, not the other way around.

"You also bought him a ticket to Panama City, a known offshore banking community. They have tight security and are not likely to turn over records to the authorities. Furthermore, Evans accompanied Brian to New York and Panama. The second time, after the robbery, Brian went to Panama alone. He drove to Brownsville. There's no record of him after that until he flew out of Panama and back to Brownsville. Here's another fact for you to ponder on. For your information, his credit cards are not maxed out."

"No, you're wrong. There has to be another explanation. Brian...Brian, he wouldn't hurt Susie or Laurel. Why would he lie to me about needing money? We've been friends since kindergarten."

"Davis, listen to me. You don't realize what's involved. We're talking about possibly ten million dollars in diamonds. Maybe Brian didn't do the actual killing, but he knows who did. Don't you realize he's implicated you in this business? You bought him the tickets."

"All I did was buy him the tickets. He said he didn't have any money. You've got this all wrong."

"I don't think so. When I went to visit him, there was a black Tahoe in his shop's backyard. The same Tahoe that's been following me around. Someone in this identical Tahoe took a shot at me. When I checked, your friend's making his rent and still doing restorations. Brian and Hollis played you."

"You're crazy, man. I know my friend. Money doesn't mean that much to him."

"Davis, people grow up. Life changes everyone. Susie was Brian's girl and then you took her. You're going on to college. Life is looking good for you. On the other hand, Brian is trying to keep his head above water with a failing business and no prospects.

"You've seen his condo. How do you think he makes the payments? And another point, car restorations cost a lot of money. There's no guarantee you'll get your money back. Don't tell me he doesn't know the value of money or want his share.

"All I'm asking for is your help. If he's innocent, no harm done. If not, then he needs to pay for what he's done."

Davis rushed at me, but his heart wasn't in it. I held out my hand and blocked him. I turned him around and held his arms down by his side. When I turned him loose, all his anger drained from his body, and he hung his head with his limp arms at his side.

"Get off my property before I call the cops. I don't care what you say. Not Brian...no way." He made his way to a lounge chair and collapsed on it.

"Ok, ok, I'm leaving. You've got my card if you want to talk. Think about what I said."

I pretended to leave and parked up the street. I noticed a vacant house with an overgrown lawn on Davis's street less than five hundred feet away. I parked in the drive and opened my laptop. Making my way to Davis's apartment, I placed two wireless cameras outside his basement apartment. One was looking through the window toward the sofa, and the other had a good view of the Mustang.

The special software Josh had installed gave me a split screen. I watched and watched and watched some more. Davis returned to his apartment, but nothing happened. He fell asleep on the sofa. Several hours later, I was about to doze off myself. Unexpectedly, Davis jumped up from the sofa, picked up his cell phone, and punched in a number. He was shouting and waving his free arm around with his fist clenched. He was out of sight for a while. When he came back, he had changed his clothes and combed his hair. He ran outside and jumped in his car.

I backed out of the drive and followed him. No doubt about it, he was headed for Brian's place. It looked like he picked up his phone again. Abruptly, he slammed on the brakes and made a U-turn in the middle of the street. I pulled in the auto parts store parking lot and turned around.

He went back to his house. I parked in the vacant house's drive again and watched the equivalent of paint drying. He sat down on the sofa and put his head in his hands. He left my view and came back with a bottle of beer. Before long, I watched him polish off an even dozen bottles. I recovered my webcams and left soon after that. No way was he going to be doing anything else tonight.

It was time to poke the hornet's nest. Paying another visit to Brian might be the shove he needed. I made my way over to his shop, but he wasn't in. I went to his apartment in Vienna, but no Brian. I called Charlie and went to his home. It was necessary to get on record what I thought had gone down at the lab. Charlie would give me an unbiased opinion.

When I arrived at my friend's home, Joyce answered the door and gave me a hug. Charlie and I shook hands. We made our way out back to his deck. Joyce brought a tray with iced tea and an assortment of nibbles. We sat in his backyard drinking our tea and enjoying the peace of the evening.

"Glad you came by. You're awfully quiet tonight, Chance. What's on your mind?"

"I wanted to talk over with you what's been happening. I'm trying to decide where to begin and how to protect my client. Will you listen to what I have to say as my friend and not as an officer of the law?"

"Chance, we've known each other for over twenty years. I've always been your friend first and a police officer second. What's on your mind?"

I explained what I had found out so far. "I know I don't have much. For the most part, it's circumstantial. I'm convinced Hollis Evans and Brian Moore are involved. Someone trashed my office and house, and I think that someone was Brian at my office and Evans at my house. I can only guess at the reason. There's again no proof.

"I have a webcam in my office but whoever did this spray-painted the lens before it took a clear picture of the perpetrator. I don't like to think it involves a brother officer in anything as bad as this, but I can't rule the sheriff out either."

"Yeah, I see what you mean. I think you're on the right trail but tread cautiously. If either one or both are crooked, you most likely won't live to prove it. So far, you've given me nothing I can run with. The state police will require more evidence before they act, particularly against a fellow officer. I can't even bring anyone in for questioning."

"I figured that one out all by myself. That's why I'm telling you. You're the only one I can trust. I'm going to poke Moore a little if I can find him. I'll watch and see what happens. Is there any way you can check ballistics on Evan's pistol? It would be dim-witted to use his service revolver to commit a crime, but you never know. My guess would be he used an unregistered firearm.

"I'm thinking he's the one who shot those people. He would be the one most likely to have access to an unregistered firearm. It was stupid to shoot them since they were in no position to report the robbery.

"Have you ever met him? I swear he's one sandwich short of a picnic with a quick temper," I said.

"No, I've never met him. If he has guns, he in all probability has unregistered firearms at home in a safe place. If he has one grain of sense, he'll have destroyed that gun by now. The ballistics for his service revolver would be on record, but surely, he would not use it to commit a robbery. Without a warrant, there's no way to get a look at his collection. For now, you only have suspicions or theories, nothing a judge would consider."

"Yeah, I know. Do you remember what make of pistol was used to shoot those people?"

"Let me see. Wait here. I'll log on to my computer at work and find out." He came back a little later and sat down. "It is believed to be a Smith and Wesson M&P Shield .45 automatic. It's usually used for concealed carry. Some officers carry a backup. If the murder gun was his, it was possibly his backup gun."

"Do you think you can let me know when no one would be home? I've got an idea about how to find out if he still has the gun."

"Chance, don't tell me things like that. I'm sure you were talking through the hole in your head and not intending on doing what I think you are. He must have security cameras everywhere in and around his house. There's no telling what he might do if he thinks you were at his house. If he's as crazy as you think he is, he'd come gunning for you."

"Charlie, you know me. I talk a lot. The way I feel now, I don't care if he does recognize me."

I reached into my jacket and handed him the slug from my truck.

"This is from someone taking a potshot at me in the Do Drop Inn parking lot. Maybe you could run a check to see if it was from the same gun that killed the scientists. If it is, we'll at least know he still has the gun."

"Yeah, I'll do that. Chance, you're taking too many chances. I'll see what I can find out, but I'm asking you not to do what I think you're planning to do. Evans is a dangerous man."

I nodded my understanding. Charlie didn't know how dangerous he actually was. When a person is unpredictable, it's hard to guess what they'll do next.

Chapter 12

I left shortly after my little talk with Charlie and headed to the computer store. I needed two more laptops. Buying two laptops for the office just fried my grits. The money I'm getting for this little job has already been spent and then some. I could have reported the damage to my insurance company, but I would need a police report to collect. If the police found my secret room and that went in the report, I could expect another unannounced visit.

I took my new laptops up to the office and left them in the safe room. Josh would set the laptops up next time he was in. My subsequent stop was Brian Moore's repair shop. As I turned in, I saw his '47 Ford truck parked out front alongside the aforementioned black Tahoe. A more prudent person than me would have waited to see who drove the Tahoe. I was a little too ticked off to be cautious.

As I was getting out of my truck, an old saying of my father's ran through my head. "You will do foolish things, but do them with enthusiasm." He said that to me when I graduated from college. He knew me a little too well. I'm sure he didn't mean for me to goad a suspect in his home territory.

Since Brian's truck was here, he must be working. I tried the front door and found it locked. Next, I called his name and knocked on the door again. All I heard was banging in the back lot. I went around the shop office and found the gate unlocked. That should have been my first clue. I walked through and called Brian's name.

From out of nowhere, someone stepped out of the shadows of the shop shed. A pipe struck me across the stomach. I doubled over in pain, unable to move. I could barely breathe through the pain. Two strong sets of arms picked me up and dragged me into the shop. Brian tied my hands behind me with rope, and someone used me for a punching bag. The fists came so fast I couldn't see who the other person was. Thankfully, the punishment stopped. They must have worn themselves out punching me, or I passed out, or both.

My next memory is of someone bending down and whispering in my ear. I felt his hot spittle spraying my ear. My eyes were out of focus. I kept opening and closing my eyes, trying to get them to focus. I couldn't see who my assailant was, but I didn't have to try too hard to make an educated guess. There was no mistaking that guttural voice.

"You stepped in it this time, Peeper. Why are you snooping around my cousin? He's got nothing to say to you. If you keep pestering him, you're asking for it in my book."

My assailant kept shouting at me. I was in so much pain his words had no meaning. After my eyes came into focus, I looked into the cold, steely eyes of Hollis Evans.

"You don't have a camera this time. You can't go crying to the sheriff about anybody. Brian will swear I was with him the whole time on the other side of town."

He punched me again. He'd hit me so many times I didn't feel the blows anymore.

I heard Brian yell at him, "Hey, hey, let up. Don't kill him. This isn't some nobody. He's got friends on the force."

"Yeah, Brian, I told Lieutenant Parks I was coming here. That'll be a little hard to explain away if I come up missing." I somehow managed to get that out, right before I threw up.

My eyes came into focus for a second, and I saw Brian grab Hollis's arm and pull him back. I must have passed out again. When I came to, I heard Evans talking.

"I'm not gonna kill him. I'm just gonna make him wish he was dead."

His sadistic laughing rang through my ears, and he did a little dance around the chair where I was sitting.

I must have passed out again. When I came to next, I was alone in the shop. My swollen eyes made it hard to see. My face was so puffed up when I tried to peer out, all I could see were the tops of my cheeks. I turned the chair I was sitting on over. I must have hit hard on the concrete floor, but I was past the point of feeling pain. The back came off the wooden chair when it fell over from my weight. I worked my arms around until they were off the chair back but still tied.

Across the room, I saw a sharp piece of metal. Crawling and dragging myself across the floor, I made it to where the piece of metal stood against a table. I worked feverishly and cut the ropes along with the skin on my wrists. With my hands and legs free, I found a piece of pipe to act as a crutch. With circulation returning to my legs, I hobbled my way to the side of the shop. I pushed the door open a crack. I had no idea how long I'd been in Brian's shop. When I peered out the door, the sun was coming up. I must have been here all night.

I listened, but the place was as silent as the grave. I made it to the gate in the fence while keeping to the shadows. Brian's truck was gone. My truck was still there and so was the Tahoe. My swollen hand felt in my pocket for my keys, and sore fingers closed around them. I eased the gate open and stepped to the side of the office, keeping in the shadow of the building.

Trying not to cough too loudly, I spit up a few droplets of blood. What I wouldn't give for a drink of water. I peeked through the window into the office and looked to see if anyone was there. As luck would have it, Evans was asleep at the desk. He had his legs propped up on the trash can and his hand resting on the gun lying across his chest.

I eased my way over to my truck and opened the passenger door as quietly as I could. Sliding over to the driver's side, I put the key in the ignition. I wasn't sure it would start. A thought ran through my mind that they could have disabled it. The sound from the engine turning over was music to my ears. I reached across the seat and slammed the passenger door shut as Evans woke up. He came running out of the office with a gun in his hand. I backed out as fast as I could.

I didn't look for oncoming traffic. I threw her in drive, pedal to the floor, and headed to the hospital. From my side mirror, I saw Evans running for the Tahoe, but I didn't think he would risk a street battle or follow me into the hospital. The red emergency room sign shone brightly up ahead. My truck came to a stop under the canopy. I did not have the energy to open the door.

As the attendants were helping me out of my truck, I glanced up the street and saw Evans. He stopped behind the railroad trestle, turned his truck around, and left. My teeth were loose and my face was swollen, but I felt a smile spread across my face despite the pain. I would be safe for the time being, while they fixed me up.

Two orderlies rolled me back to one of the cubicles. Doctor Digman came in to see me.

"Well, Mr. Sunday, we've got to stop meeting like this. First your friend and now you. Mind telling me what immovable object you came up against this time?"

"It-it was a mugging, Doc."

"Yeah, that's your story. If it was, you should have just given the mugger your money."

"I guess I'm selfish that way. What's mine is mine." He shook his head and stared at me for a moment before he motioned for the people with the stretcher to take me.

"We'll know more after the x-rays. For now, the nurse will give you something for pain after she takes you down to x-ray. We have to make sure there's no internal bleeding first."

He wrote on his clipboard and hurried to the next patient.

They brought me back an hour or so later. The doctor walked in and threw my x-rays up on the screen. He kept looking and going, "Umm."

"It's worse than it looks, Doc." I tried to laugh and felt the pain radiating all over my body.

"I don't see how it could be, Mr. Sunday."

Doctors have no sense of humor.

"However, nothing appears to be broken. There isn't any internal bleeding I can see. How that's possible, I don't know. You look like you've been in one of those mixed martial arts contests and lost. You will be in a lot of pain for the next couple of days. I've got a prescription here for you to help with the pain and nausea. Do you have someone to drive you home?"

"Not here. I'll need to call someone."

"I can't let you leave until you do. Give the nurse your friend's number, and she'll call for you."

When they released me, I found Charlie reading a magazine in the waiting room. The nurse wheeled me out. Charlie glanced at the nurse and me, but he didn't recognize me. As we came closer, he looked me up and down. Abruptly, he jumped up with his mouth open. I was hard to recognize with a swollen and bruised face.

"Chance, is that you?" He put his hand across his mouth and continued to stare at me.

He followed the nurse out to my truck and helped her put me in. Once he had me in the truck, he drove down the street two or three blocks and pulled over. "What happened?"

"I walked into a whirlwind. Evans and Moore were waiting for me. Evans gave me the going over. I passed out, and they left me alone in the shop. With a little luck, I escaped.

"As bad as it hurts, I know I'm on the right track now, but I have to find out for sure. His excuse, he said, was because of the video and my bothering his cousin. Maybe that was all it was, but it seems an extreme reaction."

"Chance, let the police handle this. You've done all you can. I'll write up a report and have them questioned," Charlie said, and shook his head.

"Charlie, both of them will swear they were somewhere else. It'll be their word against mine. I'm this close to finding out who did the murders. I can't stop now. If Brian and Hollis are in on this, I have to find out. I'm not satisfied as to the identity of the third member of their gang.

"The longer I look at this, the more I'm convinced Laurel is innocent of the murders, but there's something she's not telling me. She knows something, and I intend to find out what it is. Either she's afraid, or she doesn't want to rat out her friends. Whatever she knows could get her killed. She was lucky the first two times she had a run-in with these people. She might not be so lucky next time.

"Brian won't expect me to come back after what they did to me. I need to get him alone. I think he's the weak link in all of this."

Charlie shook his head and frowned.

"Don't look at me like that, Charlie. I promise I won't do it today. Maybe tomorrow," I said, and tried to grin, but it hurt too much.

"If I have to lock you up, I will for your own good. You're gonna get yourself killed."

"Were you able to match the slug I gave you to the lab killings?"

"Not yet. Ballistics has it, but I should know soon."

"The longer we have to wait, the more chance he has to get rid of the gun.

"Charlie, just listen, OK? Here's what I plan to do when I feel better. I'm going by Moore's apartment. I'll Skype you first and leave my cell on record. You'll be listening and recording along with me. I think I can get him to confess. I know it's not admissible in court, but you should be able to bluff a confession out of him. He doesn't think I can do anything. It's the only way I will clear Laurel and find out who killed Susie."

"I don't like it, Chance. I have one stipulation. Call me before you do anything. I want to be close by when you confront him. It may be the only way to solve this."

Charlie took me home, and his wife Joyce was waiting outside my house with their car. Joyce brought a container of homemade chicken noodle soup and crackers. They both stood and watched while I made it to my recliner.

I looked up at them and saw concern written all over their faces. "Don't worry about me. I'll be OK. Phil will check on me."

"Yeah, I talked to him when we brought you home. I hate leaving you here. Maybe I had better stay."

"Charlie, you've got better ways to spend your time than being my nursemaid. Go on home. I promise to rest and not do anything foolish for at least a day."

"Talk like that scares me. I hope you're joking. I wish I could believe foolish was out of the question," Charlie said, and grinned.

They waved goodbye, and I was on my own again.

I stayed in my recliner the rest of the day and the next. Phil came to check on me and brought food. Today I felt better, and the swelling has gone down some. I still have a black eye and numerous bruises covered by my shirt. When I stand up, I no longer double over in pain. I still have pins and needles in my arms and legs.

Soon I would have to confront Brian. I couldn't wait much longer, or they will have left for parts unknown—if they haven't already. I'm not sure why they were hanging around unless they're lying low until this blows over. They must think they've pulled off the perfect crime and they can afford to wait until the fuss dies down.

The next day I told myself I felt better. My only option was to search Evans's house for the gun that killed the people in the lab. I had no proof of anything otherwise. Brian could wait until I found the gun. I called the sheriff's office and found Evans had taken a vacation day but would be on duty tomorrow.

Most of my pain was gone. Thanks to the pain pills the doctor had given me, I didn't feel too bad. I needed a testing block to get a spent bullet for ballistics. The only way to do that was to enter Hollis Evans's home. If I could find his stash of guns, and find the murder weapon, I would turn my evidence over to Charlie and let him take it from there. My test would not stand up in court. If I found the gun and the bullet matched, the police could get a warrant based on information from a source.

Mixing the gel block to do the testing is easy to do, but it does require a lot of elbow grease, space, and time. You need a strong powdered gelatin, approximately 1 to 2 pounds per gallon of water. You also need distilled cold water, a large stock pot, a plastic 2-gallon bucket, a thermometer, a high-capacity scale, a stirring stick, a strainer, a stove, a mold, and space in a refrigerator. It had been a long time since I'd made one, but I knew what to do.

I was still sore and weak from my beating. Phil came up to help with the heavy work. I weighed out the correct amount of gel and set it aside. Phil put a two-gallon bucket on the scale and poured in eight pounds of water. Next, I stirred in the gelatin. It looked a little like mashed potatoes. I put the lid on the bucket and made room in my refrigerator. Phil set it in the refrigerator for me. It would need about four hours. I had to remove several cans of beer, but anything for a good cause.

Phil had a propane deep fryer turkey pot that he let me borrow. I put a spacer in the bottom of the pot so the stockpot wouldn't come into direct contact with the heat. I then filled the cooker with water until my bucket of gel was almost covered. I turned on the heat to low so the gel would melt but not boil.

When it foamed, I had to skim that off. By this time, it was time to put the gel in a mold. I had a plastic storage container that would work as a mold for my purpose. I let the mixture cool to room temperature in the mold before Phil put the mold in the refrigerator. I turned the temperature down to thirty-four degrees. Usually I keep my refrigerator set at thirty-six degrees, but I didn't think the drop would hurt what beer I had left in there.

When the mold was set and ready, Phil took it out of the refrigerator. I made four bags packed with polyester fill material and a metal plate to put behind the mold. I needed the polyester bags to catch the bullet if it passed through the gel and the metal plate would stop the bullet if it made it past the sacks. Phil made me a wooden frame to hold everything. The next day we loaded all of this in the back of my truck, and I was ready to head out to Pinedale. Phil wanted to come with me, but if Murphy's Law tells you anything, it's that you don't want your friends involved.

I knew Evans's wife worked as a teacher during the day and Evans was on duty. This was my chance. I took my Beretta and put it in my shoulder holster. I plugged his address into my GPS and headed for Pinedale. Finding his house was easy enough. It was in the curve of a cul-de-sac.

Backing my truck up to the garage, I parked under the shade of a large oak. I had mud smeared on my license plate covering up the number. I stepped out and fastened my tool belt like any other laborer. No one at the neighboring houses appeared to be home. I scanned the area and didn't see anyone peering out of a window. If anyone was, I looked like any other workman, and that should satisfy most nosy neighbors.

Most people have security systems nowadays, and Evans did, as I expected he would. Typically, people only put the sensors on the first floor. He had cameras in front of the garage, the front door, and the back door, and sensors on the first-floor windows.

I kept my hat pulled low over my eyes, dark glasses on, and my face away from the camera. He would know who broke in, but I didn't think he would report it. I walked around the house and saw a small window on the second floor. It was most likely a bathroom window, and it was open. Evans had stored a ladder by the side of his toolshed. I used it to climb on the roof, where I could look in the second-story windows of the bathroom and bedroom. They did not have sensors.

Once in the house, I checked out the upstairs and found a lockbox gun case. It was open, and the gun was gone. I made my way downstairs and checked those rooms. The only place left was the basement. I had to hurry. I could set off an alarm and not know it. In the basement, I found his workshop. Still no guns. I knew he was the type to have guns somewhere in his home. I had to find his hiding place. There had to be at least one rifle. I looked around the room, and realized something wasn't right with the width and length.

I fumbled around until I found the latch that released the back of his work bench. It moved forward, and there was the collection. The Smith and Wesson I was looking for was there. It was loaded and recently oiled.

What were the odds he would have two guns just alike or have kept the incriminating gun? If he had kept the gun I was looking for, he had an overdeveloped sense of security. My guess is he had the pure arrogance of the person who believes he is smarter than everyone else. He thought a mere mortal could not catch him.

I took the gun outside to my truck, where I'd left the testing block, and fired into my gelatin mold. Climbing in through the window again, I reloaded the gun and replaced it. I put everything back like I found it. I climbed outside the same way I'd gained access with the help of the ladder. After I put the ladder beside the shed, I walked around the house, got in my truck, and headed home.

On my way through Pinedale, I saw Evans in his cruiser. He didn't see me, but he was hot footing it in the direction of his house. I must have tripped an alarm. I made it home and dug the bullet out of the mold. Placing it in a plastic bag, I left to have Charlie check it.

Charlie was leaving the office as I ran up the steps. "Chance, what are you doing here? How you feeling?"

"I'm fine for the shape I'm in," I said and tried to laugh.

Charlie shook his head. Sometimes I think he despairs of me and my messes.

"By the way, I ran ballistics on the bullet that made a hole in your truck, and it doesn't match the ones that killed the scientists."

"Thanks for doing that. I've got another one for you to check. This one came from a Smith and Wesson belonging to Hollis. Can you run it for me and put a rush on it? If it's from the same gun, we have him. When he finds I've been in his house, he may get rid of the gun. If it's not the gun, then I have to keep trying until I connect all the dots."

"At some point we will have to get a warrant. This means you will need to stay out of this before you get yourself killed."

"I know, I know, but I've got this one last T to cross. I promise after that to leave it to you." Waving goodbye, I hurried away before he could stop me.

My next step was to pay Brian a visit. I waited in my office until time to deal with him. He would most likely be alone and home in the evening. I cruised by his apartment building and saw his old truck parked in his space. A light shone through the crack in the curtains of his apartment.

I called Charlie.

"Hello, Parks Residence."

"Charlie, it's me. I'm at Moore's apartment building. His truck is parked in front of his condo and there's a light coming through the curtains. I put my cell in my shirt pocket. Do me a favor and bring up Skype. Tell me if you can see and hear."

I waited for him to call me back on Skype.

"Hang on. Yep, I'm hearing and seeing. Be careful. Give me thirty minutes before you go in. I need to advise Vienna PD of the situation, and they need time to get to the condo complex. And Chance, I don't need to remind you that a cornered person is dangerous. Evans could even be in the condo with him."

"Yeah, I thought of that too. I'll do a recon. Let me know when you're in place."

I hung up and walked around the parking lot looking for Evans's SUV or the Tahoe. I didn't see either. Charlie confirmed he was on his way there. I waited the thirty minutes it took him to get to Brian's apartment and called Charlie back on Skype. I put the phone in my shirt pocket and walked up to the door. Taking a deep breath, I knocked. Brian must have been expecting someone. He threw open the door on the first knock.

"Where you been...?"

When he realized it was me, he tried to slam the door, but my foot in the opening did the trick once again. If I lost my PI license, I could get a job as a door-to-door salesman. I'm getting good at putting my foot in the door. I put my shoulder to the door and pushed my way into the room.

"Hello, Brian. Surprised to see me? We've got some unfinished business, you and me."

I looked around the room. "Where's your old buddy, Hollis?"

He held up his hands and backed into the center of his living room. "Look, I swear I had nothing to do with beating you up. I didn't know he would do that. It was all Hollis's doing. I told him we shouldn't, but he said he had to teach you a lesson. We wouldn't have killed you. He said we would keep you tied up for a while and then dump you and your truck at the beer joint you're always going to. By the time someone found you, we would be long gone."

"That doesn't cut any ice with me. You were there, and you did nothing to stop him. You even helped tie me up. By the time someone found me, I would have been dead. Didn't you think of that, or didn't you care?"

"There wasn't anything I could do. It doesn't do to interfere with Hollis when he's in a mood. He wanted to shoot you...shoot you. I talked him out of that. That should count for something. You shouldn't stick your nose in where it doesn't belong."

"Maybe so, Brian, but you shouldn't have killed those people in the lab or had one of your friends killed. You couldn't stop there, could you? You set up Laurel to be killed. Were you going to let Laurel and Davis take the blame for everything? You tried to blow Laurel and myself to kingdom come. What about that, Brian? That's all on you."

"No, no, honest, I didn't do that. Sure, I knew where Laurel was holed up. Susie told me, but I didn't try to kill her. You can't pin that one on me, no, sir. I had the phone on speaker when Susie called me. She told me where Laurel was. Hollis was standing beside me and heard. I didn't know he was gonna kill Susie, I swear. I never would have let him do that." He stuck his chin out and backed up a step.

"The fact remains Susie's dead. You knew what kind of nutjob your cousin is. You did nothing to warn Susie or Laurel. My guess is Susie was getting nervous. She could put the finger on you and Hollis. Hollis couldn't let that happen, could he? You even called Susie to make a date after Davis left. What did you think Evans would do? Shake her hand?"

I took a step toward him, and he backed up another step, keeping his hands up.

"Look, I'm not Hollis's keeper. If he did it, that's on him. I swear I didn't know he would do anything like that." He licked his lips and wiped his hands on his jeans. "What're you going to do?"

"I haven't decided yet. Where is Hollis?"

"He'll be here in a few minutes. You better leave. I can't be responsible for what he might do if he finds you here. He said he's cleaning up loose ends, and he'll be here when he's through."

For the first time, I noticed Brian had his bags packed and sitting by the door.

"I can take care of myself. Now, let's talk, shall we? I know you and Hollis were the ones who robbed and murdered the people in the lab. Who was the third?"

"What do you mean, me and Hollis? You can't prove that. As soon as Hollis gets here, we're leaving the country."

"Brian, Brian, old man, you two beat me up for sticking my nose in your business. That's as good as a confession. It had to be the two of you. Who was the third?"

He was sweating profusely. His eyes darted around the room. "What do you want? A cut?"

"A cut would be nice, but I don't think Hollis would approve. What about your other partner? Who was the third man? Was it Davis?"

Brian laughed and sidled along the wall toward the kitchen. Once he knew I was on to them, he thought there was nothing I could do about it. The whole story unfolded. He puffed out his chest and grinned. He was actually proud of what they had done.

"Not that do-gooder. I never even asked him if he was interested. I knew he wouldn't do it. He'd rat us out."

200

"He bought you the tickets to New York and Panama. Why'd he do that if he wasn't involved?"

Brian said nothing. He stood there with a self-satisfied smirk.

"Oh, I see. You made a patsy out of him, didn't you? If anyone checked and didn't ask questions, he would be the one blamed for the robbery. Why would you do that? He's your best friend."

He put his finger to his nose and winked. "Why shouldn't I? He took my girl. All of them are moving on, leaving me behind. Davis, Laurel, and Susie got what they deserve." He chuckled with his head down.

"Who was the third man?"

"You fool, some detective you are. Can't you guess, Sherlock? It wasn't no man. It was Susie." He bent over laughing and holding his side.

"Susie! Why would she want to throw in with you two maniacs?"

"She wanted to marry Davis, didn't she? She told me she was pregnant. His folks would have cut off the money if they got married. She wanted to be free from her parents and his. Susie liked a rush. Sex, drugs, it didn't matter. It was all a game to her.

"Besides, we didn't have to talk her into it. She knew Laurel's password for the back door. She wouldn't give it to us unless we promised to take her with us and give her a cut."

"You mean Laurel wasn't involved? How'd Susie get her password?"

"One night Laurel was over at Susie's and laughing about what an insecure password system they had. She told Susie what it was. Susie could be a flake, but she knew more than you'd think. She said we had to let her come along. If you tell any of this, I'll deny it. It would be your word against mine."

"Yeah, yeah. I have one more question. Why'd you kill those people? People who couldn't report the robbery for obvious reasons."

"That wasn't planned. We went on a night when we thought Laurel wasn't working. Everything went like clockwork. Susie kept watch by the door. Hollis held a gun on them and made them unlock the safe. I gathered up the diamonds. We were ready to leave. Hollis passed by that Mr. Leslie. He reached up and jerked Hollis's ski mask off. Hollis had to shoot him because he could identify him."

"That still makes no sense. Why shoot someone who couldn't report the theft?"

"You don't know as much as you think. Leslie knew Hollis worked for Sheriff Henry."

"I still don't understand. Even if he worked for the governor, Mr. Leslie would be a fool to report the robbery when he was also doing something illegal."

"That's the kicker. The sheriff ain't so lily-white as you might think. Leslie and the sheriff have been friends since they were kids. Hollis eavesdropped on the sheriff and Mr. Leslie talking about the diamonds one evening at the sheriff's home. The sheriff took a consulting fee for telling him where to take the diamonds to sell in New York.

"Hollis didn't want them complaining to the sheriff. His father-in-law didn't like him very much as it was. If he thought Hollis was cutting in on his business, there would have been hell to pay."

"Someone killed your third partner. It looks like someone didn't want to share."

"I swear I didn't do it. Hollis did it. Laurel went to Susie for help. Susie told me where she sent Laurel, and Hollis heard her tell me. He said she could identify us. He said Laurel was a loose end. I thought maybe he would kill Laurel, but I never thought he'd kill Susie."

"It was OK to kill Laurel but not Susie?"

"When you're backed into a corner, you have to choose. Hollis made me call Susie and make a date for when Davis left. He went in my place. He said he would warn her to keep her mouth shut. That was all. I swear that's what he told me.

"I asked him later when I found out she was dead. He didn't deny it. Susie was my girl once. He shouldn't have killed her. She wouldn't have talked. I told him, but it was too late." Brian kept edging behind the counter, into the kitchen. "You want a cup of coffee? I made a fresh pot." He opened the cabinet door and took down two cups.

"No thanks. One other question..."

I didn't get to finish. He took a gun out of the kitchen cabinet and pointed it right at me.

"Brian, put that gun away. I didn't come here alone. This is the end of the line for you. You need to give yourself up. If you go to the police now, maybe you can cut a deal. You don't want to go down for the murders. The robbery alone with a gun will get you twenty years, and the murders could be life without parole. Forget Hollis. You better think through your options."

"I don't believe you came here with anyone. You're not that smart. We'll wait 'til Hollis gets here. He'll know what to do. You should never have come. You couldn't leave it alone, could you? Now you're going to pay. I can't do anything to help you."

"If you wait until Hollis gets here, it'll be too late to make a deal. You know what Hollis is capable of doing. You'll have another body on your hands. And you can consider yourself a loose end. Hollis has already killed four people, and I would be five. You think he wants you around to tell the tale or share the money?"

"Hollis will be here any minute. He said he had a few loose ends to take care of, and then he'd be over here. We're leaving tonight and never coming back. Hollis knows how to do stuff. I'm his cousin. He'll take care of me."

He didn't say it as confidently as he should have. I had him thinking.

At that moment, the door crashed in and Charlie came through with the Vienna S.W.A.T. Brian dropped his gun and held his hands up. They rushed at him, kicked his gun out of the way, and handcuffed him. All the officers had heard what Brian said. I had it recorded, and so did they. Three of the Vienna police waited outside and hid in the parking lot, waiting for Hollis to show. One stayed inside in Brian's apartment.

I walked into the parking lot to get a breath of fresh air. Charlie followed me out.

"We'll wait in the apartment for Evans. I have lookouts along the street to let us know ahead of time when they see him."

"Brian said he was taking care of loose ends. What do you suppose...?"

I couldn't finish the sentence. My heart started thumping like a tom-tom, and I couldn't breathe. I knew what loose end he was talking about. He planned to take out Laurel. When I could breathe again, I grabbed Charlie.

"He's going after Laurel. He's friends with the Weston Police. It won't be too hard for him to find out where they're keeping her. Call the DA or the police chief, someone. Tell them to get reinforcements over there ... now!"

I left Charlie dialing his cell phone.

Chapter 13

I jumped in my truck and gunned it out of the parking lot with Charlie yelling for me to come back. I don't think I've ever driven through city streets as fast as I did that night. Not even when in pursuit of a criminal. I turned on Highway 50 and prayed there were no deer strolling across the highway. When I looked at the speedometer it said a hundred. I kept the pedal to the floor.

Luckily, Highway 50 is four lanes, but it has some squirrelly curves. Somehow, I made it to Clarksburg, and in record time too. As I turned on I79, my cell phone started ringing. I fumbled on the seat for my phone and answered on the fifth ring while doing everything I know I shouldn't. I should have pulled over to answer the phone, but Laurel was running out of time. Trying my best to stay in my lane. I put the phone on speaker.

"Hello," I said, out of breath.

"Chance, Chance, is that you?" she asked in a high-pitched, panicked voice.

I didn't have to ask who it was. "Laurel, what's wrong?"

"Chance, something's not right. My two bodyguards are outside in their car talking to someone. I can't see who it is. I'm afraid to go outside. One officer usually stays in here with me, but both have been out there for over an hour. It looks as if one bodyguard is slumped in his seat. I can't explain it, but I think something's wrong. Can you come?"

"I'm on my way. Stay away from your bodyguards. You need to get out of there now. You're in danger. I've just passed Clarksburg and turned down I79. It'll be fifteen or twenty minutes before I get to where you are. Can you go out a back door?"

"No, there's only one outside door. The door to the next room is locked."

"How about a window?"

"Yes, there's a window in the bathroom I can crawl through. Why are you coming here? What's happened?"

"Good, good, try the window. I'll explain everything when I see you. There's no time to lose. Go through the window now. No time to talk now. I'm driving. Keep the phone on. You need to hide in a tool shed, a crawl space, or anywhere you're out of sight.

"When I get there, I'll drive around the motel. When you see my truck, wait until I get out and talk to you on the phone. You can tell me where to find you. I'll check the area and tell you if it's safe to come out of hiding."

"Please hurry. I'm going through the window now."

"I'll be there as quick as I can."

I made it to the Weston exit ramp. It was all I could do to slow my truck down. The ramp is a 25 mph curve. My tires squealed out their protest at my recklessness, but I made it more or less on two wheels. I straightened the truck out and turned right.

I prayed I had made it in time to save Laurel. The motel was two miles away. As I turned right into the drive before the shopping center, the Snuggle Inn Motel came into view. I let out the breath I had been holding. The motel looked peaceful. I calmed down, took my foot off the gas pedal, and scanned the area. Unhurriedly, I turned into the motel parking lot. With trembling fingers, I picked up my cell again.

"Laurel, are you there? Are you all right?"

"Yes, where are you?"

"I'm in the parking lot now. Stay where you are. I need to do a recon. What is your room number?"

"It's number t-twelve. Chance, I'm so scared. Someone entered the room as I was going out the window. I think it's Hollis Evans. I can't breathe. I'm shaking all over."

"I understand, but it's important you remain calm. I'm here now. I'll pick you up as soon as I check the area. I see your room. The car parked in front has two men in it. Continue to keep your phone on while I check."

I stepped out of my truck with my pistol down by my side. The two men did not move as I neared the car. I recognized them from the church when I'd turned Laurel over to the Weston Police. I walked up to the car. Still nothing. I knocked on the passenger side window, but they remained motionless. The hairs stood up on the back of my neck. I opened the passenger side door, and the officer fell out into my arms. He felt warm. I felt for his pulse, and happily, he had one.

The other officer was in the same condition. They appeared to be drugged. My guess was it was in the coffee they still had in their cups. I used their radio and called for an ambulance. The door to Laurel's room stood ajar. After making my way to her room, I eased the door open wider, holding my pistol at the ready. The room did not look disturbed. I went into the bathroom and saw the open window Laurel had crawled through to the outside.

Hollis Evans had to be here somewhere. Who else could have drugged the officers? They would have trusted a fellow officer. No doubt he'd brought the coffee. He'd expected to be long gone after he took care of Laurel and before someone discovered the officers.

The hairs stood up on the back of my neck. Weston police should have been here before me. Charlie was calling them as I was leaving the parking lot. I jumped back in my truck and started a slow recon around the motel. I made my way behind the motel. There was a driveway between the motel and the river. Driving by the river and around to the front again, I still did not see anything out of the ordinary. There was no sign of Hollis's truck.

"Laurel, I don't see anyone. Where are you?"

"I'm in back behind the storage shed."

"I'm coming back there again. Watch for my truck. I'll stop the truck beside the shed. First, I want to look around the area. When I give you the word, come out at a run and jump in the truck."

"OK, hurry. I'm so scared. Someone was walking around back here before you came. I couldn't see who it was from my hiding place." She whispered so low I had to strain to hear her.

There were only a few places to hide. The shed stood by itself with bushes and brush on either side with the river in back. My headlights scanned the shed and the brush. I saw nothing. I stopped the truck, stepped out, and scanned the area around the motel. Still nothing. It made no sense. Where was Hollis? Why go to all the trouble of drugging the guards and not be waiting for Laurel to make an appearance? I made my way around to the other side of my truck with my gun by my leg. I opened the side door of my truck for Laurel to get in and walked toward the shed.

Speaking into my cell again, "Laurel, are you listening?"

"Yes, I'm here."

"It looks clear. Come out now!"

She stepped out of the bushes and walked at a snail's pace toward me.

"Laurel, hurry. Get in the truck!"

"Chance, I can't. You see the other side of the shed? Hollis has a gun trained on you. I'm sorry, so sorry. He said he'd kill me and my family if I warned you."

Hollis stepped around to the front of the shed. Moving behind Laurel, he put his pistol into her side and kept behind her. It was all I could do not to throw caution to the wind and wipe that smug grin off his face.

"Well, well, Peeper, we meet again. I still have the advantage. Step away from the truck and move over by the river."

I moved to where I stood on the edge of the river bank.

"Oh, by the way, drop that gun you're carrying by your side."

Not taking my gaze from Hollis, I laid my gun on the ground. I straightened up and found Laurel staring at me. She tried to break free, but he held her with his arm around her shoulders and the gun still in her side.

"Laurel, were you the third member after all? You should be an actress. You played me extremely well."

"I swear it wasn't me! He found me hiding in the shed. He knew you were coming. That's why he waited. He heard me talking to you. Susie was my friend. Believe me, I wouldn't have done anything to hurt Susie."

He held his arm across Laurel's shoulders in a vise-like grip and pulled her with him as he made his way in front of me.

"Shut up, I'll do the talking."

Hollis eased his grip on Laurel and waved his gun around while he talked.

"Hollis, what's your next move? I hate to rain on your parade, but this place will be thick with cops before long. Your cousin is in police custody as we speak. I called the Weston PD and an ambulance when I found the two men you drugged."

"Shut up. I don't believe you. You'd say anything to save your hide. This is all your fault, you know."

"How do you figure that? I'm not the one who murdered four people."

"You scared Susie when you told her what would happen to her if she had information and didn't come forward. She didn't want to go to jail. I told her I'd fix it, but I could tell she would spill everything she knew with a little persuasion. We should never have used her.

"That blast was supposed to kill you and Laurel. With both of you dead, I had no worries. I could scare Susie worse than you did. In the end, she had as much to lose as Brian and I did. But no, you had to keep nosing around. You've led a charmed life until now, but your luck has run out."

"Sorry to be such an inconvenience. You must know I wouldn't come here on my own. I've told the DA, Sheriff Henry, and the Parkersburg police. You can't get away. Your cousin will rat you out to save his neck."

"I don't think you told anybody. I was on duty and took the call to check out the motel. I knew where Laurel was being kept. Nothing gets past me. I told dispatch I'd take the call. So, you see, your luck has run out.

"As soon as I dispose of you, I'll be on my way, enjoying all that lovely money. Daddy-in-law won't have any hold on me. I can do as I please."

"I know you planned on taking your cousin with you. He had his bags packed. What about Laurel? Brian said you were tying up loose ends."

"For now, I need Brian. After that...who knows? Plans change. Don't worry about little old Laurel. If what you say is true about Brian, I'll need her more than ever. I will let her go once I get out of the country—that is, if she wants to leave."

His eyes raked over Laurel. He grinned and shrugged when she didn't respond.

"That doesn't bode well for Laurel. Displease the person behind the gun and become a liability. You're gone also."

Laurel looked up at me. There was nothing but hopelessness written across her face.

"Shut your stupid mouth," Hollis yelled and raised his gun, ready to fire.

I could hear the ambulance siren in the background. The siren distracted him for a second. He turned his head to look in the direction of the siren. I took the opportunity to dive into the river.

I felt the wind go past my face as the bullet missed me by an inch. It was good the river was deep and fast-moving. Hollis fired several more rounds into the water where I had gone in the river. I stayed underwater until I was far enough downstream.

I worked my way toward the bank of the river. It's not a great idea to stand up in fast, deep moving water with a rocky bottom. The chances of getting trapped are good. I floated until I could get close to shore and more shallow water. Dragging myself out of the cold water with the swift current was tough. The water was ice cold this time of year. I dragged myself up the bank cold, wet, and shivering. The next sound I heard was more police sirens.

I made my way back to the motel. The ambulance had taken the two officers away, and the Weston police chief and sheriff's deputies were questioning the motel guests. Several officers were walking around my truck. I didn't see a car or truck for Hollis when I cruised the parking lot. Where and how had they disappeared? He must have parked in the shopping mall parking lot next door. With all the confusion, it would be easy to slip past in his patrol car.

All eyes were on me as I made my way to where the sheriff stood. My wet clothes weighed a ton, and my feet squished as I walked. I felt foolish, but I was alive to tell the tale. I guess that was something. I would like to wipe the smirk off the sheriff's face, but I didn't have the energy.

"Well, well, Mr. Sunday. Good of you to join us. You turn up in the darndest places. Been swimming?"

"Pleasant night for it. You're not going to like what I have to say, but your son-in-law, Hollis, has Laurel. He did the killing at the lab. Brian, his cousin, admitted that much. I'm positive he drugged the officers guarding Laurel. Do you have any idea where he'd take her?" My gaze locked on Sheriff Henry.

He stared at the ground and shook his head. "Parks told me, but I still can't believe it. My daughter trusted him. Hell, I trusted him. I don't know what I'm gonna tell my daughter. She truly loves that piece of dead wood."

"He said he'll let Laurel go once he's out of the country, but I don't believe him. He didn't say where he's headed. All he said was he's leaving the country. My guess would be Panama. I believe a

211

Panamanian bank is where they stashed the money. Once he has the money, he'll disappear."

The sheriff and Weston's police captain stared at me. Henry was the first to speak.

"What do you mean, once he has the money? What money are you talking about?"

"I thought someone had told you. Hollis and his cousin Brian were part of the robbery at the lab. It has been alleged Mr. Leslie and the other two scientists in the basement lab were smuggling diamonds in from Africa."

The sheriff swallowed hard and paled. I couldn't help enjoying his predicament.

"Although I have no proof, I believe Hollis and Brian took the uncut diamonds to New York. Brian left for Panama a few days after the robbery when he returned from New York. I'm almost positive he took the money from the sale of the diamonds and put it in a bank in Panama. Both Hollis and Brian visited Panama a week before the robbery. There would have been no reason to visit Panama twice or even the first time. They certainly didn't go there on a vacation to travel all that way and stay two days, then come home."

"Wait a minute. Hold on. You're saying Hollis and Brian robbed the lab and killed those people, and now he's on his way to Panama. How can you know that? What about my daughter?"

"That's precisely what I'm saying. Brian admitted as much. Your daughter wasn't mentioned. I don't know what her involvement is, if anything. Susie was the third person. If you have any idea how we can find them, now's the time to tell us, sheriff."

It felt good to put him on the spot for a change.

"I'm as much in the dark as anyone. It never crossed my mind that Hollis would do something like this, or that he could be involved. He answered the 9-1-1 call for the lab. I arrived a short time later. This is too awful to wrap my head around."

I didn't mention the fact that the sheriff was also implicated in some underhanded dealings. That was for the DA and the state police to sort out. I'm sure if they caught Hollis, he would rat out his father-in-law. If he didn't, Brian would. There was no love lost on either side.

"I've put an APB out on him and Laurel. We're setting up roadblocks and watching all the airports, public and private, for miles around as we speak. We'll get him. Was the McIntyre woman involved in this with him?" the Weston police chief asked.

"It does not appear so. She looked genuinely scared, and he was holding her at gunpoint. Mrs. McIntyre needs to be notified of this latest development."

Yet another promise I couldn't keep. I'd promised Mrs. McIntyre to keep Laurel safe. I was at a loss what to do next. I have more minuses than pluses on my rap sheet of life.

"We've got that covered. Your friend Lieutenant Parks is on his way there now. I suggest you go on home and get out of those wet clothes before you catch pneumonia. We'll be in touch. We know where to find you if we need you. For now, you're in the way. You can come into the Weston or Pinedale office tomorrow or the next day and give us a statement."

"Always a pleasure, sheriff."

I saluted and turned to go.

There was nothing left to do but get in my truck and head home. I turned on the heater full blast and shivered all the way home. Abiding by the posted speed limit, I arrived home an hour and a half later. I didn't know what else I could do. I couldn't help worrying about Laurel. There was no reason to kill her since everyone knew what Hollis had done, but he didn't seem to reason logically.

Turning in my drive, I felt all of my energy drain from my body. Phil was coming out of the woods by his cabin. He waved and continued walking. By the time I got out of my truck, he was standing near the garage door.

"Glad you're home. Rain's coming. Closed your windows."

He turned and left. Sometimes it's good Phil doesn't like to talk. I didn't have the energy to say one word. He doesn't expect me to talk either. I could tell he noticed my wet clothes, but he would never ask how they got that way.

The water in the shower was hot and warmed me as nothing else could have done. Taking the longest shower I've ever taken, I hated to turn the water off and step out of my watery cocoon. I dressed in lined khakis and a flannel shirt, and went into the living room to start a fire. Once the room warmed up, I'd let it die out.

More often than not, I would have made coffee, but for some reason, I wanted hot chocolate. Not the kind in packets, but the kind you make yourself from cocoa powder and milk. Once it was ready, I sat down to read and enjoy my cup. I fell asleep before the fire went out, shortly after I took my last sip. I slept through the rest of the night and into the next day. Waking up long enough to eat a leftover dinner in the refrigerator, I went back to sleep.

Someone rudely woke me by roughly shaking me until my teeth chattered. To my dismay, I looked up into the stone-cold eyes of Hollis Evans.

"What the hell? What are you doing here?"

When he saw my surprise, he laughed.

"Well, well, Peeper, I bet you never expected to see me again. To tell the truth, I didn't expect to see you once more either, dead or alive. I figured the river would get you. Too bad. You will have to put up with me a little longer."

He pranced about the room, waving his pistol, very amused with himself. I lowered my recliner and followed him with my eyes. He must have seen the disbelief on my face. Walking over to the fireplace, he posed in front of it with his arm on the mantle and one foot propped up on the hearth.

"I bet you want to know what I'm doing here?"

I nodded, too stunned to say anything.

"That's better. I have your attention. Look at it this way. I know how the police think. What with APBs and roadblocks, I needed a safe place to hole up. We were holed up in a barn a little ways down the road, but we needed a better place to wait this out. What better place than your cabin? Not even dear old daddy-in-law will think to look for me here.

"Incidentally, I love what you've done with the place," Hollis said as his eyes scanned the room.

"Why did you come back for Laurel? You had your money. You could have been long gone before anyone missed you."

"Yeah, well, I never did like loose ends. Besides, I had to pick up Laurel."

"Was Laurel in on this with you? I thought it was just Susie and Brian."

"It was in the beginning. I have Susie to thank for Laurel figuring it out. Laurel was never meant to know anything about the robbery."

"Are you crazy? You can't stay here. They'll come looking if I don't show up."

I glanced around the room and came back to Hollis. My heart pounded in my ears.

"Where's Laurel?"

"Outside in the truck. I'll bring her in when I'm ready. Say, you got anything to eat?"

"I keep very little food here. There's coffee, Cokes, beer, and oatmeal pies. Hollis, you need to turn yourself in. You're only making it worse."

"Turn myself in? You're a riot. How could it get worse? Thanks to Brian, everybody knows what we did. How stupid do you think I am? They'd put me under the jail.

"No, you see, I got me a plan to slide right on out of here. They don't have the money or manpower to keep all those men searching for too long. In the meantime, I will stay right here until I get my call, and

215

then I'm leaving. No one, I mean no one, would expect me to hole up anywhere near you."

"What about Laurel? Is she still alive?"

"She's my insurance."

He motioned with his gun for me to get up.

"You come with me, and we'll go get her. Try anything, and you'll be the first to go down."

I stood up and waited.

Hollis poked his head out the door. When he didn't see anyone, he stepped aside and motioned for me to go by him. I looked around for Phil, but he was nowhere in sight. Not seeing him didn't mean he wasn't there. I had no idea what he would do if he saw someone holding a gun on me, or if he might walk in on the situation unaware. One thing for certain, Hollis would not hesitate to shoot him.

Sweat beads formed on my forehead and ran down the side of my face. Hollis was smart enough to stay well behind me so I had no chance to take the gun away from him.

On the far side of the garage, I saw his Tahoe. The window was down, and I could see Laurel handcuffed to the steering wheel. She was draped over the steering wheel and not moving. I stopped when I saw her.

Hollis gave me a shove.

"Move one of your vehicles from the garage and put my truck in. They'll most likely have helicopters up before long."

If Laurel had not been there, I would have backed the Jeep out and kept on going. Let the bullets fly, but I couldn't take the chance he wouldn't kill her. Once I had my Jeep out and parked, I moved to the Tahoe. Hollis gave me the key, and I undid Laurel's restraints. I drove the Tahoe inside the garage and helped Laurel out of the truck. I took her arm, and she leaned on me, too tired to stand on her own. I helped her into the house and to the nearest chair. She sat down with a sigh.

"Are you all right? He didn't hurt you?"

She shook her head slowly. Hollis moved behind her chair and put a hand on her shoulder.

I looked up at Hollis.

"I don't have any food here. I get my meals from the Do Drop Inn. I'll have to go down there to get food unless you intend to starve."

"How dumb do you think I am? You're not going anywhere. I can't take a chance like that. You get that handyman of yours to go, but let me make myself clear. If I see one badge, Laurel will be the first to die. Next will be your handyman. I'll make your death long and painful."

He held out his hand.

"Give me your cell phone."

"I understand."

I gave him my phone, which was useless anyway since I live in a dead zone.

"He's got thirty minutes to get down there and back. You tell him about us, and Laurel's the first to go."

"No need to repeat yourself."

I watched through the window until Phil came down the trail. Banging on the window to get his attention, I stood in the doorway.

I felt Hollis's eyes bore into the back of my head as I stepped out on the porch. Phil came over with his rifle across his chest, resting on his left arm. I heard Hollis step closer to the door so he could hear what was being said.

"Phil, could you do me a favor?"

Phil nodded.

"I have two guests and no food in the house. Could you go down to the Do Drop Inn and get us three of their specials? Tell John to hurry it up. We're starving."

Phil nodded again.

"Wait here and I'll get you some money."

I went back in, almost tripping over Hollis, and searched for my wallet. Pretending to find it behind the counter of the bar, I took two twenties out. While I was searching for the money, I found a small sticky note and wrote on it, 'SOS, tell PPD & CP.' I fixed it to the back of one of the twenties and stepped back outside.

I hoped he would read my message and know what I meant. I had to get word to Charlie about what was going on. I didn't trust the sheriff to be discreet. His temper was already at the boiling point. I expected the sheriff would come in with guns blazing.

A short time later, I heard Phil going down the drive and opening the gate. After several minutes, I heard gravel crunching and a truck come to a stop in front of my house. Phil arrived back at the house with five minutes to spare.

As I started for the door, Hollis shoved me up against the wall.

"He sure took his own sweet time. You think I don't mean what I say?"

I pushed back.

"How would he know you gave him thirty minutes? He had to drive down there, and he was not the only customer they had. You didn't want him to draw attention and make anyone suspicious, did you? He acted normally because he doesn't know what's going on. John and Elsie always want to talk. He couldn't brush them off."

"Yeah, yeah, all right. Don't push me. I'm not any happier about being here than you are having me."

I went through the door and took the dinners from Phil.

"Thanks for doing that, Phil."

He nodded, handed me my change, and stepped off the porch. I took the dinners in and set them on the counter.

Hollis looked around the room until he caught Laurel's eye. He motioned with the gun for her to come up to the kitchen island. We sat down at the bar and opened our dinners. Laurel picked at hers. I ate mine, although my stomach was turning over with each bite. Hollis wolfed his down like it was his last meal. I hoped with all my heart that it would be. Before we finished our dinner, there was a knock on the door. My stomach tightened, and chills ran up my spine.

"Go see who that is."

He picked up his gun and laid it beside my head. As he whispered in my ear, I felt his hot, moist breath against my skin.

"No funny business."

There was another knock. Hollis grabbed Laurel and moved against the wall away from the door. He motioned for me to answer it.

My heart jumped up in my throat. I could see through the door's window. It was Phil. With my heart beating out of control, I opened the door and stepped out.

"What's up?"

"Chance, do you need anything before I go to my meeting? Better make sure your windows are closed. There's a chance of rain. As red as the sky is tonight, it could rain hellfire on the wicked before the night's out."

"Thanks, Phil. No, I don't need anything. You're right about the sky. I've never seen it so red."

He nodded and turned to go.

He turned back and said, "Oh, I heard over the radio that there's a statewide search for that Deputy Evans and Laurel. Sorry to hear that. Well, I'll be seeing you."

He tripped as he turned to go.

I pointed at his feet.

"Phil, your shoelace is undone."

He bent down to tie his shoe and slipped a knife in the outside cargo pocket of my pants leg, so slickly I almost didn't see or feel it. I thought he was talking too much for Phil. He had seen or read my note. I don't know why I'd doubted him; he didn't miss much. He stood up and waved before he stepped off the porch.

I moved back in the house and closed the door, letting out the breath I'd been holding.

Hollis grinned. "You handled that real fine, Peeper. Keep everything cool, and you and that handyman might just make it through the night. I got fake passports being made for me, Brian, and Laurel. I don't plan on being around too long. As soon as they're ready, I'm out of here."

"You're taking Laurel with you? If she had nothing to do with this, why not leave her here?"

He looked at her with a gleam in his eye.

"Why would I leave her? She's my girl. Who do you think I did all this for? She said she wouldn't date a married man. I might get me one of them quickie divorces and marry her. I couldn't have done this without her."

Laurel cringed and pulled her sweater tighter around her. Something was going on beneath the surface. Laurel gave the appearance of being a hostage, but was she? I had seen them with their heads together, and Hollis watched every move she made. She had no way to escape even if she wanted to. He could shoot her before she made it out the door. If she wasn't a hostage, there was no need to watch her like a hawk. When he was ready to leave, I would not bet on either one of our chances of making it out alive.

I hoped Phil would wait for Charlie before he did anything, or this could be a bloodbath. I had no doubt he had called him when he mentioned hellfire raining down before the night was over. Since this wasn't in Charlie's jurisdiction, I hoped he would call the state police and not the sheriff. The minutes ticked by, and the night dragged on toward the morning.

Hollis paced the room waving the gun as he muttered more to himself than us. What he said didn't make a whole lot of sense. I think he was chattering to hear himself talk. Eventually, he ran out of topics to talk about and dragged in a chaise lounge from the patio. He positioned it where he could watch both of us, sat down, and leaned back.

Laurel sat at the bar and drank tea. Sitting in my recliner, I tried to read. I read the same page ten times and still didn't know what it said. I put my book down. There was no hope of sleeping.

There were two ways to come in the house undetected. The basement had an outside door. It would be possible to enter it without being seen from the house. The door was locked, but Phil had a key. The other possibility was to climb in the second-story window that was unlocked. Phil had hinted at this way in when he mentioned closing the windows earlier. I remembered his telling me when I came home, he had closed the windows. I never locked my second-story windows. There was nothing worth stealing anyway.

I closed my eyes and tried to rest. When I opened them, I saw Hollis's and Laurel's reflections in the glass door of the fireplace. They had their heads together whispering. Laurel shook her head and tried to pull away. Hollis had a tight grip on her wrist. She broke her wrist free and rubbed the feeling back in it. I pretended to sleep. I was getting an uneasy feeling for both Laurel and myself. Our life expectancies were getting shorter with each passing minute.

Laurel came over and sat on the hearth. I watched her through my half-closed eyelashes. She kept rubbing her wrists and looking at Hollis.

"Hollis, I'm tired. There's a bed upstairs. Do you mind if I lie down for a while?"

"Yes, I do mind. Lie on the chaise. It's comfortable. Don't go getting any bright ideas. I'm not letting you out of my sight."

Laurel leaned against the fireplace and closed her eyes. I waited for Hollis to walk over to the front window and peer out again before I spoke to Laurel.

"How do you know Hollis?"

She opened her eyes and stared at Hollis before she looked back at me.

"I met him through Brian. He hung around with us some when he was at WVU."

She stood up and moved by my recliner. I reached out and took her hand. I felt her tremble.

"Laurel, you're not involved in this, are you?"

"Hands off, Peeper. No talking."

She glanced at Hollis and back at me.

"Let go, I want to lie down."

I released her hand, but I guess I had my answer. She moved to the chaise and stretched out and heaved a sigh, but she didn't close her eyes.

Hollis would have to sleep some time. I had to watch and wait for an opportunity. Laurel looked worn out. If I found a chance to jump Hollis, would she be a help or a hindrance?

I stood up and walked over to the counter. I made another pot of coffee and heated water in the coffeemaker for Laurel. She came over to the bar and sat with her elbows on the bar, and her head in her hands. When the coffee finished dripping, I poured myself a cup and handed Laurel a tea bag and a cup of hot water.

I sat beside her and watched Hollis out of the corner of my eye. He kept looking at his watch and peering through the slats of the window shutters. While his back was turned, I tried again to talk to Laurel.

"What's your connection with Hollis?"

I watched her shake her head.

"Don't lie. I know it's more than being a convenient hostage."

She raised her head and spoke so quietly I had to lean in to hear her.

"We ran into each other last December in Pinedale. I was coming out of the bank, and he was going in. He stopped me and started talking. You know how it is. I haven't seen you in a while. How you doing?

"I met him two more times. One thing led to another, and he asked me out. I swear I didn't know he was married. By the time I found out, it was too late. I fell in love. Crazy, huh?"

She shook her head and glanced across the room at Hollis.

"I must have been demented."

She kept turning her head and watching Hollis before she spoke again.

"People always say a girl looks for someone like her father. My real father died before I was born, without benefit of wedlock. The only one I know as a father is a first-class, A-1 bastard. Hollis is living up to my expectations, or down, depending on how you look at it."

She smiled forlornly and took a deep breath.

Wrapping her hands firmly around her cup, she lifted it to her mouth with both hands and sipped her tea. She set her cup down and stared into the liquid. She raised her head and glanced at Hollis.

"Being with him was like riding the curl of a wave or being addicted to drugs. He caught me up in a whirlwind, and I couldn't get enough of him. It was so wild, so unpredictable. I couldn't think for myself. I told myself I had to stop, but he kept calling me. He kept telling me he loved me and couldn't live without me.

"I didn't have the good sense to see what he was doing. When I was around him, I couldn't think. I never thought I would have an affair with a married man. Not in a million years."

"What was the real reason you switched the day you worked at the lab?"

She gave a half-laugh and closed her eyes.

"Just one bad decision after another. I switched my usual day of working at the lab because I wanted to go home and give myself time to think. To get away from school and Hollis. I told him I was through with him on the weekend before everything happened.

"When I told him I was through, he got so mad it scared me. He didn't know I would be there that night. No one did. I've never been as scared as I was when I saw them coming in."

"I have to ask you again. This is no time to lie. Were you in on the robbery at the lab?"

"Good lord, no. Those people had all been so nice to help me. I could never do anything like that."

Hollis still had his back to us.

"I thought I recognized Hollis, but I couldn't be sure. It could have been Davis. Both are about the same size, same color of eyes. When I saw the peace symbol on his hoodie, I couldn't think. I thought it had to be Davis. I didn't want to believe any of my friends could do something so terrible. That's the real reason I went to Susie. I thought she was still dating Brian, and she could tell me what was going on."

Hollis paced in front of the window. Laurel kept watching him. He walked around the room, got a cup of coffee, and went back to standing and looking out the window.

Laurel took a deep breath and continued her story.

"Susie denied everything at first, but eventually she admitted she was in on it. She said she'd give me a place to hide if I promised not to tell on her. She promised me she wouldn't tell anyone where I was, but she did. You know the rest."

She swallowed hard.

"If I hadn't had cabin fever, I wouldn't be here now. After someone tried to blow me up...and you too, I hitched a ride into Parkersburg and went to Susie's apartment. I didn't know what else to do. I told her what had happened. She wouldn't believe it. She tried to convince me it must have been an accident. I told her I knew better.

"She told me she'd only told Brian. I thought it was Brian who tried to kill me at first. I'm ashamed to admit it, but I got her stoned so she would tell me the whole story. She admitted Hollis killed those people in the lab and tried to kill you and me."

Laurel jumped when Hollis kicked the wall a couple of times. He didn't look our way but continued to stare through the window slats.

"When I learned that, the shock sobered me up. I never meant to see Hollis again. I couldn't trust him anymore or any of my friends. It was hard to believe he'd tried to kill me after all we had meant to each other.

"That's the real reason I went with you that night. I had to get away from there before any of my so-called friends came by the apartment. One thing I don't understand. If Susie was a part of the robbery, why did he kill her?"

"Hollis was getting rid of loose ends and getting a bigger share of their take. Susie started getting nervous and became a liability. At first, she thought of the robbery as a game, a rush. It rapidly became something much worse. I think Hollis was afraid she would talk.

"I don't think Brian would have made it once they were out of the country. If Hollis takes you with him, and you upset him, he would not hesitate to kill you. The Vienna police picked Brian up. You have to understand, we're on borrowed time."

Tears formed in the corners of her eyes and spilled onto her cheeks.

"Before all this happened, he said he was leaving his wife, and we would go away together. He claimed he loved me. He was always complaining about his father-in-law and his wife. I never dreamed he meant to do what he did. How could I love such a person? But sadly, I have no one except myself to blame."

She hiccupped and stared into her teacup.

"I'm sorry, Laurel. You must be strong now. We have to find a way out of this."

"Do you think he only said he loved me to get information out of me about the lab? Do you think he ever truly cared for me?"

"I'm sorry, but I think it very unlikely. People like Hollis only love themselves. Did you tell him anything?"

"No, no, I would never do that. I did let my password slip when I told Susie about how to get in the back door of the lab. I was just letting off steam. I never meant to tell her. It slipped out. When I asked her about it later, she said she didn't remember. Fool that I am, I believed her. Now she's dead. Everything that's happened feels surreal. I feel like such a ninny."

"Don't give up hope. If I see a chance, we have to take it. You must be ready to move."

With her eyes wide with fright, she nodded her head.

Chapter 14

"What are you two talking about? Didn't I tell you no talking? You won't like it if I have to tell you again."

Hollis yelled across the room, then strode over to us.

He waved his gun around, pointing from one of us to the other. Grabbing Laurel's arm, he swung her around on the barstool. I jumped up. Hollis pushed Laurel against the bar, almost knocking her off her stool. Keeping his hand on Laurel, he stepped up in front of me, pointing his gun at my chest. I sat back down.

"Hollis, calm down. Why are you so upset?" Laurel asked. "Please let go my arm. You're hurting me."

"We're just talking to pass the time. You want a cup of coffee?" I said.

He slammed his gun down on the counter, then pushed Laurel off her stool. She moved over one, and Hollis sat on the stool between Laurel and me.

"No more talking. You got something to say, you say it to me. Laurel has nothing to say to you. Got it?"

"Yeah, Hollis, I got it. When am I going to be rid of you?"

"I got a phone call to make in a while, and then we'll see. What's the matter, Peeper? You're not enjoying my company?"

"I want you out of my house is all I meant. I don't want my friend, Phil, hurt. He can't keep going after food and not be suspicious when he sees no one except me."

"Whether or not Phil gets hurt depends on you. Take your coffee and go over there. I don't want you two talking. Understand me?"

"Yeah, I understand. Don't do anything foolish. We'll be quiet."

"Well, see you do. I can't think with all this jibber-jabber going on."

His hard, cold eyes bored into me. I noticed beads of sweat on his forehead. He kept blinking his eyes and then staring at Laurel. I felt a chill like someone had walked over my grave. I took my coffee and moved to my chair. There was nothing else I could do for now. I thought it best to do as he said for the time being.

After two more tense hours, the clock struck midnight. Hollis stepped over to the phone and dialed a number. I could only hear one side of the conversation.

"Hello, Mike. You got what I want? You can forget Brian's. He's not coming. Yeah, yeah, you'll still get the same money for two as three."

He'd planned to take Laurel with him all along. She appeared to know nothing about this. Surely this was not some elaborate charade for my benefit. I glanced at Laurel, but she had her eyes closed.

"I'll be there by seven in the morning. The documents better be flawless for what I'm paying you....Yeah, yeah, see you do."

He turned to us as he hung up, with a smile on his face.

His whole body relaxed, and he quit waving the gun around and muttering to himself. He settled in to watch by a window. He peeked through the window slat and kept watch on the driveway. By turning his head a little, he could see what was going on in the living room by the reflection from the mirror by the stairs.

Several times we'd heard a helicopter pass overhead. After dark, the pilot used a light to search the area. The clock chimed one AM Hollis jumped up and looked around the room. He shook Laurel to wake her up. I was awake anyhow. He motioned for me to stand.

"All right, let's go, Bubba. We'll be taking your Jeep. We're going down old logging roads to my friend's house. From there, Mike'll drive me and Laurel to where we can catch a plane out of the country. To a real accommodating country without extradition.

"Your job will be done, Peeper. I'll tie you up and leave you somewhere. If you don't give me any trouble, you might make it out of this little mess alive."

I didn't believe a word. I could identify this Mike, and I'm sure he wouldn't want that. Hollis didn't care what happened after he was on his way and received his documents from Mike.

"Why don't you take my Jeep and leave me here?"

"I know back roads and bare trails that the Jeep will come in handy on. But there's a long stretch where we'll be on the main highway into Clarksburg. If there's a roadblock anywhere, you're my ticket through it. We'll hide in the back under a tarp. No one is going to inspect your vehicle."

When we stepped out on the porch, I looked up and watched the clouds moving in. The weatherman had said we could expect torrential rain with a chance of flash flooding. I could hear thunder rumbling off in the distance and see flashes of lightning. The gathering clouds covered the moon, making it dark, and then all of a sudden, the clouds cleared, and it was almost as bright as the day.

As we were getting in the Jeep, I looked at the moving clouds one last time. There was an eerie cloud underneath the moon giving the appearance of icicles. Chills ran up my spine. I looked around for Phil, but I didn't see him. I knew if he didn't want to be seen, he wouldn't be. I would have felt better if I could catch a glimpse of him. He was unpredictable. He could be on patrol for all I knew. It might be much later before he realized we were gone.

At the end of the drive, I stopped the car and waited. Hollis said nothing. He looked up and down the road without saying a word. We sat there for what felt like an eternity.

"Well, which way? I'm not a mind reader."

"Keep your shirt on. I'm just checking. Turn left and drive for about three miles. On the left, there's an old forest service road leading into Turpin's Woods. Turn onto that track and keep going until I tell you to stop. Do you know where that is?"

"Yeah, I've hunted in Turpin's Woods, but I don't remember a service road."

"I may be the only one that knows about that road. You can believe me, it's there. Don't you worry about it, Peeper. I know what I'm doing. I checked everything out before I decided on this little adventure."

"You can't be serious. You couldn't have picked a worse time to try a rough mountain road. Even in the best of times, mountain dirt shifts easily. With the rains we've been having, I'm afraid my Jeep will mire down in the muddy dirt if we don't slide off the mountain first."

"You better hope it can make the grade."

He settled back in his seat with the gun resting across his stomach and pointing at me. I glimpsed Laurel in the rearview mirror biting her nails and staring out the window. The rain started splattering down in huge drops.

At the so-called service road, I pulled over to the opposite side of the road.

"Well, go ahead and turn. There's the road."

"I see it, but you can't seriously expect to make it up the mountain? That's not a road. It's little more than an animal trail. We'll never make it. It's nothing but mud and shifting rocks. With this rain pouring down in buckets, we'll be stuck in the mud before we're halfway up the mountain."

Hollis leveled his pistol at me. He had a strange glint in his eyes.

"As they say in the seminars, every problem is an opportunity waiting for a solution or something like that."

The words of the Dalai Lama kept running through my mind. "If a problem is fixable, if a situation is such that you can do something about it, then there is no need to worry. If it's not fixable, then there is no help in worrying. There is no benefit in worrying whatsoever."

For some reason, I felt reassured. I'm not sure why. My situation couldn't be worse. I didn't have the wisdom, not to worry. I looked up the trail and saw nothing but disaster.

"Peeper, I'm talking to you. Now, I hate to keep repeating myself. I said, turn on that road."

He waved his gun around and let it come to rest on the back of the seat in Laurel's direction.

"You better pray we make it, Peeper, or you and Laurel will push this Jeep all the way to the top."

I searched his face. He was not joking.

"Have you ever been up this trail?"

"Of course, I have. Do you think I haven't planned for every contingency? No more talk. Start up the trail. Now!"

He reached in the back and grabbed Laurel by the nape of her neck, putting the gun to her head.

"OK, OK, let's all calm down. Put the gun away. I'm turning onto the road."

I took a deep breath and started up the trail.

"No more backtalk and questions. I'm tired of questions. I don't have to explain anything to you. When I say jump, you say how high."

He chuckled to himself.

I felt the wheels grab in the mud and gravel as we started up this wide spot in the forest. I relaxed when I saw him take the gun away from Laurel's temple. She fell back in the seat and closed her eyes. The road felt like driving on never-ending speedbumps. With this rough trail, I hoped the gun didn't go off by accident.

After I turned onto the so-called service road, the wind picked up. I kept driving up the roughly rutted trail and prayed I didn't get stuck. The trail was getting more muddy and slippery as the grade steepened, with the rain pounding down. Wind-blown limbs and brush flew across the path.

The mixture of wind and rain bent the trees almost to the ground. The rain flew at us in a slant now with ice crystals bouncing off the windshield. Tree limbs were hitting the Jeep. The air cooled rapidly. I had the Jeep in four-wheel drive low and hoped it would make it through.

About halfway up the mountain, a tree blocked the trail. I got out and looked. Lightning had struck the tree, and it was still smoking. I tried to move it, but it was too heavy. The rain poured down in buckets. With the wind, torrential rain, and thunder, it was deafening. The air was electric. I became disoriented and had to hold on to the Jeep to keep from falling. Several boulders rolled off the mountain across the trail. Scarcely able to see, I wiped the rain out of my face and got back in the Jeep.

"Well, what's the matter?" Hollis asked.

I turned and stared at him. "You might have noticed there's a tree across the road. I can't budge it. This is as far as we can go. We could be struck by lightning any second. The air's so thick you could cut it with a knife."

Hollis laid his pistol on my arm. "I don't have time for this. You get out and move it. I got some place to be."

"I can step out, but I can't move the tree by myself. Shoot me if you want to, but I can't move that tree by myself. Both of you will have to help me."

Hollis scowled at me and muttered under his breath. He motioned for Laurel to get out. All three of us stepped out in the pouring rain. The three of us strained to move the tree, but that was not going to happen. It might as well have been a brick wall.

I took a rope out of the back of the Jeep and tied it around the fallen tree and looped the other end around a thick oak. I gave the end of the rope to Hollis. He had to pull on the rope when I had the tree moving. Looking around, I found a sturdy limb I could use. With the help of a nearby rock, I used the limb and rock as a lever. Laurel helped me, and Hollis tightened the rope as the tree moved. We shifted it enough for the Jeep to pass by. Lightning streaked across the sky, and thunder crashed overhead.

Even with our jackets on, the rain ran down our necks, and plastered our hair to our heads. My pants were drenched. They couldn't have been wetter if I had been swimming in them. Not to mention muddy. We looked worse than survivors coming out of the wilderness. Sporadically, lightning streaked straight downward as an arrow in front of us rattling the Jeep. The higher we climbed up the mountain, the more danger of a lightning strike. Regardless of what old wives say, a car is not the safest place to be in a lightning strike.

My shoes were so wet and muddy they slipped off the gas pedal several times. We made it to the crest of the mountain with no more mishaps. I can't imagine how some of those boulders rolling across the trail missed us. Hollis came out of his trance as we made it to the top of the mountain. He sat up for the first time and looked around, alert.

"Hold it. Don't go down the other side. It's not time yet. Turn left. There's a hunter's shack over there. We'll stay there until it gets light."

I turned and saw the shack up ahead. I would never have guessed there was a hunter's shack here. Someone had painted the shack green and enormous pine trees leaned over the drive to the shack, hiding it effectively. We made it to the shack and stepped out of the Jeep. Sloshing through slipping, sliding, oozing mud, we made it to the door.

It had a padlock on it. This didn't bother Hollis. He took a lug wrench from the Jeep and broke the padlock away from the wood of the shack. With our energy spent, Laurel and I stood on the porch and stared at the broken lock. Hollis seemed none the worse for wear. Where was he getting all his energy?

"Well, don't just stand there. You waiting on an invitation? Go on in." He glanced around the area and motioned impatiently with his gun.

We moved into the shack. It was orderly but dusty. Gusts of wind rattled the walls and whistled around the windows. It wouldn't surprise me if the wind picked up this old shack and threw it off the mountain with us in it.

"How'd you know about this shack? I've hunted all over this area, and I never saw it."

"We got a call about some hunters up here a year or so back. One of them shot himself accidentally. I came with the rescue squad. We came up the other side, but I noticed the trail. While the EMTs were busy, I checked it out. No one would ever guess, but the road is passable, as you found out. We made it, didn't we?"

Laurel and I could do nothing but stare at him.

Yeah, by the grace of God, and four-wheel drive, we made it.

"I stored that little piece of information away for future use. You never know, do you? Who would guess anyone would try it in this weather? No one. The rain and wind will wipe out any tracks. I know where all the roadblocks are placed normally. This is the only way to avoid most of them."

He grinned at me and waved his gun around again. "Enough chatter. You, Peeper, get a fire started. It's freezing in here. There's a stack of firewood behind the shack."

Laurel stood in the far corner staring at the floor. Once again, into the elements. I gathered wood from the wood pile behind the shack. Hollis came out with me and watched. We heard the front door slam, and both of our heads turned in the direction of the sound.

I glimpsed Laurel as she made a run for the trail. Hollis turned to go after her. I threw my armload of wood down and tackled him. We wrestled for the gun and hit the ground hard, knocking my hand loose from the gun. He thumped me on the side of the head with it and stunned me. Jumping up, he sprinted after Laurel. Before I could get my senses about me, he appeared in front of me with Laurel, both covered in leaves and mud.

"Either one of you tries something like that again, and I'll shoot the pair of you without a second thought. I don't have time for this."

He gave Laurel a shove through the door of the shack. She stumbled and fell. I stood and shook my head to clear it. He motioned with his gun for me to pick up the wood and come in the shack. When I made it to the porch, he gave me a shove as I started through the door.

Using the dry kindling stored inside, I managed to get wet wood burning in the woodstove and looked around for something we could eat. In the cupboard, there was a tin of coffee, some cans of soup, and those dinners you add hot water to in foil pouches. Survivalist-type stuff that lasts twenty-five years. I found an old percolator coffeepot. There was an old-fashioned water pump on the back porch. Beside the pump was a jar of water with a laminated note, *prime the pump before use.*

I primed the pump, not expecting anything for my efforts. I couldn't believe it, but after many up-and-down cranks on the handle, water poured out of the spout. Refilling the prime jar, I replaced the note. Next, I filled the coffeepot and sat it on the stove.

Laurel stood up without saying anything and held onto the back of her chair. She stared fixedly at Hollis, making me nervous, but he did not seem to notice. There was a storm cloud of emotion gathering behind those staring eyes. Her eyes were getting narrower every time I looked at her. She had something on her mind. Hollis was oblivious to the danger signs.

She cleared her throat and called Hollis's name, but he ignored her. She moved into the middle of the room, edging closer to him. When she broke the silence of the room again, her voice sounded high-pitched. Not her usual speaking voice. She cleared her throat and raised her voice again. She had his attention, and he looked up with a frown.

"Hollis, did you ever love me? You said you did. You promised you would divorce your wife and marry me. Did you mean any of it? Was it all just a trick to get information out of me?"

"No point in lying to you now, is there? You were a necessary convenience. I'm not divorcing my wife. That was never part of the plan. She knew I had to get to know you and get as much information out of you as I could. She didn't care how I did it. You didn't tell me that much, but I got a feel for the layout listening to you talk about your friends. If Susie hadn't known your password, I maybe wouldn't have tried it."

He chuckled to himself and looked at me, and then at Laurel. "Naw, I would have anyhow. It was too sweet a setup not to try for it. Besides, it felt good to get one over on the old man. He doesn't know I know how he paid for that little retirement condo in Belize.

"When this all dies down, my wife'll sell the house and meet me wherever I wind up.

"Don't get me wrong. You're eye-candy all right and an amusing piece in the sack. Can't say I didn't enjoy our little tryst, but I'm not leaving my wife for you. My wife, now, there's a woman who can satisfy her man."

Laurel's face turned four shades paler than it already was. "I believed everything you told me. How could you lie like that? We made plans for a life together. For a family! Now you tell me everything was a lie. You're lower than dirt." She crossed her arms over her chest and turned her back to him.

Hollis shrugged and grinned. "Guilty as charged. I'm a natural, you might say."

Quicker than the blink of an eye, Laurel turned around and flew across the room with her fists clenched. I stepped in between them, blocking her before she reached Hollis. She landed a few punches on my chest before I caught her arms. I swung her around and saw Hollis's eyes were wide and his mouth a cruel slash. He reached back and meant to slap Laurel before I dragged her out of his reach.

Keeping my body between them, I pulled her away and back to a corner. I had a hard time holding her, until finally the fight drained out of her. When I turned around, I saw Hollis's shoulders relaxed. He wiped the saliva from his chin and walked around the room loosening his shoulders.

She held her head to one side and stared at him. "If you're not leaving your wife for me, why are you taking me with you? I thought you came to kill me at the motel."

"Sure, I thought about killing you, but lucky for you, I decided not to. How many times do I have to say it? You're my hostage. I have to have companionship until my wife can get clear and join me. You try any more stunts like that, and I'll reconsider. When I get to where I'm going and my wife comes, I'll release you. I'll even send you back on a plane first class."

"Gee, thanks, Hollis. You might as well shoot me now. I'm not going anywhere with you." She crossed her arms over her chest, and turned her face away.

"In case you haven't noticed, I'm the man with the gun. You do what I say when I say. You got that? Look at me when I'm talking to you."

Her head slowly turned, and she stared laser beams at him.

I could see her body tremble. At least, she knew the truth. Thinking the fight had gone out of her, I led her to a chair by the fire. Faster than a cat can lick its whiskers, she flew across the room. With her hands in the shape of claws, she headed in a straight line for Hollis. Her fingernails raked across his face. He punched her in the stomach, and she bent over in pain. I ran over to her and helped her up. Hollis pushed me aside, stepped between us, and pointed the gun at my head.

"Leave her be! If I didn't still need both of you, I'd end it all right now."

He reached up and felt the blood on his face where she had scratched him. He took out a tissue and blotted the drips. "You stupid cow."

He drew back his foot to kick her where she lay on the floor. I moved between them, deflected his boot, and helped her up. He sat down in the nearest chair and laughed.

"Quick on your feet, Peeper. She tries anything like that again, and I'll fix it so's neither one of you bother me anymore. Perhaps I don't need you after all. Yeah, maybe I don't." He grinned at us and nodded.

"When's that food gonna be ready? I'm starved."

It took all the self-control I possessed to turn around and walk toward the stove. I wanted to smash his face in even if it meant he would use his gun. I had Laurel to consider and knew I must appear calm. Instead of going for him, I turned and added more wood to the fire. The water was getting hot. With my back turned, I tried to keep my eye on Laurel and Hollis out of the corner of my eye. Laurel slumped in her chair. The fight had drained out of her, at least for the time being.

Hollis stretched his legs out in front of him and lit a cigarette. I could feel his eyes bore into my back.

"You want a piece of me, don't you, soldier? Don't forget I'm the one with the gun, and it's up to me if you make it out of this alive to tell the tale." He laughed and turned toward Laurel.

I shook my head to clear it. The coffee perked. I fooled with the coffeepot to give myself time to calm down. We had to drink it black. The shack warmed up a few degrees. There was nothing left to do but wait for sunrise.

The sky began to lighten up a little after six, but visibility was still poor. Hollis shook Laurel awake and motioned for us to move. We loaded up, and I had to back the Jeep on to the main path. The tires spun at first, and I held my breath. When I thought I might have to get out and push, the mud released its hold. We were on our way again.

As we started down the mountain, I could feel the Jeep sliding. I put it in low gear and low four-wheel drive, but I didn't have much control. The trail was scarcely wide enough for the Jeep. Several times I stared out over a rock cliff and prayed the Jeep would stay on the trail.

The conditions were the same as when we'd came up, but we were headed down. The rain continued to pour, making the going more treacherous with each minute. My hands were locked on the steering wheel. If we made it to the bottom of the trail, I'm not sure I could release my hands. The pain from holding on so forcefully ran up my shoulders and the back of my neck.

I forced my hand off the steering wheel in order to wipe my foggy windshield until I could see the highway up ahead. When it came into view, I relaxed my white-knuckle grip on the steering wheel and put on the brakes. There was nothing to hold the Jeep back. We slid to a stop in the middle of the highway. I put it in reverse as quick as I could and backed up on the service road, just as a car came over the rise in the highway.

After the car passed, I put the Jeep in two-wheel drive and pulled out on the highway. The rain was coming down in sheets again, with the wind blowing at a slant. My Jeep swayed from side to side with the wind. The windshield wipers, even on high, were not adequate for this downpour, but the rain was washing the mud from the windows. With the defroster running on high, the windows were clearer now, but visibility was still poor.

"Hold it!" Hollis shouted, and sat up straight in the seat. "Pull over, quick!"

"What is it now?"

"This is the main road into Clarksburg. There could be a roadblock. Me and Laurel will get in the back under that tarp. You drive carefully and no funny business, or I shoot both of you. If we're caught, I got nothing to lose."

"You don't need to remind me again. I know what's at stake."

To say I was getting a little tired of these threats was an understatement. I get grumpy when I'm dead beat and haven't had much sleep. Nodding I understood, I watched them climb over the seats and cover up with the tarp.

Chapter 15

The Jeep was mud-splattered, and I was tired from the tense driving. It was hard to see out through the downpour, but sure enough, up ahead not more than two miles from the trail I saw flashing blue lights. A police officer stood by the side of the road directing traffic.

"I'll have to stop. There's a roadblock up ahead. Don't panic and don't do anything stupid. I'll do my best to get us through this."

"See you do," Hollis said in a muffled voice.

By this time, I was sweating bullets. I practiced deep breathing to the count of five and exhaling to the count of five. Willing myself to remain calm and act innocent, I pulled up to the roadblock and looked in my side mirror. I recognized the policeman coming toward me from the back. It was Charlie in uniform. I took a deep breath and rolled down the window.

"Hello, Officer."

He walked around the Jeep, came back to my window, and held up two pictures.

"Have you seen these two people?"

"Sorry, Officer." I shook my head and rolled my eyes toward the back.

Charlie nodded.

"Looks like you've been four-wheeling. Please step out of the vehicle, sir."

"Is something wrong, Officer?"

"Step to the rear of the vehicle."

I walked around to where he was standing. He pointed to a perfectly good taillight.

"Do you see that? You're driving around without a brake light on the left. I'll have to write you up. You have ten days to get that fixed."

With his back to the Jeep, he looked at me and mouthed the word "argue."

I nodded. "There's nothing wrong with that taillight. I replaced it less than a month ago."

Charlie nodded. I had said the right thing, but I didn't catch on why he wanted me out of the car. He motioned for one of the officers to come over. I held my breath.

"Sergeant, get in the driver's seat and apply the brakes. Watch your brake lights, sir. What do you see?" the soft-spoken Charlie said louder than was necessary.

"I'm sorry, Officer. You're right. It's out."

He took out his ticket book and wrote. He handed me the ticket to sign. I took the ticket book from him and signed.

"Thank you, sir. I advise you to get the taillight fixed at the earliest. If you see the two people we're looking for, please notify us."

"Yes, sir. I will."

I got back in the car. There was a small Smith-and-Wesson pistol lying against the seat back. I slid into the seat and slipped the pistol into the back of my jeans. I put the Jeep in drive and the police officer motioned for me to continue.

"You had me worried there for a second, but you did good, Peeper. You do have a problem with taillights," Hollis sniggered. "We'll stay back here. Drive toward town. On the left before you reach town, pull in at the Country Roads General Store. I'll tell you where to go from there."

I had to make a move soon, before we reached the store. His friend must live near the store. Once we made it to his friend's house, I would not be useful to him. Worse of all, I would have seen his friend's face. He had no problem in telling us his plans. That meant we were fast losing our usefulness to him.

"You can make it to your friend's house from here with no trouble. Let me and Laurel out anywhere along the highway."

Hollis raised the tarp and pointed the gun at me. "I said drive to the Country Roads General Store. I hate repeating myself. No more talking. I got to think."

"All right, all right, I'm driving. Relax."

I watched in my rearview mirror as he slipped back under the tarp. I heard Laurel whimper.

There's a picnic park on the right before the general store. This would be my last chance. When I make my move, I hope he'll be so interested in catching me he won't hurt Laurel. If he's angry enough, he would not think to use Laurel to draw me out. The road curves before the park, and past the bend is the drive down into the park.

I picked up speed as we rounded the last curve, then took my foot off the gas, pulled the hand brake and turned the steering wheel hard left. This action sent the Jeep into a 180-degree spin in the gravel berm. I released the hand brake and counter-steered to keep from flipping the Jeep.

As the Jeep slowed, I threw open my door and rolled out. Stumbling to my feet with pain shooting through my shoulder and arm, I sprinted for cover toward a cement block building, the park's restroom. I made it behind the building before Hollis could get out from under the tarp and out of the Jeep, as I counted on. Leaning against the building, I tried to catch my breath before making another run for it.

I heard a car door open, and Hollis yelled something. He fired a shot in my direction without aiming. The bullet hit the restroom wall and ricocheted into the trees.

I peeped around the building on the opposite side and saw Hollis dragging Laurel out of the Jeep. She looked up at him, closed her eyes, and went limp. She appeared to faint. I hoped she was only pretending. Whatever the reason, it was a good move. He could not cart around a limp body and come after me at the same time.

Her dead weight was too much for him to drag even in his rage. He let go of her shirt and raced toward me. With my last glimpse before making for the tree line, I saw Laurel jump up and run toward the highway in the direction of the general store, less than a quarter of a mile away.

He was so focused on me, he didn't notice her running for help. Now it was time to save myself. Holding on to my limp arm, I ran for the woods and the cornfield beyond, giving Laurel as much time to get away as possible. His footsteps were close behind me.

"You can't get away, Peeper. When I find you, I'm going to empty this whole clip into you. You've cost me valuable time. If I miss my flight, I don't know when I can get another."

I stopped behind a huge rock and leaned against it to catch my breath. Hollis stopped also. I listened, but I didn't hear anything. He must be waiting for me to say something or make a noise, so he can get a fix on my location. I took off my belt and made a sling for my arm.

Crawling and sliding through the underbrush as quietly as I could, I tried to make my way to the cornfield and the highway beyond. The rain was still coming down, making it hard to see or move, but it helped deaden the sound.

I slipped down in a drainage ditch with several inches of water. Slipping and sliding, I tried to make my way out of the ditch and up the hill to the cornfield beyond. Looking back, I saw Hollis standing on a rock. I ducked and rolled into the brush.

Crawling behind a tree, I stopped and scanned the area to see where Hollis was now. He was still standing on the rock, his eyes scanning the brush for me. At my feet, there were several small rocks. I grabbed one. When Hollis turned and looked in the opposite direction, I tossed it behind him. Just like in the movies, he fired into the brush toward the sound.

I took this opportunity to run, but he was too quick. He turned back and fired in my direction. Bullets were buzzing all around like a swarm of bees. One bullet grazed my hurt shoulder.

I was so tired. My shoulder was bleeding now. I found it hard to put one foot in front of the other. I felt dizzy, but I had to keep moving for my sake and Laurel's. If he caught me, I'd be dead. He'd turn his attention to Laurel then.

There was no cover between the edge of the cornfield and the highway. I could hear sirens in the distance. I had to make my stand here. I sat on the nearest rock and pulled the gun out of the back of my pants. There was nothing to do but wait for the inevitable. It was quiet. I couldn't hear a sound. What was he doing? I looked around the tree to my left, but I couldn't see him. When I turned back around, he was standing in the cornfield with his gun aimed at me.

"Hollis, put the gun down. You can't get away. You must hear the sirens. Put your gun down and maybe both of us will walk out of here alive."

"Well, well, looks like we got ourselves what ya might call a Mexican standoff. I have no intention of being taken. If I have to go, I'm going out in a blaze of glory. I don't plan on going alone either. This is all your fault. I think it only fitting you share eternity with me." He chuckled and grimaced. "You know what's waiting on me if I give myself up? I don't look good in prison stripes."

He lowered his gun a few inches. At last, he was running out of energy. He couldn't run on sheer nerves for much longer. He took several steps toward me.

"You're all that's standing between me and freedom. I've killed four times. One more won't make that much difference. The first one was an accident. The others were necessary. The first time I didn't even hear the gun go off. I never killed anyone before Leslie. I saw him fall. It was almost like he fell in slow motion. Everything slowed down. I could think clearly at last, and I knew I had to kill the rest. You can't leave witnesses behind, now, can you?"

Hollis raised his arm again with his gun pointed at me. I raised the gun I had down by my side, took my shot, and rolled to the right. Fell off the rock would be more accurate. He fired at the same time as I did. His bullet missed me and ricocheted off the rock.

His gun hand went limp, and he dropped his gun. He looked at his hand with blood running down his arm and dripping off his fingers. He looked up at me with surprise written across his face before he collapsed. I limped to where he fell and kicked his gun out of the way.

He was still breathing. My shot had hit him in the shoulder. The sirens were louder now. I sank to my knees, my energy spent. The rain hasn't let up, but I didn't feel it hitting my face. My shoulder was hurting. My arm fell out of my homemade sling and hung limply at my side. My next memory was of Charlie running across the field, gun in hand, with the rescue squad trailing behind him.

He knelt down beside me. "Chance, old man, are you all right?"

"I've been better, but I'll get over it. Is Laurel all right?"

"Yes, the EMTs are looking her over now. She's bruised and scratched but nothing that won't heal. Central patched her through to us from the store, but we were already on our way. We didn't want to crowd Evans. We've been watching you at a distance since last night. While we had you stopped at the roadblock, I put a tracker on your vehicle. We wanted him to lead us to wherever he was making you drive him. We figured our odds would be better if we caught him as he made it to his destination."

"Laurel had nothing to do with the robbery and murder. It was Brian, Hollis, and Susie. Hollis admitted he was the one who killed those people at the lab and Susie. He also rigged the explosives at the cabin. Laurel was a hostage same as I was. Unfortunately, she was having an affair with Hollis. He made her think he was leaving his wife for her."

"Yeah, Brian admitted that much to us. Of course, he's laying all the blame on Hollis."

"What about Hollis? Will he make it?"

"Yeah, it looks like it. You hit him in the shoulder. You didn't hit anything vital. More's the pity. Come on, we need to get you to the hospital. The guys with the stretcher are coming for you. I'll call Phil and tell him. He wanted to go charging in there at your house last night.

I had to threaten to arrest him before we could convince him to let us work it out. Hollis was crazy enough to kill all three of you."

Everything around me was growing dim. I closed my eyes. When I came to, I found myself in the back of the ambulance on my way to the hospital. This was getting to be a habit. I hoped I didn't run into Dr. Digman. This one would be a little harder to explain.

* * *

It's been four months now, and all the hoopla in the newspaper has died down. I took time off to recuperate and do a little fishing. To my surprise, Phil agreed to come with me. There's nothing better than fresh trout cooked over an open fire by a stream. Phil seemed to enjoy himself. The peace of the mountains was good for both of us.

I'm back at work, and Boomer is by my side as usual. Phil's on his rounds at night, and all is right with the world.

Laurel and her mother came by today to thank me and give me a check for my services. Laurel is receiving counseling. She will go to summer school to finish her degree. I asked her about what she planned to do with her diploma. She said she had not decided. She thought she would take some time off to decide. The trial will be next month, and both Laurel and I will be called as witnesses.

When the dust died down, thanks to Hollis, the sheriff had some explaining to do. He refused to cooperate and resigned. I haven't heard what the DA has in mind, if anything. Last I heard, they could not find a condo in Belize in the sheriff's name.

A search of the sheriff's house turned up no cash or incriminating evidence. I didn't expect them to find anything. The sheriff has been around the block a time or two. When the dust settles, I expect he, his wife, and daughter to disappear. They only have Hollis's word for what the sheriff did.

Sipping a cup of coffee, I waited for my two o'clock appointment, something to do with a missing husband and a divorce. It doesn't sound too exciting, but it pays the bills. Another client may be taking a chance on Sunday.

CPSIA information can be obtained
at www.ICGtesting.com
Printed in the USA
BVHW031533100921
616542BV00004B/298